MW01520013

# Fire Lake

**Adam and Grace**
**Book Three**

By J.C. Paulson

ISBN 978-0-9959756-4-4

# Chapter One

*Somalia, 1993*

ook down, and shut up," Abukar Dualeh told the
children, as he blackened their teeth with sooty wax.
The boys' faces blended into the deep desert night.
Only their eyes and teeth gleamed in the starlight, and the
leader of the group, just fifteen but authoritative beyond his
years, threatened them with beatings if they spoke or smiled.

Dirty wax helped obscure open mouths, but a glint off a
shiny molar could still give them away. Sunglasses or night
goggles would have been more helpful than simply looking
down, but the Somali children could neither access nor afford
such luxuries. Indeed, had such things been available, along
with sufficient food and clothing, night raids would be entirely
unnecessary. Eyewear was first on the list of must-steals if
found in the Canadian camp.

The little band of six boys slipped into the open desert
from the nearby village and took positions before dark. Tension
knotted Abukar's shoulders as he remained on constant alert,
ensuring no one had followed them to their hiding place.

Flattened on the cooling earth, bodies rigid, they waited with simmering impatience for the sentry change.

The Canadian Airborne Regiment took its camp security seriously, but the change brought a split second of divided attention. A blink. A breath. Abukar saw his advantage and led the silent boys over scrub and sand toward the supply tent. Heads down. Mouths closed. They quietened their breathing, preparing to slide into the cache of treasure.

A strong hand seemed to come from the sky. Before Abukar could react, it lifted him by the scruffy collar of his threadbare black shirt, and a voice said softly, in broken Somali, "Little one. Who are you?"

The smaller boys turned and fled. Abukar, even at fifteen a skinny, starved "little one," squirmed and kicked in the soldier's grasp, but said nothing.

"Listen," said the soldier, sotto voce. "Do you understand English? Stop wriggling. I won't hurt you. Stop, now."

Abukar nodded. He spoke English quite well and understood a great deal more. He had learned it in school, before the civil war began.

"Go back to your village. This is very dangerous. You do not understand how dangerous. Do you hear me? Go, and don't come here again. I may not be here the next time."

Abukar peered up at the enormous brown man who held him effortlessly and perceived that he pleaded not only with his voice, but his eyes.

"Little one. Be careful. Now go. I will watch you. Do you understand?"

The soldier put him down and gave him a gentle shove. Abukar hit the sand running. He could feel the Canadian corporal's gaze burning into him, and he did not look back.

# Chapter Two

Grace glanced out the front window of her tiny bungalow for the seventeenth time in the last hour, and again checked her watch. Eleven o'clock in the morning, and the moving van should have been there by now, on the street, ramp down.

How much did Adam really have to pack? He had sold all the furniture in his condominium, decided to leave behind the appliances and thrown away scores of books, ancient linens and sundry other items. Where was he? And the moving van?

With an effort, Grace abandoned her vigil, uncurled her lithe body, slipped off the couch and padded into the kitchen. Coffee. She would make fresh coffee. No way would she call Adam and ask him what was going on. She refused to nag, complain, or even suggest that she was becoming very impatient. But she did peek out the window again.

Nothing. No van. No one.

Focus, Grace Rampling, she told herself. Make the coffee. Then sit down and read a book or the newspaper or something. Don't think about Adam for five minutes, if you can help it.

Two short weeks ago, she had asked Adam Davis to move in with her, and he had said yes. To this moment, she couldn't believe she had done that — even in the throes of passion, Adam inside her, filling her, declaring his love for her. She hadn't regretted it for a second, but was still surprised at herself, the quite remarkable nerve she had displayed that night. What if he had said no? Or that he had to think about it? Her heart would have shattered right there, along with her pride.

But he hadn't said either of those things.

*Grace. Oh, God, yes. I will come and live with you.*

When she thought about his words, her entire body shuddered with arousal and joy in equal measure. And today, he was coming. To stay. It had all been planned, yet Grace couldn't help feeling nervous. What if Adam had changed his mind at the last second? Experienced cold feet? Made a run for the border?

They had only known each other since March, although their relationship had really begun in June. Grace experienced its rapid development as a fire coursing through her body. It burned away all thought of anyone, and sometimes anything, else. His face, etched in her mind, could distract her in the middle of an interview she was conducting for the newspaper. A meeting with the boss. A laugh with a friend.

Where was he?

That Adam was theoretically moving in so soon after all this transpired was largely due to excellent timing beyond their control. The Saskatoon real estate market of late 2006 through 2007 was steaming hot, even as the summer had been. Few listings and a spectacular number of people seeking to expand the booming city's population meant homes of all kinds, including beautiful condos like Adam's, flew off the market. In some cases, sales took a day or two; occasionally, a week or two; and only the seriously awful product lagged for a month or two.

Adam's downtown condo attracted four bidders and sold for fifteen thousand dollars over the list price in two days flat. He would have moved into Grace's Buena Vista bungalow a week earlier had he been able to rent a truck large enough for his remaining possessions. That he found one at all was only because it was the middle of September and not the end of the month.

The phone rang, making Grace jump. But the number on her screen wasn't Adam's.

"Hello? Mom? Dad?"

"Hello, my girl," Wallace Rampling said, in his characteristic affectionate rumble. "How are you doing?"

"Hi, Dad. I'm fine. And you?"

"Fine, too, honey. I'm calling to see if you're busy next weekend."

"No more than usual. What's up?"

"Your grandmother. She's having that hip replaced Friday; Mom got the call this morning."

Her grandmother Margaret had been on the waiting list for some time, hoping to sneak in ahead of the competition for precious operating room time if she was ready to go at a moment's notice.

"So we're off to Regina for a week or two," Wallace continued. "Can you handle the cabin, sweetheart? You know the drill. I can ask David if you can't make it, but Hope is busy with adoption meetings. She's close to a decision on a child. It could wait until Thanksgiving, but we could also have a foot of snow by then. I'd rather not take the chance. Remember last year?"

"Yeah, that crazy blizzard. It was impossible to get in there. Sure, I can go, Dad. And I'll call Gran today sometime. I'm so glad she's getting that hip. Say hi to Mom."

"Will do, Grace. Thanks for this. See you soon."

Closing the cabin, as Grace well knew, was no small or unimportant thing. The small, rustic but comfortable three-bedroom, perched lakefront in Saskatchewan's mid-northwest, was not winterized. Frozen water pipes were not a threat but a

7

sure thing in a climate that reached thirty and even forty below on a regular basis, every damned winter. Grace's brother David was busy finishing his degree, and her sister was working on an adoption; so, she was the best person to go.

Besides, Grace hoped that if Adam indeed moved in, and hadn't caught the morning plane to Mexico, he might be able to come with her to the lake. Unlikely, considering how busy he was putting together evidence for two murder trials, but she could always dream. She couldn't wait to take him there, to show him its beauty, to slip naked into the water with him under cover of early, warm darkness.

The coffee pot spit, gurgled and made a small beeping noise, announcing the completion of its duty. Grace poured herself a mug full just as the door flew open; she jumped and spilled a few drops of the cup's contents.

"Good morning, Babe," Adam said, striding in, a grin sliding up one side of his stubbled, chiselled, beautiful face. He flung his arms around Grace and kissed her soundly, two-day beard scratching her cheek and upper lip.

Grace felt her heart hammering against him. *He's here. Not in Mexico, cold toes buried in hot sand. Here.*

"Sorry to be late." Adam loosened his grip so he could look at her. "We stopped for a bite, and the truck wasn't ready until nine."

"As long as you're here, and not in Puerto Vallarta." Grace hugged him in relief and buried her face in his chest.

"Puerto Vallarta? Why the hell would I be in PV?" Adam asked, sounding honestly puzzled.

"Never mind. Just my goofy imagination. Want some coffee?"

"No, thanks. I'd like to get this done. Three men waiting outside probably feel the same way."

"Who's out there?" Grace asked, trying to look over Adam's shoulder and failing, even on tiptoe.

8

"James, Bruce and Lorne Fisher." Adam cocked an eyebrow. "This shouldn't take long."

Grace laughed. No, it shouldn't. This could be the shortest move in history, considering the men on the job: James Weatherall, Adam's right hand in the police detective department and as fit as a human being could be; his spouse, Bruce Stephens, approximately the same substantial height and build as Adam; and superhero-sized Constable Lorne Fisher, the biggest and strongest man Grace had ever seen in real life.

"Tell me what I can do to help."

"Nothing. Direct traffic, maybe. Refill your coffee cup? Sorry. I think I startled you."

"I was . . . woolgathering."

"You're not used to another person barging through your door. I should have knocked."

"No. This is your home too, Adam. Barge away."

"My home too," he echoed.

Adam's face softened from the bright, excited expression he wore when he had indeed barged in. Navy eyes darkened, and he bent slightly to meet Grace's forehead with his own, his arms sliding again around her waist.

"You're home, Adam," she whispered, and touched his lips with hers.


*****


Untamed auburn curls tumbled around the box as Grace bent over it, musing about where its contents should go.

Packed inside were Adam's framed diploma from the University of Saskatchewan and other illuminating mementoes. Summa cum laude, eh? I knew he was smart, but that's ridiculous, thought Grace, considering Adam's brain in a new and more brilliant light.

9

The box also contained a university ring and evidence that Adam had contributed to a Huskies' Vanier Cup win, as a receiver on the squad; the national university football championship trophy didn't often land in Saskatoon.

Those long legs were gridiron weapons. He ran like a hungry animal on the savannah; Grace had seen him in full flight more than once.

Grace unpacked a tiny golf trophy. Unearthed commendations from the police service. Discovered a certificate verifying that Adam had completed police training. Found a letter welcoming him to join the local force — in fact, insisting upon it — from the chief of police.

Bloody hell, thought Grace. How will I keep up with Mr. Athlete of the Year? Detective Sergeant Superman? Shaking her head, she picked up the box, took it into the living room and cleared space on the bookshelf. There, she carefully arranged the degree, the tiny trophy, the police training certificate . . .

"What are you doing?" Adam's big, booming baritone rang out behind her, and Grace gave a start.

"God, you scared me, Sergeant. For someone so big, you can sure creep up on a person." That was another excellent attribute in a cop, she thought — the ability to sneak up on folks. "I'm putting up your commendations and things. Adam, for heaven's sake — summa cum laude?"

He coloured a bit, then regained his composure.

"And you, Grace? Did you fail horribly at journalism school? Or in political science?"

"Well . . . no, but . . ."

"What was your degree designation?"

"Magna."

"You do realize that many of my classes were in science, yes? Objective, not subjective?"

"Your point, mister?" Grace asked.

10

"It's pretty easy to get an A if the answers are fact-based. You, on the other hand, were writing for subjective marking. Stories and essays and so on. Very different."

Grace's eyes widened. She was even more impressed, and horrified at the same time. He got those marks in *science* classes? At a university known for failing more than half of its first-year biology students?

"You don't have to put that old stuff out on a shelf."

"I'd like to."

"Why, Babe?" he asked, walking over and putting his arms around her.

"It's nice to look back on the good things, the milestones. And it lets me in on a little piece of your life, before . . . you know, before . . ."

"I think 'us' is the word you are looking for. Before *us*."

He wrapped his arms around her more tightly, tugging her into his chest.

"We are now us, you know. You can say it out loud, Grace. In front of anyone you want, including me."

His voice lowered half an octave and reverberated as he swept a hand through Grace's wild curls and pushed them back to touch her cheek.

"You are mine." Adam's blue eyes met Grace's slightly-troubled chocolate gaze. "Believe it."

"There may be a small IQ differential."

"No. But there is definitely an EQ differential. Who's the genius at three in the morning, when I'm thrashing around and gasping like a fish on the beach? You're not really worried about this, are you, Grace? It's just a bloody piece of paper."

She looked down. Grace feared that Adam was both more intelligent and more attractive than she was; that he would tire of her, and find other, more alluring women.

"Grace, my God." Adam broke into her thoughts, clearly reading them correctly. "You are worried. Quit it. You are the most intelligent, fearless, beautiful and erotic woman I have ever met, or even seen."

Grace shook her head slightly, still troubled.

"I'm going to have to prove it, am I?" Adam growled.

He swung her abruptly into his powerful arms, buried his lips in the soft skin at the base of her throat and bore her off to the bedroom, taking the short hallway in a few strides.

He didn't put her on the bed, as Grace both hoped and expected. Instead, he placed her carefully in front of the full-length mirror and stood behind her.

"This flaming glory," he said, swirling her mane to one side and staring at her in the glass. "These eyes, so deep, so thoughtful. This skin, rich and soft and white as magnolia blossoms."

Grace went pink, belying his comparison, and tried to turn around. "Oh, Adam . . ."

But he held her firmly between his thighs, unzipped the rather filthy old fleece she wore for unpacking, and ran his fingers along her collarbone. "These delicate wings."

Long fingers slipped lower, touching high swells. He unhooked her bra, slowly, deliberately, and soon she stood naked to the waist as he cupped her breasts, stroking the nipples, still watching her face in the mirror.

"And these. These defy description. Look at them, Grace. Silken and soft, and hard and high and so, so beautiful. I remember our first night. I couldn't wait to see them. I still can't, every damn day."

Grace stared back, mesmerized and writhing; speechless, and aroused.

Adam reached down and slipped her casual pants over her hips and down to the floor. "Step out," he demanded, before standing again.

Now completely naked, she peered shyly at herself in the mirror, and then up at Adam's face.

"Do you see, Grace? How beautiful you are? Smooth and sleek and succulent. Wild and windblown. And that, love, is just the outside."

His hands roved softly over her breasts and belly, her thighs and buttocks, as he gently forced her to watch by placing his cheek against hers. Grace could feel him rising as he pressed into her back; she thought her knees might give way. When he finally slipped a hand between her legs, they buckled. Adam picked her up again and his mouth crashed into hers, tongue plunging in, his own desire getting its way.

"For God's sake, Adam," Grace whimpered around his kiss, gripped in his embrace. "Please. I need you inside me."

"Or what, Grace?"

"Or you," she panted, hands raking his hair, "will have to move out."

*****

"Adam?" Grace said tentatively, after his loving had yet again moved her, body and soul.

"Babe," Adam answered, cuddling her against his chest.

"I have to head up to the cabin next weekend. Have I told you about the lake yet?"

"Not much. It's up near Meadow Lake, right?"

"Yes. My grandmother is getting a hip replaced, and Mom and Dad are heading down to Regina for a couple of weeks."

"Is this your namesake grandmother?"

"No, this is my mother's mother, Margaret. Honor is Dad's mother's name."

Grace was known by her middle name. Her parents had thought it was an excellent plan to give her two names to live up to.

13

"Dad called to see if I could go up and close the cabin, since it often snows at Thanksgiving and he won't get there for a few weeks. Last year, we couldn't get within miles of the place — do you remember that October blizzard? Thirty centimetres, I think we got, and even more up north. We had to hire someone to plow his way in and winterize it."

Adam groaned at the memory. "Oh, yeah. Hell of a storm. Made policing super easy, too."

"I bet. I was wondering . . . do you think there's any chance you could come with me? I'd love to show you the place. It's beautiful. I've practically grown up there, and I'd like you to see it. Or maybe you've been up that way before?"

"We went up to Lac Des Isles once, when I was a little kid. That's nearby, right?"

"Fairly. Lac Des Isles is quite different, though; more of a prairie lake. Ours is a remnant of glacial retreat, surrounded by forest. But yes, it's maybe half an hour from there." Grace paused. "Is there any hope you could come? I'd really like to go for three or four days, but two will work if necessary."

Grace held her breath, thinking there was nowhere on Earth she'd rather be than up north in a cabin with Adam. Alone, by a lake, in the pristine wilderness.

"I'll check with the chief on Monday, but I'm pretty sure I can figure it out," Adam said. "I don't know if I can manage four days, but I'll try."

"I'll take what I can get." Grace burrowed into him. "It will be so quiet, so peaceful. You'll love it. I promise."

# Chapter Three

Grace and Adam had become a three-vehicle household: one small, older Honda sedan; one rather ancient but otherwise perfect BMW; and one big, black, fairly new truck. The truck seemed the right choice for the lake trip, higher gas bills notwithstanding.

Adam worked like hell all week, justifying two extra days off to create a four-day long weekend. The trial for the man who killed the city's Catholic bishop in March was a month away, and he was still finalizing documents and answering the Crown prosecutor's constant questions. Adam did not resent the seemingly endless case, even as he did resent murder. It had brought Grace into his life.

Working on a late-breaking story for the daily newspaper, the StarPhoenix, she had stumbled over Bishop Howard Halkitt in the cathedral and alerted police to his gory corpse. Adam and Grace met, literally, over his dead body. And Adam's life changed in that moment. He would never forget seeing Grace for the first time, emerging from her hiding place between two pews, her wild auburn hair, gleaming brown eyes and pale face followed by the long, elegant rest of her.

He was also completing the horrific details of the case against a serial murderer of at least five women, also the perpetrator of vehicular manslaughter and a dog killer. The violent man almost succeeded in ending the life of Grace's friend Suzanne Genereux. Looking back, it had been an unusually crime-ridden spring and summer.

Grace wheedled an extra two days out of her boss, Mark Williams, the managing editor of the StarPhoenix. Mark tended to give Grace anything she wanted. She had almost left the paper, and Saskatoon, for good two and a half years ago when her Australian boyfriend talked her into following him to Canberra. But Mick Shaw turned out to be a jerk and a bounder, and Grace, self-esteem in shreds, came home. Mark often told her not to ever try that again; she was one of his best reporters.

The hell she would now. Wherever Adam lived, there she would remain. If he left Saskatoon, she would follow; but he showed no interest in moving away. Indeed, Grace had a feeling that Police Chief Dan McIvor would do his best to keep Adam in Saskatoon, even if it meant promotion.

On Friday morning, Adam and Grace quickly packed a large cooler of food, wine and beer, clothing and sundry other items into the truck's box.

"It's four hours," Grace warned.

"Bullshit," Adam said, grinning.

"No, really," Grace protested.

"We'll see, Babe."

Adam managed to maintain one hundred and twenty kilometres an hour most of the way to North Battleford, but had to admit defeat between the small city and the resort town of Cochin. One lane of bumper-to-bumper traffic, facing a similar snake of vehicles coming south, almost drove him mad. Grace could tell.

But Adam relaxed into clear sailing, or rather speeding, after that. Few vehicles traversed the closely-treed highway from Glaslyn to Meadow Lake, in large part because it wasn't a summer long weekend. They made it to the lake in three hours and forty minutes, despite the slower speeds demanded by the winding, narrow trail that led to the lake from the Waterhen River crossing.

"I see why it's so tough to get in here after a blizzard," Adam said, after a few kilometres on the gravel road. "You'd need a good plowing first, for sure."

"It's also very safe and easy to navigate after three days of rain."

Adam laughed at her sarcasm. "I can see that, too. But this truck will take most roads, in most conditions. We're good, even if it does rain."

The truck easily wound around curves that suddenly gave way to vistas of blue water sparkling in the fall sun; this part of Saskatchewan was known for its countless rivers, streams and lakes. Deer nibbled grass in the narrow ditches, and yellow leaves swirled in the soft breeze. The weather was fine for September, sunny and dazzling.

Grace watched Adam as he drove, wondering if the wild beauty of the place had the same effect on him that it always had on her. She placed a hand lightly on his thigh, feeling the muscles tense slightly as he changed speeds on the winding trail.

"Almost there."

"I hope so," Adam said, in the deepening voice that always betrayed his arousal. "Oh," he added, as her hand slipped higher. "I do have to drive, love. Unless you want me to pull over and ravish you right here."

Grace simply smiled, and pointed to a sign that read Ferguson Lake, one kilometre. First came the turnoff to the campground and store; then another five hundred metres, and they turned into the peaceful crescent of cabins nestled among pine and aspen.

"We're halfway down the front road. Here. To your left. The greyish brown one."

He backed in the truck, braked and turned to Grace.

"Wow," he said. "I can't wait to see the lake. So what's the protocol?"

"I love that you know there's a protocol. First, we unpack and turn on the power. Plug in the fridge. Then we grab a drink and head down to the lake. Once at the shore, we exclaim about the water level. Oh, the water's so high! Or, of course, low. Ready?"

"Very." Adam kissed her and jumped out of the truck.

Grace slipped down from the high vehicle, grabbed her suitcase and unlocked the cottage door, flinging it open to let the breeze blow fresh air into the rather stuffy space. Adam followed her, bearing the cooler and the beer.

"It's not, you know, fancy or anything," Grace said seconds later, flicking on the electricity in the little bedroom that housed the breakers. "Feels like home to me, though."

Adam seemed not to hear her. He strode to the front door, swung it open and stepped onto the expansive deck.

The lake glittered a few metres ahead of him, waves softly susurrating on the shore, just beyond a narrow, sandy path and a thick copse of mixed trees. Late in the season as it was, no power boats marred the quiet; only a sailboat and a kayak could be seen in the distance.

Grace came up behind him, slipped her arms around his waist and laid her cheek on his warm back. She didn't ask. Finally, Adam spoke.

"God, Grace, really? This is spectacular. No wonder you love it so much."

"I hope you will, too."

"Already do. Let's grab those drinks and go down to the water."

"Nope. We have to get the rest of the stuff inside first. I'm way too superstitious to break with tradition now."

Loading in the food and luggage took only a few minutes. Drinks in hand, they wandered single file down the skinny, shaded path and the little incline that led to the beach. The lake wasn't a huge body of water but contained a couple of small islands to the west, near the opposite shore. Beyond the islands, although it could not be seen, was a little bay thickly populated with Northern Pike. White sand covering the public beach stretched along the eastern shore. Directly across the lake there was nothing, or so it appeared, but dense forest.

Grace shielded her eyes against the blazing sun and looked around, as caught in wonderment by the sight of her lake as always.

"Is the water up, or down?" Adam asked.

"Up. About two feet from last year. There's been a lot of rain here, and the lake refills from little underground springs that come off the river system."

"That's why it's so clean."

"Yes. It's rare that it becomes weedy or murky."

"Even this summer? It was so damned hot."

"Apparently. But it is September. The cool nights and the lack of boat traffic help."

"Hey! Grace!"

Grace's head snapped around to see who was calling her from the path above.

"Hi, Gord," she responded, with warmth.

The older man's face lit up with a welcoming smile as he approached Grace, and he greeted her again with a hug.

"Nice to see you. Haven't been around much this summer, hey?"

"No, I'm afraid it's been very busy. Gordon Allbright, I'd like you to meet Adam Davis. Adam, this is Gord, from over there," she said, pointing west to a log cabin.

"Nice to meet you, sir," Adam said, offering his hand.

19

"And you, Adam Davis. Tell me, do you have designs on our Grace?"

Grace blushed. Gordon was a favourite neighbour of hers — indeed, she had known him all her life — but he did like to discomfit whenever possible.

"I do," Adam replied.

The older man scanned Adam with frank appraisal and nodded.

"Good. Very good. How long are you up for, Grace?"

"Four days. And you?"

"Another week, I hope. Been up since harvest. Can't beat the weather for September, and who knows what'll happen in October? Make hay while the sun shines, I always say."

As does everyone else, Grace thought, but smiled. The farmer had earned the right to use the cliché as if it were his own until the cows came home.

"Well, come for a drink later, once you're settled," he said. "Tillie'll be glad to see you."

"We will, Gord, thank you. See you later. Give my love to Tillie for now."

The older man wandered off, waving over his head.

"I think you passed muster," Grace told Adam, once Gord was out of earshot.

"Thank God for that."

Grace sighed. "I'd rather stay at the cabin tonight. Maybe we could get away with a quick drink? Do you mind very much?"

"Not at all. Looking forward to getting to know the neighbours."

\*\*\*\*\*

After dinner, they wandered in the gloom of dusk toward the little log cabin, twinkling with tiny lights. Gord and Tillie saw them coming up the path and met them on the porch.

"Grace!" Tillie said, throwing ample arms around Grace's slim shoulders. "We haven't seen you in over a year. How have you been? And who is this?"

"Tillie, this is Adam. Adam, Tillie." Grace didn't think she needed to elaborate on who, exactly, Adam was.

"Nice to meet you," said the tall, greying older woman. "Come in, come in. What can we get you? Beer? Scotch? Wine?"

"A little wine, please. Adam? Scotch?"

"That'd be great, thank you."

As Gord poured the drinks, Tillie settled into her corner chair beside the glowing fireplace and Grace could sense a storm of questions brewing.

"What's new around here?" she asked quickly, forestalling them.

"Well," said Tillie, and launched into a long gossip about who had birthed babies, who had been divorced, and who was making too much noise on the lake.

"And a strange thing happened about a week ago," she went on. "A man who said he was selling satellite dishes came on by. It was so strange. That never happens way up here — people soliciting door to door."

"No," Grace said, brow furrowing. "That's never happened at our cabin. That is weird."

"Well, at first I believed him," Tillie said. "He had all the right pamphlets and such like. I told him we had satellite already, and we weren't interested, but he did go on. This service was better. The Roughrider games would be so clear, it would seem like they were in the room with us. And on and on.

"But then he began asking questions about who was up at the lake, and did we know anyone who didn't have a satellite

21

dish, and what were their names, and did anyone have cabins across the lake."

Tillie finally took a breath, and Grace jumped in.

"What did you say?"

"I said no." The two women exchanged meaningful glances.

"What did he look like? Did you call the RCMP, or the satellite company?"

"He was tall, very straight shoulders — I noticed that, particularly — and he had a tattoo peeking out of his shirtsleeve. Couldn't tell much about it. I told him to get away, and I did call the police."

"What did they say?"

"Thanked me for letting them know. I haven't heard anything back."

"I wonder what he was up to," Grace mused. "Anything else you remember? In case I see him around?"

"He wore a ball cap. Wouldn't take it off. That really annoyed me, because I couldn't see his eyes very well."

Grace's own eyes opened wide, and she looked quickly at Adam.

"Well, I'm glad you mentioned it, Tillie. If he comes around, I'll consider myself forewarned, and not let him in the door. How are Tom and Pat?"

Tom and Pat were the Allbrights' children. Grace still remembered the night Tommy went missing in the dark when she was a child of six. Tom, about ten at the time, had not come home at curfew after playing with the other pre-pubescent boys on the crescent. Searchers gathered at her cabin instead of at the Allbrights' because it was much larger. She lay shivering with delicious fear in her bunk bed, little sister Hope below her; baby brother David was in a crib in the other room, shared with big brother Paul. Had a bear eaten Tommy? she remembered wondering. Had a moose dragged him off into the forest, to be consumed later? Had a very big fish gripped him in his teeth, and taken him away into the bay?

At midnight, a man had appeared out of the thick, velvet darkness — there were no outdoor lights around the cabins in those days — with Tommy in tow. He delivered the terrified boy to the cabin, turned and walked away without a word. The incident forever after was the mystery of Ferguson Lake. Who had found, and probably saved, Tommy Allbright? Tommy himself had no idea; the man came from nowhere, grasped him by the collar, and silently marched him home.

Ten years later, a similar thing happened to Grace. But that turned out to be quite a different story.

She shivered again at the childhood memories, shook her curls and brought her attention back to the present. Tillie had been saying something about how Tom and Pat were doing, but Grace missed most of it.

"We should go," she said to Tillie. "It's getting late. See you tomorrow?"

"For sure. So good to see you again, honey."

Adam paused at the door.

"Mrs. Allbright, did that satellite salesman give you a name or a business card?"

"Call me Tillie. And no, I don't believe he did. Now, isn't that strange?"

\*\*\*\*\*

Curled on the sectional couch in the cabin, Grace leaned against Adam, internally purring with contentment. She was at her favourite place, with a man she loved like no other, safe in his strong arms.

She did, however, find herself wondering if Adam would dream tonight. His nightmares, born of post-traumatic stress disorder after being shot six years ago, often surfaced when he was in a new environment. Usually, Grace would climb on top of him, soothe him, make love to him and send his demons back to hell.

Sometimes, that didn't work. A few weeks ago, he had lurched out of sleep, pushed her forcefully onto the floor, and crouched on the bed like an animal ready to spring. He had awakened, then, but had been so disturbed by the event he had refused to sleep with Grace on several nights when he sensed the horrors rising.

It wasn't the event itself but his refusal to spend the night with her that sent Grace running to the confidential confines of Dr. Anne Blake's office. Anne was both friend and psychologist, and Grace craved her expertise on PTSD.

"I love him, Anne. I want to live with him. But he thinks he will hurt me one night," Grace told her, after explaining what had happened. "I need your help to help him. And me."

"Well, he's right, you know. He could hurt you. He did, actually, when he flung you to the floor and you bruised your hip."

"It was nothing."

"No. It wasn't. But yes, I can help you. It'll mean you'll have to change your tactics, though. You might not like it."

"Bring it on. God, Anne, this has to work."

"You can tell when the dream is happening, as I understand it."

"Yes, he cries out, shakes and thrashes around. Weeps and sweats, as well."

"But he's still asleep."

"Yes."

"The best thing is not to touch him. Wait," said Anne, finger raised, as Grace opened her mouth to object. "Don't touch him. Speak to him quietly but firmly, and say 'Adam, you're dreaming. Adam, you are safe. It's me, Grace. You're in our bed, and you are safe.' Use his name, and your own, and tell him he's safe and only dreaming. Got that?"

"Yes," said Grace. "Oh, God. Poor Adam. He's frightened, of course, in his awful dreams. He needs to be reassured that he's safe, is what you're telling me. And he'll hear me?"

"Yes. Keep saying that until he either quietens and falls back into a real sleep, or until he awakens. Then, judging by your experience so far, you can apply your love approach. Remember, don't touch him until you know he's awake. He may not know it's you soothing him when he's asleep. He could perceive that it's someone in his dream, trying to hurt him."

"Or trying to hurt me."

"Or that."

Grace hadn't had to use the tactic yet, but she thought about Anne's advice as she gently ran her fingers down Adam's powerful chest and muscular stomach.

"Would you like another drink, Adam?" she asked.

"No, thanks," came his rich baritone, dropping into bass territory. It vibrated in Grace's bones, and elsewhere. "I'm going to make love to you now. I've been waiting all day. All my life."

He stood up, took her hand, and pulled her into the bedroom.

# Chapter Four

Adam was making love to Grace with his tongue but she, as always, took him by the shoulders and tugged him up to her face, asking him to be inside her.

Why, Adam wondered, would she not allow him to bring her to orgasm with his mouth? She would let him go down on her, but not to the end.

He decided he had to ask her. Was he doing something she didn't like? He wanted to give her, he knew, the most intense pleasure available to women. But he didn't want to inflict anything on Grace; he didn't want to insist on something that obviously made her uncomfortable. Now, as she moved under him, was not the right time to ask. But tomorrow, maybe, would be.

Despite his concerns, Adam slept like a boulder of granite, after the long day and the late loving. Refreshed, he leapt out of bed, kissed Grace and announced he would whip up his famous omelettes for breakfast.

"I'll do toast and tomatoes." It was already one of their frequent rituals; herb omelettes and toast, no matter the time of day, accompanied by orange juice in the mornings, white wine in the evenings.

They took their coffee out to the lower deck after breakfast, to contemplate the day. And Adam plunged in, trying to keep his voice even.

"Can I ask you something, Grace? Something intimate?"

"Yes, of course, Adam."

"I, ah, I'd like to be able to talk about everything with you, Grace, including, you know, making love. Is that okay?"

"Yes," Grace answered, although to Adam's ears, she sounded a little unsure.

Go easy, he told himself.

"I, well, as you know, I want you. All of you. And I want to make love to all of you with all of me. To, ah, a satisfying conclusion."

Grace flushed a deep pink and looked away. She obviously got what Adam was driving at.

"You always pull me up, ask me to be inside you. Why?" Adam asked as gently as he could. He couldn't let it drop, despite Grace's obvious discomfort. "Did something happen? Don't you like it when I do it, or how I do it?"

Grace's breathing changed.

"I do like it, Adam. Very much. But I'm afraid my powerful thighs will break your neck."

Grace's weird humour. Her way of dodging the question. Adam took her chin in his hand, then, and made her look at him.

"No, Grace. Not now. Tell me the truth."

Her face crumpled, and Adam felt like a jerk, especially since he had obviously wrecked Grace's contented mood; but he had to know.

"What is it, love?"

"I don't know if I can explain."

27

"Please try. Don't be embarrassed with me, Grace. Please tell me."

"It's, well, I guess I was kind of thrown by Mick. I don't want to tell you."

"Tell me, Grace."

"Mick would, well, afterward, you know, he would . . ."

"What, Grace?"

"He would . . . laugh at me, tease me. He'd crow about putting me out of control, exclaim about what a great lover he was, talk about how strung out I looked afterward. But he also bragged about it. To others. I found out from one of his friend's wives. It made me feel very embarrassed, very small. I had to stop it. But it wasn't enough. I had to stop the whole relationship."

Good thing that Mick person is in Australia, because if I ever find him, I am going to rip him into small pieces as slowly and painfully as possible, Adam thought viciously. God, what an asshole. What a thing to do to Grace, of all people. It was worse than insensitive; it was abusive. Adam felt fury contorting his face, knew his eyes were narrowing and turning black. He fought it, because he needed to comfort Grace, not display his own feelings.

He gently pulled Grace up from her chair, picked her up and sat back down, cradling her in his lap.

"I'm sorry I made you tell me, Grace. I'm so sorry he did that to you."

Grace whimpered a little, rosy with shame, her face half-hidden in Adam's shoulder. Adam couldn't understand how someone could do anything so damaging to such a beautiful woman. But he wondered, was he the asshole now, making her tell him the story?

He stroked her hair and back, being careful not to make it feel like a sexual advance.

"Grace. Listen to me," said Adam into her hair. "You are the most beautiful woman I have ever seen, body, soul and big, big brain. Every time you have an orgasm, I am overwhelmed. I can't believe you've chosen me to share those moments with you."

He couldn't go on about how much watching and feeling her come turned him on, made him crazy for her. It had to be about her, and considering the conversation, as non-sexual as possible.

"Grace, can you try to trust me? I want to make you happy. Insanely happy, if possible."

"You do make me happy, Adam," Grace said, her voice muffled by his shirt. "Very."

"You know what I mean, love."

Adam felt he had to use his words wisely. He did want her to lose control, to experience almost unbearable pleasure under his touch; and while he couldn't even imagine reacting like Mick, he didn't want her to connect his words with Mick's. Or to connect anything about him to Mick. So, he left it there, for now.

"Are you all right, Grace?"

She snuffled.

"I don't like thinking about him. I'm also very embarrassed right now."

"Don't be. Do you want to show me the lake? I think we've had enough protein for a long paddle."

Grace brightened. "I'd love to show you my lake. Let's get out the canoe. Let's go."

They collected the paddles from the back porch, dug the life jackets out of the closet, and went back outside to pick up the canoe from its home beside the cabin. Grace couldn't remember it ever having been so easy to take the heavy, sturdy craft down to the lake. With Adam at the other end, she barely felt the pull of the canoe's weight on her arms.

They slipped the slender boat into the water. Both were expert paddlers, and they skimmed along in a smooth rhythm watching the shoreline and its many wonders. Adam commented every moment or so on its beauty, or asked Grace a question about the wildlife rampant in the provincial park. An eagle's nest topped a tall tree. An otter slipped in and out of the waves. Within twenty minutes, they had reached the smaller of the two Islands, and surprised a beaver near the shore. He dove under the surface after a slap from his tail.

"No one has a cabin on these islands, do they?" Adam asked. "I found myself wondering that after last night. The satellite salesman asked Tillie that question. But I don't see how you'd get services in here."

"No, there are no actual cabins here." Grace paused. "There's a story behind that, though. I'll tell you about it sometime."

"Can't tell me now?"

"It's a long story. I might not get it out while I'm paddling. I'll regale you with tales of adventure later."

Grace directed Adam, steering from the back of the canoe, toward the bay. They could see the pike darting deep under the water's surface, alarmed by the canoe's shadow. A beaver lodge loomed on their left; lily pads covered the water to their right. Human silence reigned, allowing them to hear the chatter of the birds and the occasional bellow from a larger animal.

All told, the canoe trip took two hours. Grace, unused to paddling that long, felt the knots in her shoulders as they eased up onto the shore.

"Ow," she said, rubbing the muscles. "But that was great. I haven't been around the lake in at least five years. Feeling it, I'm afraid. And I'm hungry. Lunch?"

"Lunch. And beer."

Grace cut Black Forest ham and Swiss cheese sandwiches, threw together a green salad and brought the food out to the deck. Adam followed with beverages. They ate, and stared at the lake, and made vague comments about the squirrels and deer passing through the yard, which ignored them completely.

"Adam, I think I need a nap," Grace said, after a while. "Apparently, my daily run is not enough to keep my upper body in shape for a two-hour paddle."

"I have paperwork, sadly. Have a nap. I may doze off too."

Grace rose, and kissed Adam. "See you in an hour."

"Love you."

"I love you."

Grace took off her clothes, pulled on a nightshirt and managed to read a few pages in her novel before falling asleep.

An hour and a half later she awakened, softly, slowly, stretching happily in the big, comfortable bed. The door opened a crack, and Adam poked his head into the room.

"Are you awake, love?"

"Barely. It's so comfortable, I wasn't ready to get up yet. How are you?"

"Great. Had a nap, feel energized."

Grace sat up and rubbed her neck.

"Is your neck still sore?" Adam asked.

"A little."

He came over and sat on the bed beside Grace. "Would you like a massage?"

"I'd be crazy to say no. Thank you."

She turned away from Adam, so he could reach her neck.

"If you lie down, it might be better," he suggested. "And I can rub your shoulders, too."

Grace turned and burrowed belly-down into the bed as Adam arranged pillows around and under her to support her back. He put some gently scented lotion on his hands. Climbed onto the bed and straddled her backside. Pulled off the shirt she had slept in.

31

Grace melted under his big, strong hands as they slid up her back to her neck, working and smoothing the muscles. His hands pushed back down, up the large muscles, down her spine, along her sides.

"Mmm," she murmured. "Are you a massage therapist on the side? I wouldn't think you'd have time."

"No, but I did take a couple of classes."

"You did?"

"Yes. When I was in L.A. in July."

Grace was quiet for a moment.

"Why did you do that, Adam?"

"Because I wanted to understand how to touch you. In every way."

He continued to prod and smooth, in long, slow, deep strokes.

"Adam, how sweet of you . . . oh . . ."

He had slipped the sheet down to expose her buttocks and started to stroke them.

The awareness that Adam was focused on her backside, completely bare to his view, sent an erotic spear through Grace's body. This wasn't just a back rub, she realized.

She didn't realize she had said it out loud.

"No," Adam said. "Not just a back rub. Unless you want it to be."

His fingers traced the line between her buttocks, then slid along the shape of them, below, around, back to the top. Grace's hips responded, thrusting into the pillow underneath; she squirmed, her backside coming up involuntarily toward Adam.

"Oh, God," she gasped. "Adam."

He began to breathe heavily, and Grace tried to turn over and start making love to him, but he had her pinned down.

"Babe," said Adam, in a husky growl. "Let me. Anything you don't like, tell me. I promise to stop. God, though, you have the most beautiful ass on Earth."

His hands went further down, massaging the backs of her thighs, then came back up slightly short of where Grace hoped he was going.

"Touch me, Adam."

"Not yet."

He stood up, turned Grace over and removed his jeans, allowing her to see his hardness; he wanted her to know exactly how he was feeling, to be as vulnerable to her as possible under the circumstances. He climbed back onto the bed to straddle her again, and began smoothing her neck muscles from the front, his hands sliding over her shoulders, down the sides of her breasts, across her stomach.

Grace reached for him, but he took her hands away.

"Don't, Babe. I won't make it. Hold on."

Avoiding the most obvious erogenous zones, Adam continued the massage until Grace wondered if she was going to survive it. Would she have to beg? Her body writhed and her brain swirled in an aroused fog. And still he touched her everywhere. Almost everywhere.

"Adam, God, Adam, you're making me crazy," she said. Aloud? She was no longer sure.

His head came down then. He sucked one nipple while he caressed the other, and Grace thought she might lose her mind, melt into another dimension. Her back arched, and she began to keen and pant. But Adam didn't stop.

Some strange immeasurable time later, with both hands on her breasts, Adam travelled down her body with his tongue and lips, slowly, slowly, and met her at the point of pleasure, kissing at first. Tongue flicking. Backing off, blowing gently.

Grace lifted her head from the pillow, looked down to see his head between her legs, his hands on her breasts, and vaguely wondered when it would end. Did she want it to?

"Adam. What are you doing to me? God, Adam . . . stop . . . oh don't . . ."

Adam returned to her with his tongue, using it slowly until even he couldn't stand it anymore.

"Come for me now," he whispered.

His lips tugged, his tongue curled, and Grace cried oh, oh, oh . . .

Her hips flexed down hard, then rose again as she thrust her hands into Adam's hair, and she was screaming his name and writhing and sliding up on the bed. The spasms went on and on and Adam stayed with her, hands firmly clasping her buttocks, following her as her body twisted and exploded.

Finally, it subsided. She slowed and lay limply, breathing hard.

Adam crawled up Grace's body and entered her immediately, felt her clutching him, so aroused he came suddenly and violently. And Grace came again, straining against him, crying out, clinging to his shoulders with her arms, his hips with her legs.

Adam waited for her to relax a little, and for his own breathing to become somewhat normal. He removed his face from her neck, braced himself on both arms and looked her in the eyes. He saw the tears, the cords in her neck standing out, and felt her ragged breathing against his chest.

"Grace. You're beautiful and erotic, and have never been more so."

*And that, fuckhead, is how you make love to this woman,* he added mentally to Mick Shaw.

Grace couldn't speak yet, wonderment at the experience leaving her without words. She tried to find them, but they wouldn't form in her mind.

"I've wanted to do that ever since the day in your kitchen, when you touched my lips and we kissed like it was the last thing we'd ever do," Adam went on. "You made me crazy. I wanted to make you crazy, make you want me as much as I wanted you."

Grace searched his eyes, then took his face between both hands and kissed him fully, for a long time, tasting herself on his lips.

"I have never, ever, been so aroused in my life," she said, sometime later. "Oh, Adam. I didn't know it was possible."

"Were you . . . afraid, at all, Grace?"

"A little," she admitted. "But. I . . ."

"What, Grace?"

"I was too far gone to care. And I think . . . I had to know. How it would be. Afterward."

"And?"

"I trust you, Adam. My body tells me so."

Adam's mouth curved into a crooked smile.

\*\*\*\*\*

Grace had long thought her reaction to Mick's boys-will-be-boys lovemaking was over the top, although she felt telling all his friends about it was going too far. But she couldn't help it. He made her feel like shit.

What if Adam had responded the same way? Crowing, tumbling her around in the bed, bragging about his technique and laughing at her? She would have shattered from disappointment and embarrassment.

Yet Adam took her very seriously when she told him about Mick, and had responded with that . . . what? That mind-disintegrating, erotic love massage, to take her out of herself

35

and allow her to feel the most intense pleasure she had ever experienced.

Sex was just sex with Mick. But with Adam, it was something else. Something life altering. Something more than physical. It terrified and transported her. It tore her apart, and melded her back together, more whole than before.

They fell asleep as one that night, tightly curled together, in that rare perfect rhythm of breath and exhaustion, peace and fulfilment.

Until Grace awakened with a start in the Stygian darkness, not knowing why. A sound? A strange, sharp, yet muffled sound.

Restlessly, she turned and through the open bedroom door, through the picture window, through the soaring trees, she saw a glimmer of red and orange — a small, shimmering dot of hot colour.

She leaped out of bed, grabbed her clothes and struggled into them as she sped out the door into the living room.

"Grace! What the hell?" Adam asked, waking. "What are you doing?"

"It's on fire, Adam. It's on fire! I have to go find him. I have to go."

# Chapter Five

G race had tugged on her jeans, pulled on a T-shirt, thrust her feet into sandals and grabbed a life jacket before Adam could take a breath.

"Grace, stop. Let me at least get my jeans on. What the hell is going on? Grace! Stop!"

She hesitated at the front door, already thrown open. Adam, struggling into a shirt, covered the distance between them in six long strides and took her by the arm, as gently as he could.

"Tell me what is happening," he said as calmly and deliberately as possible.

Grace simply pointed.

Adam then saw the flicker of flame in the distance, faintly painting the shadowy trees crimson, across the lake to the west.

"What do you plan to do about that? You can't put it out. We have to call the park's fire line."

"You don't understand," Grace cried. "He could be in there! He could be hurt. I have to go and see. Try to help him."

"Who could be in there?"

"There's no time to explain," said Grace, eyes huge and wild, pulling her arm out of Adam's grasp. "Let me go."

"No. I'm coming with you. But we only have a canoe, Grace. How will we get there in time to save . . . whoever? Even in a boat, it's unlikely."

"I have to try. We'll take a neighbour's boat. There are still a couple down at the water." Grace turned, flew down the steps and ran for the beach.

Adam grabbed his cellphone, took the flashlight off the shelf, pushed his feet into deck shoes, and raced down the path to catch up, unseen black branches scratching his cheek. *Duck*, he advised himself.

Starlight offered a little more illumination down at the water; the moon had long since set, but at least Adam could see a bit of something at the beach. By the time he caught up with Grace, she had indeed found a boat and was yanking the motor's throttle. Another glance at the island, and Adam perceived that the flames did not seem to constitute a forest fire. So far at least, they appeared localized and near the ground — not climbing into the canopy. His police sergeant's brain clicked, whirred and said *arson*.

But what the hell was on fire?

The motor chugged into life, then roared, and Adam jumped into the boat a moment before Grace gave it a surge of gas. In a second, they were flying across the water. Communication made nearly impossible over the noises of wind and motor, Adam simply watched Grace steer, terrified eyes huge under her whipping mane of hair, and tried to fathom what might be happening. His mind returned to what she had alluded to while they were canoeing.

*"I'll regale you with tales of adventure later,"* she had said. Something to do with the island. His abdominal muscles painfully gripped his stomach. Did Grace have a mysterious lover in her past? Was she racing to save him? If so, what in hell was he doing on that island?

They neared the island in a scant few minutes and Adam felt the heat from the flames, burning higher and hotter. Grace slowed the boat, navigating it to the west side. It skidded into the shore and Grace jumped into the shallow water, screaming over the roar of the fire.

"Elias! Elias!"

Adam, right behind her, bellowed at full volume.

"Grace, stop! It's a fire, for God's sake. Stop!"

He simultaneously tried to dial the RCMP; he had their number stored on his cellphone, although not the park fire line. Grace kept striving to cross the sand. I'm going to have to actually grab her, he thought; and as gently as possible wrapped an arm around her waist.

"Grace, wait. Let me call the damned RCMP, okay? This is dangerous."

As he spoke, he spied the remains of a tiny hut tucked into the trees, almost in ashes except the crumpling frame and twisted metal door. Did someone actually live in this minuscule cabin? Ridiculous. Or . . .

"Grace, is this a fishing or trapping hut or something? Do you know whose it is, then?"

"Yes! Elias's. Elias!" she shouted, again.

With one arm around her shoulders, holding her back from the flames as she struggled in his grip, Adam stepped backwards and pulled her with him as she tried to wriggle away. A voice crackled on the RCMP line, and the cop who answered obviously recognized the name on his call display.

"Davis. Al Simpson here. What's going on?"

"Fucking hell, Al, I'm in the middle of Ferguson Lake standing in front of a fire. Get someone out here now. Grace — ah, my girlfriend — says someone lives in a cabin on this island. It's actually no more than a hut, and it's on fire. The flames are starting to spread a bit to the trees, but it is an island and there's been lots of rain. That's not a big problem, but she thinks someone might be in there. Get out here."

"Got it, Davis. You sure as hell are getting into your share of trouble this year."

"Just call the fire people and get out here, Al," Adam yelled, and hung up.

He turned his attention to Grace, wrapped her in his arms and refused to let her approach the burning cabin.

"Okay, okay, take it easy, Babe. We have to be ready to move if that spreads, and what if they send a water bomber? We'll be flattened. Besides, if anyone is in there, it's too late. We can see from here there are no signs of life."

"I have to know if he's okay, if he's on the island." Grace pulled away again, this time successfully, and made for a path around the back of the hut, now a glowing husk. The fire was waning, and the trees were damp enough that it had not spread beyond a few nearby pines.

Adam smelled accelerant. Close behind Grace, he evaluated the forest fire risk and decided the flames were unlikely to erupt into a conflagration. Thank God, because Grace was tough to dissuade when she was determined.

He wished he had his firearm.

Still calling "Elias," Grace jogged around the side, looking everywhere, going deeper into the brush. Adam trained the flashlight on the ground ahead of her, hoping she wouldn't trip over the tree roots that crawled along the surface.

"Grace, for God's sake. You don't know what's going on here. Someone started that fire. He may still be here."

But Grace didn't register his words.

"Oh, no. Oh, my God. Elias," she whispered, and sank to her knees.

In front of her, on his stomach, lay the body of a tall man, long hair wrapped into a thick braid, blood pouring from his

40

head. Adam could see Grace shaking; he crouched beside her and took the man's pulse.

"He's dead," Grace said.

"Yes."

"But not from the fire? He's bleeding. Unless something fell on him inside the hut? And he wandered off?"

"No, Babe. Not from the fire. Come away now. The RCMP are on their way; there's nothing you can do for him."

Grace's eyes, brimming with sadness and fear, met Adam's in the beam of the light. Yet she turned back and touched the man's face.

"Goodbye, Elias," she said quietly. "I'm so sorry. Thank you for everything."

"Don't touch him anymore, Grace."

"You think he's been murdered."

"Yes."

*****

Job one, thought Adam, was to make sure Grace was safe, not to mention that he was. Whoever set fire to the hut and shot Elias in the back of the head could still be nearby: Adam was sure the fire had been set mere moments before Grace had awakened.

Had she, somewhere in her sleeping brain, registered the gunshot? Noise travelled clearly across expanses of water.

Adam saw no boat, but that didn't mean much. It was incredibly dark, and the island was more or less round. A boat could be stashed anywhere, around any curve.

That will teach me, he thought, not to ever leave my weapon behind. Even on civilian time. This woman of mine gets into more shit than I do.

41

Grace was momentarily tractable; she quivered from the shock of finding the dead man, and Adam was able to gently lead her back to the borrowed boat. He pushed away from the shore, started the motor and drove out into the water, praying they were out of gunshot range. He didn't have time, or enough light, to check the man's wound for a hint as to bullet calibre. They had to get away.

Back on shore in front of the cabins, Adam gathered Grace into his arms. She didn't weep, but shuddered and whimpered a bit, as she always did when deeply moved.

"I'm so sorry about your friend. Hush, now." Adam rubbed her back and kissed her hair. "Poor Love."

Grace was silent. She shook so hard she couldn't speak and hung on to Adam as if he were life support.

Waiting for the RCMP seemed interminable, but they arrived quickly considering the remoteness of the lake. Sirens blaring and lights flashing, an emblazoned SUV towing a police boat drove down the greenway. Adam climbed from the boat and shone the flashlight on the wide path, so the federal cops could find him in the dark.

The siren served as a signal; the beach suddenly came alive. Cabin owners, shocked into wakefulness, barrelled out of the cottages wrapping robes around themselves, calling to each other and to the police.

Sergeant Al Simpson greeted Adam while two other RCMP officers tried to manage the frightened little throng. A second vehicle screamed into the crescent bearing two more officers.

"What's going on, Adam?" asked Simpson.

"We found him, Al."

"Who? The guy in the hut?"

"Yeah. He wasn't in the hut. He was a few metres behind, shot in the back of the head."

"What do you think happened?"

42

"Someone was gunning for him. This was no hunting accident. The dead man — Grace says his name was Elias — probably locked himself in when the killer appeared, but the perp set fire to the hut. I smelled accelerant. It looks like he threw himself out the back window and made it a short distance before being shot. The door, when we saw it, was still partly closed against the frame, although twisted by the heat, so he didn't come out that way. If he had come out the door, he would have been shot in the face. That's my best guess."

Simpson nodded his head at Adam.

"Nice work. Okay. You'll have to come along and show us where he is."

"I would have stayed, Al, but I don't know where the killer is. I couldn't risk Grace being shot. And I'm unarmed."

"Fuck, Adam, of course not. No regrets, man."

"Thanks, Al. And maybe call off the water bomber, if they're thinking of sending one. The fire's almost out, and we don't want gallons of water dumped on us."

"Right," said Al, and turned to ask one of the constables to call the fire line again. "Let's get going. Looks like the boat's launched and ready to go."

"I'm coming with you." Grace had clambered out of the neighbour's boat they had used and come up behind Adam.

"You must be Grace," said the RCMP officer. "Nice to meet you. Are you all right?"

"No. And I'm coming with you."

"Now, ma'am . . ."

"Don't call me that. I found the body. I know who he is. And I know that island much better than any of you do."

"It's not safe, Grace."

"Please, Grace, please stay here . . ." Adam started.

"Why? How do you know it's safer here than there? What if he comes looking for me, and I'm alone? What if he saw me? You said yourself he might still have been on the island."

Deep pause. Damn it, thought Adam, she made some good points.

"I don't suppose you have any extra vests," he said to the RCMP sergeant.

"Yeah," Simpson sighed. "Two. Brought one for you, buddy, and there's always an extra one in the back."

Tillie Allbright finally broke through the tight police circle, questions pouring from her lips.

"What is going on? Has someone been hurt?"

"Ma'am. I'm Sergeant Simpson, RCMP. I'm afraid there has been an incident, but I can't tell you anything right now. I'm going to ask . . ."

He stopped and raised his voice.

"Everyone! I have to ask you all, please return to your cabins and stay inside, as a precaution. Please! Go back inside. There has been an incident across the lake. We are going to investigate now. We'll tell you what we can when we get back."

"Does this have something to do with that satellite salesman?" Tillie demanded.

Al Simpson turned confused eyes on Adam.

"We don't know, Tillie," Adam said. "But the RCMP will want to talk to you later. Right now, we really have to go. Okay? Stay inside. It will be fine."

The cottagers began to wander away from the scene shaking their heads, clearly unhappy about the lack of information being provided. But it was dark, chilly and the initial burst of adrenaline was wearing off. That worked in the police's favour.

One of the RCMP officers held out a bulletproof vest to Adam, and Simpson helped Grace put hers on. The crowded boat was pushed into the water, and Adam and Grace were speeding across the lake again.

Simpson asked Grace questions about the victim, yelling over the racket of wind and motor.

"Who was he? I understand you recognized him."

"Yes. His name was Elias Crow. He was a war veteran."

"A vet? From which war?"

"The civil war in Somalia. It wasn't exactly a peacekeeping mission, was it?"

"What the hell was he doing on that island?"

# Chapter Six

Elias Crow's body was gone.

Grace and Adam led the RCMP to the spot where he had been lying. And he was gone. Adam released an uncharacteristic stream of curses, livid at himself for not protecting the body, yet not knowing how he would have managed things differently. Whoever killed Elias Crow was still somewhere on the island, or very nearby, when they had found the body.

"He was still here, then," Simpson said softly. "Damn. That could have been really bad. Where the hell would he have gone? You said you didn't see a boat?"

"No, but it could have been anywhere."

"And we didn't hear one, although he may have made his escape while we were on our way over here," said Simpson. "Or while you were on the way back from finding him."

"He could have gone through the bay," said Grace. "Unless the motor's really loud, you can't hear a boat in the bay."

"It's pretty swampy on the other side of the bay," Al said. "Could he get through there?"

"It wouldn't be too hard to the south," said Grace. "It's firmer on that side, if he can make it over the first few metres of marsh."

"We'll have to organize a search. I don't know how much we can do before morning, though. Damn, it's so dark. No moon, either. Okay, look. We'll take you back to shore, but we're going to need more officers. Can we borrow your cabin to set things up?"

"Sure. Fine. Whatever you need, Sergeant," Grace said, wearily.

"Call me Al. I think we're going to get to know each other pretty well."

Al Simpson left the other officers on the island to investigate what they could by flashlight, and for the fourth time that night, Adam and Grace sped across the secretive, deep black water.

\*\*\*\*\*

Grace tried to make coffee but ended up spilling both the grounds and the water all over the kitchen counter. Adam gently took her by the shoulders, moved her into the bedroom, sat her down, came back to the kitchen and started the brewing machine.

Al sat at the dining room table, which would temporarily serve as office and muster point.

"I'll help you in the morning," said Adam. "First, coffee, and let me comfort Grace a bit."

"I need to know what she knows." Al looked up at Adam. "Soon."

"I realize that. I do, too."

Adam left Al and rejoined Grace in the bedroom to find her staring into space, arms clenched tightly around her body.

She gave a shudder, took a breath and without preamble or greeting started her story.

47

"Fourteen years ago, I got lost," she said. "Very lost. I don't know how it happened, to this day, really. I had been visiting my uncle and aunt at the campground. There wasn't enough room here at the cabin for them, because another aunt and uncle were staying with us. It was an extended-family weekend; my aunt was from the United States, so having her up for a visit was a rare thing.

"I didn't really want to go to the campground. I wanted to hang out with my American aunt. I loved her, so much. But my uncle wanted me to babysit his two kids, who were little at the time, while he and his wife came over for a visit with the adults.

"But they were drunk. They were also mad about being relegated to the camping area. I sure got an earful about that when I got there; he was ranting and being a jerk. It was clear even to me at the time that they were too drunk to drive and almost certainly too drunk to walk over. And it was already getting dark.

"After an hour of that, I told them I had to get back. Obviously, they weren't going to drive me; they didn't offer, either. I took off. I was a bit scared; there are a lot of big animals in these woods, as you know, and you don't want to stumble on a moose or a bear."

"No such thing as cellphones at the time," Adam noted.

"No; they weren't in widespread use, anyway. Even today, cell connection can be spotty up here.

"I headed for the path, but after a few minutes of walking, I heard something rustling in the trees; I panicked and turned away from the noise. I ended up on a path I didn't recognize — really an animal trail — and I was suddenly, utterly terrified. The flashlight didn't help at all; it threw eerie shadows and made me feel like I had a beacon shining on me."

Her voice dropped, and she whispered. "Here, bear. Here, wolf. Here I am, your dinner."

48

Grace paused, sniffed and shivered. Adam put a blanket around her shoulders.

"Do you want a drink, Grace? Let me get you some scotch or something. Wait here. Don't move."

Adam went out into the main area, made sure Al had helped himself to coffee, and grabbed two glasses and a bottle of Glendronach, his favourite single malt.

He poured two ounces for Grace. After she had downed a sip or two, she went on.

"Thank you," she said first, with a weak smile. "I'll make this as short as I can.

"After fifteen, twenty minutes of thrashing around in the dark, I started to cry. I didn't know what to do. I was being eaten alive by mosquitoes and it was getting pretty chilly. Out of nowhere, I heard a human voice. I thought my insides were going to fall out of me. Who could be out there in the dark? I stopped crying, held my breath and huddled behind a tree.

"The voice said, "Miss Grace? Is that you?" Who on Earth would call me Miss Grace? I didn't answer, although I thought about it. You know: Yes! Yes! It's me! Come save me! But I didn't know who it was, although he obviously knew me.

"Well, it didn't matter. He had found me. A moment later, I could barely make out the shadow of a man — a very big man, right in front of me. He stood there, not moving, and finally said, 'Please don't be afraid, Miss Grace. It's just Elias.'

"The whole thing clicked together. He was the man everyone called the Hermit. I thought he was a legend; a myth, would be a better word. A story was going around at the time about a war veteran who had built a cabin in the woods and a fishing shack on the island. He had come back from serving overseas with terrible PTSD and couldn't bear being around people. So, he lived this quiet life off the grid, and he was big and really messed up. People talked about him in hushed tones; they were afraid of him.

49

"He said, 'I won't hurt you. I'll help you find your way home.' And I figured he had me anyway. How would I get away from someone who knew the woods that well in the darkness? And I mean dark. It was pitch black, even darker than tonight.

"He took me by the arm without another word and led me through the forest. Eventually, we got to the path I was familiar with. He walked me to the cabin, turned and walked away."

"But that wasn't the only time you met him, was it?" Adam asked.

"No. I saw him a few more times. I went looking for him — in daylight, of course — and the first time I found him, I think I spooked him. I wanted to thank him, properly. But of course, I was also curious as hell. Anyway, when he spotted me, he ran off.

"But the second time, he talked to me. It was months later, and he was in better mental shape, for whatever reason. Maybe he had healed a bit by then.

"I asked him what all that "Miss Grace" stuff was about and told him to call me Grace. He laughed and said he used the honorific so I wouldn't be frightened. He was trying to demonstrate respect and show that he knew who I was. 'Well,' he said, 'I thought if I used your name, you'd be less scared. I thought using 'Miss' made me sound nice.' And he was nice. After that, I'd try to find him every time I came to the lake. Went fishing with him, once."

"Tell me about him. Who was he?"

"I don't know a lot, really; he didn't want to talk about his past. He was from a nearby First Nation. He was vague about what had happened to him. I looked up some news coverage later, and from the timing, I think he might have been involved in an incident in Somalia, when the Canadian Airborne was on the ground there in 1993."

"Not the Shidane Arone murder?" Adam asked. He, and everyone else in Canada, remembered with horror the death of a Somali teenager at the hands of two crazed soldiers. The brutal Arone affair led to an inquiry and the disbanding of the elite Canadian Airborne Regiment. A Saskatchewan soldier named Clayton Matchee attempted to take his own life after being charged with second-degree murder; he did not succeed, but brain damage caused by the attempt made him unfit to stand trial.

"It wasn't the Arone killing. I think it was a raid on a village near the Airborne camp."

"I don't think I'm familiar with that."

"It didn't get a lot of public notice. Neither did the case of a Somali man shot to pieces after trying to steal from the base at Belet Huen. The Shidane Arone killing seemed to take over national attention, especially since it ended up the focus of an inquiry. But I looked up the shooting at Belet Huen. An Airborne captain had decided that petty theft was sabotage, so the soldiers had a shoot-to-kill order if they caught someone stealing. They used it."

"Could he have been in Rwanda? Our forces were there at about the same time."

"It's possible. I couldn't find any really ugly stories about our soldiers there, but many of them came back having seen terrible things, too.

"I asked Elias what happened, that second time I found him, and his demeanour changed. Completely. He shook and stuttered, and I thought he was dealing with PTSD. The physical manifestations were shocking to me; he had seemed very calm until then.

"He just said, 'They saw monsters.' Over and over again. Then he said, 'They followed them. They followed them! They saw monsters.' But he said they, not 'I' or 'we.' I interpreted that as meaning he wasn't involved, but it's hard to say.

51

"What I was able to piece together," Grace went on, for a moment, and stopped. "It wasn't much. Something happened in that village."

Grace's voice cracked, and she began to weep openly.

"Stop, Babe, that's enough for now." Adam reached out to hold her.

She swallowed hard but shook her head and finished her story.

"After that, Elias fell off the Earth. He landed at Ferguson Lake, and enclosed himself in the forest. And now he's dead."

"You never did a story on it."

"No."

"Why?"

"By the time I became a reporter, all of that was well in the past. All I could go on was news coverage, before that. And I couldn't ever, ever betray Elias. He may have saved my life. The least I could do was protect his privacy. But what if I'm wrong, and he was involved?" Grace paused. "And what awaited him, if he was found?"

Grace looked up at Adam with angry, tear-filled eyes.

"Now we know."

# Chapter Seven

At four in the morning, Adam persuaded Al Simpson to grab some sleep in the tiny third bedroom off the living area. Simpson had assembled a search party, filed a report, alerted his superiors by phone and now had to wait through at least two more hours of utter darkness.

"Nothing's going to happen until dawn, Al. You might as well try to have a nap. You'll be a piece of crap in the morning otherwise."

Al capitulated. Adam returned to the bedroom he shared with Grace, tugged off his jeans and pulled her down into the quilts. He rubbed her back and tried to get her to calm down.

"This is going to be a shit storm. Isn't it." She wasn't asking.

"Yeah. Try to sleep, Grace. Chaos arrives in a couple of hours."

Adam didn't think he would be able to sleep, and doubted Grace would, either; yet comforted by the warmth of each other's bodies, exhausted by the long and bizarre night, they slipped into a dreamless, brief oblivion.

Until chaos did, in fact, arrive.

At six-thirty, uniformed men and women swarmed into the Rampling cabin. Adam awakened at the slam of the first car door. He rolled out of bed, pulled on jeans and a shirt and slipped out of the bedroom in seconds, closing the door behind him to shelter a naked Grace from the churning group of officers.

But two minutes later, Grace was dressed, unruly hair pulled into a slightly crazy ponytail, pale face as composed as possible, and out in the living area.

"Food," she said, finding Adam in the throng as she nodded politely to the other officers. "Do they need food? Coffee?"

"They might. Al will, and the officers who came with him last night. We certainly do."

"Okay. Can you put the coffee pot on? I'll run over to ask Tillie for supplies. Eggs, bread, whatever she has. We definitely don't have enough for this crew."

Grace plunged her feet into well-worn deck shoes and fled out the door, craving a few moments away from the rapidly-developing madness. Adam watched her go; saw her stop, briefly, when she reached the lakefront; saw her look out over the water to the right, tilt her head to one side; saw her look down.

"Aw, Babe," he whispered under his breath.

Then she lifted her head and hurried down the path toward the Allbrights' cottage. Tillie met her before she knocked.

"What is going on, Grace?" she said, dispensing with a greeting. "This is pretty frightening."

"I don't know how much I can say yet, Tillie. I think whatever happened wasn't random."

"It was the Hermit. Wasn't it?"

Grace nodded.

54

"I didn't tell that salesman, Grace. I didn't tell him anything."

"I know, Tillie. It's not your fault, I know it isn't. But whoever he was, that salesman, we have to find him. The RCMP are going to ask you a lot of questions. Are you ready for that?"

"Hell yes. Bring it on."

"But Tillie, I didn't come over to talk about it. I don't have time. I also don't have enough food. Could I borrow some eggs, maybe? Do you have any bread, juice, anything you can spare? I have something like ten or twelve cops in my cabin right now. At least four of them, not to mention Adam, are very hungry."

"You've come to the right cabin, my dear. And I'll come help you."

"I promise to replace the food, Tillie. I'm so sorry to have to ask."

"Forget about it. Let me find the cooler and we'll fill it up."

Moments later, Grace and Tillie were carrying the big cooler between them by its handles; it was heavy, laden with eggs, bread and butter, fresh muffins, orange juice and a coil of farmer sausage.

"I can't thank you enough," said Grace, huffing a little as they hoisted the cooler up the deck stairs.

"You can tell me what on God's Earth happened," said Tillie, breathing hard. "That's how you can thank me enough."

A cheer greeted the two women as they came through the door. Adam started the barbecue and prepared to cook the sausage. Grace scrambled three dozen eggs and melted Swiss cheese on top. Tillie made whole wheat toast, laid out the blueberry muffins and mixed the orange juice. Paper plates were filled and refilled with the savoury and sweet breakfast foods; juice and coffee were poured into plastic and pottery cups. Police officers sat on the couch, the chairs, and the deck to eat on their laps. Half an hour later, not a crumb remained.

"That's how we do it at Ferguson Lake," announced Tillie, accustomed to cooking massive meals for cottagers' meetings.

"Well, thank God it was we and not just me," Grace said, dropping into a chair.

Al Simpson took the opportunity to come and sit beside her.

"Thank you. I sure appreciate it, Grace. And you, ma'am," he said to Tillie, nodding at her. "I need to have a quiet chat with you now. Adam?" he called across the room, where Adam was chatting with the officers. "Want to join us on the deck?"

"You bet."

Settled in a far corner away from the buzz, Al sat across from Grace and Adam with a notebook and asked, "Who was Elias Crow? How did you know him, and why did you care enough about him to race across the lake in the middle of the goddamn night?"

"He may have saved my life." Grace wondered, by the way he asked the question, if he thought Elias had been her lover. "I owed him the same. It's a long story."

"Give me the short version. We can talk more later."

Grace gave Al the abridged version of what she had told Adam a few hours earlier.

"He served, as I said, in Somalia, as far as I know," she said, ending her tale.

"What was he doing on that island?" asked Al, repeating the question he had asked five hours ago.

"He had his fishing shack there. I never did find his main cabin. It was well hidden in the woods. Or is. I don't know. He may have moved at some point."

"But what was he doing there? Why didn't he live on the reserve? Did he live full time on the island and in the cabin?"

"Yes, he did. The PTSD drove him away from society. Or so I thought. Maybe it was something else that made him choose to live alone in the forest. He is dead."

56

"You think he was hiding."

"Well, he may have been, right? In light of what's happened."

"Your neighbour said something about a salesman. What's that about?"

"You'll have to ask her the details. A man who said he was selling satellite dishes knocked on her door one day, a little while ago. No one does door-to-door sales out here, Al. You know that."

"Right. Okay. We'd better get going. It's going to be a tough search."

"Grace," Adam put in, "before we go, do you have any idea where his cabin might be?"

"Well, I have some ideas. But they're just ideas."

Grace went inside and returned carrying the large map of the provincial park that hung over the couch. She showed Al and Adam the spots she had long suspected could harbour Elias's more permanent home, if you could call it that.

"It can't be here," she said, pointing to an area south and east. "There's a little lake right there, then the Beaver River. And it can't be here," she added, "because it's too close to the fire break. Too exposed. It also can't be here." Grace indicated an area she knew was particularly swampy; she had tried to walk through it and around it, with no success, more than once.

"So it's got to be here, or here, or here." Grace showed the officers areas mostly south and west of the islands and the bay. "I've noticed, a few times, bits of things when walking around there, mostly when I went looking for him. You know, things that didn't fit — not garbage; that's tourist spoor. But fish scales. A snarl of fishing line. A little piece of woolen fabric. No one comes out this way in the cold weather, or at least, very few people; you don't see evidence of winter clothes very often. And fish scales? No. It had to be Elias. So my best guess is here."

57

Grace pointed to a spot south of the second island, and to the west — a considerable distance. "I was too afraid to go that far in," she whispered.

"It's okay, Grace," Adam said. "It's okay. You couldn't have prevented this, no matter what you did."

"God, I hope you're right."

Al took the map, motioned to Adam, and went back inside to organize his people.

Five minutes later, the cabin was empty, except for piles of dirty dishes, a carpet of crumbs and a huge garbage bag full of discarded cups and plates. And Tillie Allbright, up to her elbows in soapy water.

Grace flatly refused to be left behind.

"You will never find the path without me," she argued. "That map won't help you."

Al wordlessly held out a Kevlar vest and a helmet, and moments later she was back on the lake, bumping across the water in the early light — not to save a man, but to find his corpse for the second time.

\*\*\*\*\*

Three police boats roared in horizontal formation until they neared the first island; there, they slowed and proceeded single file. Grace, in the lead boat with Al, Adam and another constable, pointed with her arm to the right and turned her wrist to the left.

Slowly, they turned around the big island, then the little one, and slipped into shore just before the bay's opening. Grace scrambled over the gunnel, splashed into the warm shallows and waded in before Adam could stop her.

She stood on the sandy shore before Al could take a breath. He raised his eyebrows at Adam.

"Wait!" Adam called, as requested by those eyebrows. "Grace, you could wait for us."

She stopped. Elias was dead, after all. And whoever killed him had had hours to get away.

"Sorry," she said when the other officers joined her. "I'm a little anxious, apparently."

"It's okay, Grace. Just stay close. We don't know what this guy is capable of, or where he is. Let's try not to get you shot today, okay?" Adam asked.

"Yeah. Okay. This way."

Grace ducked under the low-hanging branches of the coniferous trees and plunged down a deer trail. She couldn't remember where that path led, or where she had once turned off, but this was definitely the right outlet from the shore.

Bless September, she thought a bit wildly, as she alternately strode and stumbled over the uneven terrain: there were few biting insects, and the weather was crisp, warm and fine.

Moments later, she pulled up: another path, barely noticeable, led off to the right. She had never, as she told Al and Adam, followed it to the end, too frightened to be that deep in the forest alone. Being lost on the night Elias found her had not improved her nerve.

"I think this might be it," she said to Adam, who was right behind her.

"Not sure, though."

"No."

"Well, you'd know better than any of us, so let's go. We should try to be very quiet, Grace."

"Have I been crashing through the forest?"

"Maybe a little."

Adam held up an arm and pointed to the right, indicating Grace's change in direction to the RCMP officers following behind. Grace took Adam's warning to heart, and crept along the path, both arms up to keep the tree branches from poking her in the face. She kept her eyes down, to avoid tripping on tree roots and to seek bits of evidence that Elias had been there.

Half a kilometre later, she sensed more than saw the clearing ahead. The light changed from filtered to dappled; birdsong echoed instead of chirped. Fish scales glittered on the path. Bits of detritus hung from trees or littered the ground: a broken unbarbed hook, and incongruously, a pompom from a woolen hat. Like a child's hat but belonging to a grown man who had felt forced to remove himself from the company of others. Grace's eyes burned.

"We're there," she whispered to Adam.

"I can feel it," he said, letting out a breath. "Let me go first, now, Grace. But stay close behind, in case the killer is still around."

Adam stopped and held up his arm again, in a signal to the other officers. He said something sotto voce to Al, who stepped ahead of Grace. The two police officers, one municipal, one federal, drew weapons — Al had provided one for Adam — and advanced down the last few metres of the trail.

There, in a clearing, stood a cabin — small, but palatial compared to the burned-out shack on the island. An outhouse was behind it, along with a small shed. All three buildings needed considerable attention but looked sturdy enough.

Grace wondered if Elias was inside — or his killer, armed, dangerous and possibly deranged: he could start shooting immediately from the shelter of the cabin. Al made a swinging motion with his hand, and in seconds the officers surrounded the main building.

One, two, three . . .

"Police!" Al bellowed, kicking in the door at the identical moment.

It was only a one-room shack. Adam and Al determined immediately that no one was moving inside. Officers who had deployed to the outhouse and shed waited for Al's call, which came a second later.

"All clear," Al called.

"All clear in the outhouse."

"All clear in the shed."

Adam walked into the cabin and straight over to the mangled body lying on the floor.

They had found Elias Crow.

# Chapter Eight

A revolting mess of blood, splintered bone and grey matter disfigured the back of the dead man's head. The killer had gone in to dig for and remove the ammunition. He had apparently been successful.

Unless, of course, the bullet had gone straight through. Adam and Al carefully turned Elias over to see if there was an exit wound, but there was not. Ballistics wouldn't be helping them much in this investigation.

"What now?" Adam asked Al, since it was officially his case.

"We get him out of here. Fast. The body is already worse for wear."

Adam thought for a moment. How fast could they get the pathologist out here? Could they fly him out of Saskatoon in a hell of a hurry? No. Not fast enough. Did Meadow Lake have a coroner? He asked Al.

"No. No coroner; only some members of the northern major crime unit of the RCMP. Including me."

Al was right. They would have to do what they could, take pictures and get the body out of harm's way — out of the killer's reach, and of the beasts and insects of the forest.

"Got a tarp?"

"Yeah. Ellard brought one in his kit."

"Okay. Let's go."

Adam went out to speak to Grace, while Al called together his officers and began giving orders.

"Grace, Elias is inside."

"I thought he must be. You've been in there for a while."

"We're going to bring his body out and take him back. We can't leave him here any longer. Are you ready for that?"

"N – no. But I don't see a choice. I'll have to get ready."

"I'm going to help Al. I won't be long. Are you okay?"

Grace nodded, although limply.

"I'd feel better if you weren't out here, even with the other cops. God knows if this guy is still around. Could you head into the shed, maybe?"

"I'd rather be in the cabin with you."

"It will be upsetting."

"I know."

"I'll ask Al if he's okay with that. It's not exactly protocol, but it would be safer. You can't report on anything though, okay?"

Grace bristled. "Not on anything? Adam, a man is dead by violent means. It's reportable. And I'm a witness. Again."

Adam sighed. "I know."

In the end, Adam, Al and Grace agreed that she could report the death of Elias Crow, but not his name; that he was found near Ferguson Lake, Saskatchewan; that the RCMP was treating the death as a homicide. But any forensic evidence was off the record, for now.

"What about the fire? Forty people saw the flames, as they were dying, anyway," Grace argued. "That piece of news is already all over the rural municipality and the provincial park, I guarantee it."

"Fine," Al groused.

Adam permitted himself a small grin as he turned back to the cabin. Grace got her way, as usual.

"I'm going to try calling the forensic pathologist," he said to Al, as they prepared to re-enter the shack. "See if he has any advice."

"It's Sunday at seven-thirty in the morning, Adam."

"I have his home number."

"Have at it. Grace, this is pretty gory."

"So was the dead bishop I found with his head bashed in this spring."

Al's eyes widened. "You're always in the wrong place, aren't you?"

"So it seems."

Even so, Grace hesitated before entering the cabin. She hadn't known the bishop, but she did know Elias, making his death a different and more personal matter.

Adam and Al had left Elias on his stomach after turning him over, briefly, to check for an exit wound. Adam now stalked over to him and placed his big body between Grace and the corpse.

"Stay by the door, Grace," he asked. "Okay, let's see if I can get any cell service."

Adam dialled the home number of Jack McDougall, the aging Scot who headed the sole pathology department in the province; he performed all autopsies in cases of suspicious deaths. Adam hoped he would get reception for his cellphone, that Jack was home, and he wouldn't ask Adam to go to hell.

The phone worked. At least, Adam could hear ringing.

"McDougall," came a big voice with a soft brogue.

"Jack. It's Adam Davis."

"Go to hell, Sergeant. It's seven-fucking-thirty in the blasted a.m. On a Sunday. My day *off*."

"Jack, I'm standing in a shack in the middle of nowhere in northern Saskatchewan looking at a body with a big hole in its

64

skull." Adam rattled the sentence off as quickly as he could. Jack wasn't above hanging up.

There was a pause, but Jack was still on the line.

"I don't know how long I'm going to have reception," Adam added.

"Okay. You still owe me scotch from the last time. What do you need?"

Adam's lip curved upward. *Got him.*

"Tell me what to look for before we move him. We have to get him out of here. He's already a little fucked up."

"You mean apart from being, what, bashed in the head?"

"Shot, actually. And yeah, animals or birds and insects. He was also in a fire, but he was alive at the time."

"Right."

Jack talked Adam and Al through checking and preserving the wound to the extent possible, although there was little they could do with what they had on hand.

"Are there any other wounds?"

"We're checking now."

They found no more gunshot wounds, but Elias was badly burned on his hands and face, as well as scratched and bruised, likely from flinging himself out the window of his fishing shack.

"Okay. Bag him up tight and get him out of there. Oxygen is your enemy. How long before he gets to Saskatoon?"

Adam looked at Al, who could hear Jack's voice over the phone.

"Depends how fast I can get a plane and an ambulance," Al said. "First we have to get him out of here and to Meadow Lake, which has the nearest air strip and ambulance service."

Adam nodded. "Not sure how long this will take," he told Jack. "I'll keep you posted."

"Get a move on, gentlemen. The sooner, the better. Goodbye. Don't forget to take a hundred pictures. Or my scotch."

Officers took photos, wrapped the body, gathered evidence and prepared to head back. Police tape would be no help to them here, so they had to do what they could under the time constraints and accept the consequences.

Four officers heaved Elias Crow into their arms and arranged themselves to protect his mutilated head. They carried his heavy body, stiff in rigor mortis, down the narrow paths of the forest.

Grace led the way out of the clearing, back along the trails and to the water's edge. She knew she would have to file a story the moment she returned to the cabin and focused her attention on writing it in her head. It diverted her from the horror following behind.

Al Simpson had called for an ambulance before they started to wrap and move the body, and Adam caught himself praying the emergency vehicle would be waiting when they returned to the cabin area, although he knew it was unlikely to arrive so quickly. He wanted Elias's body on its way to Saskatoon, and in the hands of Jack McDougall, as fast as possible — not only for the sake of the investigation, but to release Grace from the pain his presence brought.

Finally, they made it to the shoreline and carefully placed the body in one of the boats. During a silent and sombre trip back across the water, Adam held Grace tightly, trying to comfort her against his heart.

"We're going to have company when we get back," Adam said to Al, as quietly as possible over Grace's head and the motor's noise. He nodded toward the shore.

"Yeah. I've been thinking about that."

"If you want, I can try to do crowd control while you deal with the victim."

"I'd appreciate that."

"Good luck," said Grace. She knew her fellow cottagers.

The ambulance had not yet arrived, but Tillie was there, standing on the dock awaiting them, with the others gathered behind on the beach. Grace touched Adam's face and disentangled herself from his grip.

"Let me see what I can do," she said, jumping out of the boat as it slipped onto the beach. "Give me a minute."

She took the few steps across the sand and walked onto the dock, where she put her arms around Tillie.

"You don't want to see this, Tillie. Go back to the cottage."

As Grace spoke, more cottagers began to arrive at the beach. They'd been watching from their lakefront windows, waiting for the police to return. Curiosity won over fear, and a small crowd began to form as it had in the middle of the night.

"Everyone," Grace said steadily. "Go back. Give the police some room to deal with . . . with this. Please."

She surveyed the cottagers as they hesitated.

"We need to know what's going on, Grace," said one of the men. He owned a new and fancy cottage — more of a house, really — four doors down from the Rampling place. George Best was not one of Grace's favourite neighbours; he liked to think he was in charge, and it tended to get on her nerves.

She sighed and turned to Adam, by now out of the boat and on the beach, keeping his body positioned between the cottagers and the corpse.

"I'm sorry," Adam said, his big baritone booming authority. "We can't tell you much yet. There has been an incident."

"What's it got to do with the fire last night?" George asked. "Obviously someone is dead."

"The fire was part of it," Adam said, being as vague as possible. He opened his mouth to ask them again to back away, but the scream of a siren split the air. Adam waded into the crowd.

67

"Okay, everyone, please leave the greenway. Quickly. Right now!" he shouted, as some of the cottagers stood as if frozen in place. "Please let the ambulance through."

Left with no choice but to move or be mowed down, the group split apart to give the ambulance access.

The big vehicle stopped and two paramedics leaped out, spun to the back of it, pulled out a gurney and hurried to the boat. With help from the police officers, they rapidly and expertly covered the body with a sheet, lifted him onto the gurney and back into the ambulance. And drove away.

It happened so fast, the cottagers seemed dumbfounded; but as soon as the ambulance left, a babble of voices rose again. Grace turned and ran down the path back to her cabin, leaving Adam and Al to argue with Tillie, George, and the rest of them.

\*\*\*\*\*

"Claire, it's Grace. I'm sorry to bother you at home on a Sunday."

"Hi, Grace," said Claire Davidson, the city editor at the StarPhoenix. "Aren't you supposed to be at the lake?"

"Yes, and I am, which is partly why I didn't check to see who is on call this weekend. So, I called you. Claire, I have a story for tomorrow's paper."

"From Meadow Lake? Or wherever you are?"

"I'm near Meadow Lake, at Ferguson Lake. There was a fire here last night, Claire, and a man died. But he didn't die in the fire. He was shot in the head."

There was a pause at Claire's end.

"And you know this because? Are you getting press releases on your phone?"

"We found him, Claire. Adam and I found him."

"Not again. Christ, Grace. That's two bodies you've found in what, seven months? Well, three, sort of." She paused again. "Are you all right?" she asked in a different tone.

"No, not really." Grace gave a funny little bark, a laugh choked with tears. She cleared her throat. "I knew him, slightly. The victim. It's a long story."

"I have time."

Grace gave her the short version. She wanted to get at writing the story.

"Right," said Claire. "Wow. I'll let John know it's coming. Do you know when the RCMP will send a release?"

"No, they didn't say. They were scrambling to get the body out of the forest and into Saskatoon as fast as possible for the autopsy, and I bet half the detachment was here."

"Okay. Got a story length for me?"

"It won't be very long — maybe six hundred words. Can the weekend reporter get some reax, if the release shows up in time? I can give you the details and the colour."

"No problem. Thanks, Grace. Take care of yourself up there, for God's sake. Adam's with you now?"

"Yes," Grace lied. "We'll be fine. Thanks, Claire."

Grace hung up and buried her face in her hands. She took a few deep breaths, and when she looked up again, two bloodshot eyes were staring at her through the window.

# Chapter Nine

No time nor breath to scream. Grace shot out of her chair, turned hard right, ran through the kitchen and bolted out the back door, down the driveway, out to the dirt road and turned left to the greenway.

Then she screamed.

"Adam!"

In deep conversation with Al and two other officers, standing on the slope of the beach, his head snapped around when he heard Grace's voice; he saw her sprinting toward him, hair streaming behind her. He loped up the slant and ran toward her, taking in her wide eyes and full-tilt flight.

Adam caught her by the shoulders.

"Grace, what the hell? Are you all right?"

She wanted to throw herself into his arms and cry, but Grace would be damned before showing that kind of weakness or emotion before the other officers.

"There's . . . a . . . man . . . "

"Slow down, Grace. Catch your breath."

"No! There's a . . . man at . . . the cabin," she got out. "He was staring at . . . me through the . . . the window and then tried to open the door."

"Did you recognize him?" Adam asked, motioning to the other officers.

"I don't know. It happened so fast."

Adam, with Grace in tow, strode with the other officers toward the cabin, guns drawn.

"Did you see a weapon?"

"No."

"What's wrong with this guy? Can't he see all the cops crawling around here? Dave, can you radio Al and get him over here?"

"Sure thing, Sarge."

"Where the hell are we going to put you, Grace?"

It seemed clear nowhere was safe right now. Adam stopped for a fleeting second, stared at the woman he loved, and shook his head.

"Stay behind me."

A minute later, six officers surrounded the Rampling cabin, but found no one outside, nor in the shed.

"Going in," someone said.

Two officers surged through the front door, and two came in the back. No one inside, either. The red-eyed man was gone; but he had obviously been there. Chairs had been toppled. Grace looked around wildly, worried now about her computer and cellphone.

"I'm staying with Grace," Adam told the officers. "No choice." They nodded and left to search the subdivision.

Grace dropped to her knees and fished under the table; her phone was there, tucked under the oak pedestal. She must have knocked it down in her hurry, spun it skidding along the carpet. As she rose, Adam reached for her; but she said one word and rushed to the bedroom.

71

"Computer."

Grace always hid her computer when she travelled, and that included trips to the cabin. The Rampling family had experienced one break-in, over all the years they'd been coming to Ferguson Lake; the only victim had been the liquor cabinet. Even so, thought Grace, my life is in that laptop. No point in advertising its existence.

Again on her knees, she dug it out from under the bed, and collapsed with relief.

"I have to write a story. Thank God it's here."

Adam gave her a crooked grin. "Is that all you can think about?"

"No." Grace crawled across the floor, clawed up Adam's body and pressed herself into him. "No. Oh, Adam. This is not what I had in mind."

He wrapped her tightly in his arms. "Thank God you're safe. To hell with the computer."

"To hell with peace and quiet and making love, too." A bitter tone crept into her voice.

"Hey, hey, Babe, it's going to be okay. None of this is anyone's fault; we'll find some time."

"We didn't get to California, either," Grace mumbled. It still stung that they had been forced to cancel a four-day getaway in the summer due to another violent death. Adam had been in California, hoping Grace would meet him there; but he was forced to come home, as the police service's foremost crime solver.

"I know."

The scales of guilt were balancing, but it was little comfort to Grace.

"Will you kiss me, please?" she whispered.

Adam lowered his head; his lips softened into seriousness from the sympathetic half-smile they had worn, and he gently placed them on Grace's. But Adam's kiss never failed to rouse her, and in a moment she slipped her tongue between his teeth, diving in for deeper sensation. Before long, their meeting lips stirred passion . . . and were rudely interrupted by a knock.

"Hell," Adam muttered. Giving Grace's mouth a longing gaze, he turned away with a pained shrug toward the door.

"Hey, Al," he greeted the sergeant. "Any luck?"

"No. Can I come in? I need to talk to Grace."

"Yes, of course."

Grace emerged from the bedroom, gave Al a shaky smile and invited him to take a seat in the living room.

"Coffee?"

"No, I'm fine, thanks. Tell me what happened."

"I had hung up with my editor a second before. I looked down for a minute, and when I looked up again, a man was staring at me through the window with these red-rimmed, bloodshot eyes. I took off as he reached for the door knob and ran down to the beach to find Adam. That's it."

"Did you recognize him?"

"I don't know. As I said to Adam, it happened so fast, and I didn't stick around for a second look."

"No, I guess not." Al paused. "But you said you aren't sure."

"No, I'm not sure."

"Does that mean you have a guess?" Adam asked.

"Not really. I have this sense that he was vaguely familiar. I didn't actually recognize him, though."

"Can you describe him at all, Grace?"

She furrowed her brow in concentration.

"He wore a hat; a ball cap, I think. I didn't see his hair. Dark eyes. Thin. Flannel shirt, maybe? Something bulky, anyway. Medium height. He was bending forward peering at me, so it was hard to tell. Five ten? And he was filthy."

"That's pretty good for a two-second glimpse."

"Reporters, you know," Adam said, with an admiring look at Grace.

"Oh, please," she said, although privately she loved the compliment. "Look, I have to get to work."

"I'd better get back out there." Al rose to his feet. "I have twelve officers combing the place, but I'm another set of eyes. Call me if you think of anything else, Grace. Any time. Okay?"

"Yes, of course. Thanks, Al."

Adam saw him to the door. "The killer, do you think?"

"Who else?"

"I don't know, but he'd have to be insane to show up here. And would he know which cabin was Grace's?"

Al mulled that over.

"Good point. But who else would be harassing Grace, out here?"

"No idea. But I'll ask her to think about it. Have you talked to Tillie yet?"

"Nope. Haven't had time. Something about a salesman?"

"Yeah. Strange timing for a salesman to show up here, and then for this to happen."

"Right. I'll be in touch, probably sooner than you'd like."

By the time Adam returned to Grace, the cabin was tidy and she was typing her story into the computer, at ninety words per minute.

\*\*\*\*\*

**The StarPhoenix**
Online edition, 1:24 p.m.
Sunday, Sept. 16

**Body discovered in Saskatchewan's lake country**

By Grace Rampling

of The StarPhoenix

A man was found dead near the shore of a northern Saskatchewan lake early Sunday morning. RCMP are treating the death as a homicide.

This reporter was on the scene after noticing a fire on a small island in Ferguson Lake, forty kilometres northwest of Meadow Lake. It consumed a tiny shack and several trees but did not cause a forest fire.

The man was discovered near the shack shortly afterward.

RCMP responded quickly and the body was prepared for transport to Saskatoon, where the province's forensic pathologist will conduct an autopsy.

Police said they are not providing further details at this time, including the man's identity. However, the man's injuries indicated foul play.

*More . . . .*

Grace sent the story to the newsroom by email and slumped in her chair.

She regarded Adam, reading quietly in the overstuffed armchair, waiting for her to finish. He was probably dying to get out there and help the RCMP, but he was stuck here in the cabin. Protecting her. How stupid was that?

She went over to Adam, kneeled before him and hugged his legs.

"What do you want to do?" she asked. "I can't just sit here and wonder if that man will come back, or what is going on out there. Do you think he was the killer?"

"I don't know. It's possible, but what would the killer be doing on your deck with a dozen cops running around the crescent?"

"Maybe he's screwed up. Well, obviously; he just killed Elias."

"That's a different kind of screwed up. He had the sense to remove the body and the ammunition. I don't think he's crazy; he was acting in a rational way. For a murderer."

Grace thought for a moment.

"I see your point. Then who?"

"Can you think of anyone it might have been?"

"No. Nothing else makes sense." Grace paused. "Whoever murdered Elias has also killed my peace of mind. This place has always been my escape."

"It will be again, love."

Grace wasn't so sure about that, but she nodded.

"Do you think it was that salesman?"

"Well, if he's not the killer, he more than likely has a connection to Elias's murder. Elias's army service is not the only possibility, though. You could argue that it was a family member, or it was race-related, or that someone didn't want him on that island." Adam, regarding Grace's face, stopped musing. "What, Grace? You've gone white. What?"

Face clammy with sweat, Grace got to her feet, ran outside and was violently sick in the tall, drying grasses.

# Chapter Ten

Adam shot out the door after Grace, wondering what the hell he had said.

"Grace, are you all right?" He drew her hair away from her face, as she bent retching over the deck's railing.

She shook her head, slightly.

"I'll get you some water. Hold on."

Grace sank to her knees and waited.

"Here, drink a bit of this. Small sips," Adam added, as she started gulping the water.

"Ugh. God. I'm so sorry. And so embarrassed."

"I've done worse, seen worse and cleaned up after worse. It's okay. Besides, you had just thrown up the first time I met you. I'm used to it."

She smiled weakly at that.

"What happened, Honey? Did I say something wrong?"

Grace shuddered. "Yes. Well, I know you didn't mean to; you couldn't have known."

"Known what?"

"Someone did want him off that island."

"Who?"

"I don't want to tell you."

"Grace, if this is a serious possible motive . . ."

"I know, I know." She sipped more water and leaned against the deck railing. "Once upon a time, someone wanted to buy the island."

"They don't allow that in provincial parks, do they?"

"No. But it is allowed in other northern areas, and certain people were making the argument that the government should change the policy. They tried to entice the province by pointing out that selling islands would enrich the public coffers, while they would get their little pieces of paradise. There are a few islands in these lakes. But it wasn't just the islands; they also wanted to build in other areas not approved by the government. In the back of beyond."

"What about services, though? How do you get electricity to those islands, and, as you say, the back of beyond?"

"They argued it could be done, although it would have cost a fortune. Most people around here didn't really care either way, as long as no one was displaced. By no one, they meant the Indigenous people with cabins in the woods. Some people had the right motives; they truly didn't want to see the hunters and trappers disturbed. Other people had less-admirable motives. They feared backlash from the nearby First Nations. And others simply didn't want more development up here."

"I get it so far. What about Elias's shack, though?"

"A number of cottagers knew about Elias's fishing shack. Many of them wanted to protect him. They staunchly argued against selling the island, signed a petition and sent it to the parks department. I signed it. Dad signed it. Parks took the island off the list. They're still considering other spots, but not that island."

Adam wondered where this was going.

"And so . . . who wanted that island, Grace?"

"My uncle. My uncle Howard."

"The drunk one who sent you home in the dark that night Elias found you?"

78

"Yes."

"Holy hell."

They were quiet for a moment.

"Do you seriously think your uncle could have done something like this?"

"No. I don't. But could he have been involved, somehow? He has quite the temper."

"He must not have been too happy about you and your dad signing the petition."

"Furious, would be the best word. Called us traitors. But killing Elias? I can't see it. Although my stomach begs to disagree."

"Babe, you wouldn't have thrown up if you weren't exhausted, hadn't found Elias and been gawked at by some freak with bloodshot eyes. Might have been a little much. Suspecting your uncle was just the last straw."

Grace nodded.

"Lie down for a while," Adam suggested. "Later, I'll make you a light lunch if you feel up to it."

He extended his hand; Grace took it and allowed him to pull her to her feet.

"Okay," she said. "Not much I can do right now, is there?"

"No, nothing. You're safe now. I even have a gun."

A whop-whop noise disturbed the quiet. The RCMP had brought in a helicopter to search for the bloodshot-eyed man. Adam grinned.

"They're on it, Grace. Once that thing flies over, you can have a nap."

*****

An hour later, Adam spied Al coming up the path. Quickly and quietly, he got to his feet, slipped out the door and met him halfway.

"Grace is asleep," Adam explained. "What's new?"

"I talked to Tillie Allbright about this sales guy. No idea how we're going to find him. And we haven't found your bloodshot-eyed man." Al sighed. "We'll keep looking, for a while anyway. Did Grace remember anything else?"

"Not so far." Adam had already decided to keep Grace's revelation about Uncle Howard to himself for now. "She's beat. I could use a nap myself. Bet you could too."

"Yeah." Al swiped a hand over his eyes. "I'll have to head back soon. I'll leave a couple of guys out here including Ellard; he only got up at five-thirty, not at one-thirty. He'll keep an eye on your cabin and I think maybe the Allbright place, too."

"Thanks, Al."

"No problem."

Adam held out his hand. The RCMP officer took it, shook it, nodded and walked away.

Adam stood a moment longer in the middle of the path, staring unseeing at the water, wondering how he could soothe Grace, make her feel like this was still her escape, her second home. His lips parted and curled upward.

Returning to the cabin, he found Grace awake and on the couch.

"Hey. Do you feel any better?"

"A little. Early night, though, maybe."

"Maybe we should have an early dinner, instead of trying to squeeze in lunch?"

"Good idea. I might be hungry in an hour or two." Grace's stomach growled. "Or sooner."

"So you're feeling better."

"I don't feel like I have to barf anymore."

"That's a start."

"Anything new? I saw Al leave."

"No. Nothing. Oh, except he's leaving one of the officers here — Constable Ellard — to keep an eye on things. It's going to be okay, Grace. Well, we're going to be okay."

An hour later, as they began to prepare dinner, the atmosphere returned to something like normal. Adam inserted a jazz CD into the aging portable stereo, and strains of Dave Brubeck, Bill Evans and Thelonious Monk filled the small space. Grace pulled potatoes out of the fridge, cut them into small pieces, and tucked them into a tinfoil package with spices and butter. Adam coated thick steaks with his signature rub and poured two glasses of red wine. He could hear Grace humming to the music as he popped out the back door to start the barbecue. Better, he thought. Good.

His eyes flicked around the yard. He looked inside the shed, strode out to the road, and peered through the truck's window on the way back. No one. He quickly went out front, scanned the yard, and slipped down to the beach, where he threw something into the canoe.

"Adam?" he heard Grace call as he returned. "Salad? Or barbecued vegetables?"

"Salad, I think," he replied, coming back inside. "Something green and crisp sounds good."

"Okay!"

He caught her around the waist, hugged her from behind, nuzzled her neck.

"And later," he said softly in her ear.

"Later?" Grace prompted, turning in his arms.

"I will dine on you."

*****

Grace inhaled her dinner. She hadn't eaten since the early breakfast shared with the RCMP officers, and Adam was glad to see her appetite return. As had his.

"This is so good," she said.

"I can tell."

Mouth full, she grinned back. Chewed, swallowed.

"You make a mean steak, mister."

"Thank you, beautiful."

Her face clouded.

"Hardly. I must look like grim death by now." She swept a hand through her hair. "Oh, God, what a mess. Worse than usual."

"Later, I will show you just how ugly you are."

"You're ugly, too." Grace leaned over and ran her hand up his hard thigh. "Soft muscles. Cloudy eyes. Rotting teeth. Let's not forget the bulging tummy."

Adam kissed her. "Let me whip up these dishes."

"No way. I'll dry."

Dishes done, Adam waited another agonizing half hour for their stomachs to settle and the sun to fully set. They sipped their wine and talked about what needed to be done to close the cabin.

"My favourite part," Grace said, "is crawling under the cabin to open up the wastewater valves."

"Spiders and snakes?"

"And worse. Poop. Don't know what kind. Squirrel, maybe?"

Adam laughed, glanced outside. Finally, he thought. Getting dark.

"Want to go for a walk, Babe? Stretch our legs a bit?"

"Is it okay to do that, do you think?" Grace sounded anxious.

"We'll stay around the cabin area. Ellard is lurking nearby. It'll be fine."

It was still unseasonably warm as they stepped onto the deck and made their way down to the lakeside path. Grace betrayed her nerves, jumping a little at noises; Adam put his arm around her.

"We will solve this case, you know, Grace. This will all go away, except in memory."

"It doesn't feel that way, right now. There's a black cloud over my lake that I haven't seen before."

"Take back your lake, Babe."

"What do you mean?"

Adam led her down to the lake, toward the beach in front of the cabin.

"This is yours, not his. And I am yours, as well. Take off your shoes."

Grace's head came up.

"What?"

"Take off your shoes."

"It's a little late for wading."

"Yes, it is."

Adam peeled off his T-shirt and threw it into the canoe. Grace blinked, her eyes darkening from chocolate to ebony as she saw his muscles etched hard in shadow and began to understand.

"What if someone sees us?" she breathed. A bathing suit, stripped off in the water, usually accompanied Grace when skinny dipping. Slipping in naked from the beach would be a new experience.

"They won't. It's almost dark. Have you taken your shoes off yet?" Adam kicked his loafers off.

"No," said Grace. "Adam, is it safe to do this? What if the killer is still around?"

"He's not."

"How do you know?"

"I don't. Your shoes."

Grace kicked them off.

"Your top, please."

She removed it, still uncertain, and stood quivering before him. She wore no bra, and Adam found himself unexpectedly staring at her bare breasts. He unzipped his jeans and stepped out of them; Grace mimicked him. For a moment, they faced each other, breathing as if they had been running, until Adam took the step between them and lifted Grace into his arms.

Without a word, he waded into the cold water, wincing a bit as it lapped around his legs. The lake was deep; it took only a few strides before Grace's buttocks met the surface. She did not squeal, but tensed and strengthened her grip around Adam's neck, then raised her head and touched his lips with hers.

Determined, Adam kept walking, slowly, as their bodies adjusted to the cold. Finally, he held a shivering and submerged Grace as his own body tightened from chill and passion. Adam kissed her deeply, imparting the warmth of his tongue to her mouth.

A switch flicked in Grace's brain, exchanging fear for the thrill of the risk; but Adam didn't realize it as she broke the kiss, slipped out of his arms and dove into the water, surprising and alarming him. She wouldn't swim away, would she? In the dark?

Then her lips caressed him underwater, heating him to the edge of control in seconds. The sensation overwhelmed him, the mixture of cold lake water and the juicy warmth of her mouth. It was also self-limiting; she would have to come up for air, very soon. Adam gasped and trembled, wondering when she would emerge.

Grace released him and ran her tongue up his abdomen and chest before her face reappeared.

"Jesus, Grace," he said, lifting her by the hips and curling her legs around himself.

He moved her back slightly, away from his erection, and could see her breasts just breaking the surface, buoyed by the water, nipples hard and red. One hand drifted over them, then plunged below to learn whether she was as aroused as he.

"I want you now, Grace."

"Yes, Adam. Now."

He filled her slowly, hard legs planted for balance; he hoped he would be able to hang on for more than a few thrusts. Cold water, warm Grace commingled to stretch and tease every nerve in his body.

"God, Grace . . . I don't know how long . . ."

"I'm ready, Adam. Come to me."

"This is yours, Grace. Your lake. Your place. And me. Take it all."

Adam erupted, burying his mouth in Grace's neck, biting her to keep from shouting her name. He felt her tighten around him, and his final spasm came exquisite in its pain and pleasure. Grace cried out and returned his bite in her own effort to stay quiet.

They stood, wrapped around each other in the water, still joined, shuddering from the cold and the loving.

"I do not want to leave this moment. But I have a blanket in the canoe," said Adam, finally.

"Genius," Grace chattered.

"Time to go. My intention was not to freeze you solid, Babe."

"I know. I've rarely been hotter, actually."

"Me as well."

They disengaged and, staying low just in case, crept toward the beach. Adam swung the blanket around them both; Grace gathered the clothing, and they started back to the cabin.

At the top of the incline, Grace froze. On the greenway, a dark figure stood, staring toward the water.

"Someone's there, Adam," she said, under her breath. She could just make him out, faintly illuminated by the yard light in front of the Allbrights' cottage.

"I see him."

"What do we do?"

Adam pulled her back to the waterline, and they quickly walked along the sand toward the next cabin's beach access. Confronting the apparition, naked as they were, was not on.

No light streamed from the vacant neighbouring cottage's windows, and darkness enveloped them. Adam led Grace up the path, around the back and they slipped in their own door before Grace finally took a breath.

"Might have been just a nosy neighbour," Adam said, rubbing Grace's arms to warm her.

"I don't think so," Grace said, shivering. "He was wearing a ball cap."

# Chapter Eleven

Lots of people wear ball caps, Adam pointed out, trying to calm Grace.

True, she thought, as she rapidly got dressed. In this case, though, it was not a coincidence. The person on the greenway was bloodshot man, phony satellite salesman or the killer. Or all three in one.

She said so to Adam. He had to agree.

"I'll try calling Ellard, see where he is."

The RCMP officer answered on the first ring, and Adam identified himself.

"Grace thinks she may have seen the man who came to the cabin earlier. On the greenway. We were just returning from a . . . walk." Adam grinned, lopsidedly, at Grace and shrugged.

"Okay. I'm behind your cabin. I'm heading there now."

"I'm on my way."

Adam pulled on his shirt and a light jacket, grabbed his gun and was again stymied by what to do with Grace.

"I'm safer with you," she argued, before he could say anything.

"Okay. But stay behind me."

Tough to do, thought Grace, when we're single filing down the damn path parallel to the greenway. But Adam somehow managed to diagonally shield her until they reached the main pedestrian walkway, where he extended an arm backwards and tugged her close to his back.

The whole operation took ninety seconds, and they were looking at Constable Ellard, waiting for them. No one else stood in the greenway.

"He couldn't have gone far," Adam said in a stage whisper. "I didn't hear any vehicles start. He's on foot."

"Conveniently, it's dark again," Ellard noted dryly. "Still. We'd better take a look around."

"Grace, can you go to the Allbrights'? The lights are still on."

"Fine," she grumbled. "Take care, Adam. Please."

"I'll walk you there first."

"Don't be ridiculous. It's thirty feet away. I'll be fine. We're so close we could see him from here, if he was there."

He kissed her quickly. "Okay. Go quickly, Grace."

She nodded and slipped through the trees and underbrush toward Tillie and Gord's cabin. She looked back to see Adam and Ellard disappear toward the crescent road. A chill shuddered through her. *Stay safe, Adam.*

Grace stepped onto the Allbrights' deck, but before she could knock, she felt a breath of movement. A hand slapped over her mouth; an arm violently wrenched her backward against a stinking male body. The man stepped down off the side of the deck and into the trees, dragging Grace with him.

Grace hadn't seen him, hadn't even felt his presence until the last second, nor smelled him among the aroma of pine and spruce. Where the hell had he been hiding? No time to curse herself for inattention. She couldn't scream or plead or try to reason with him, silenced as she was by his hand; her arms were held captive by one of his. Her feet, clad in flimsy deck shoes, were her only weapons. As he dragged, she lifted one foot off the ground, bent her knee and kicked her heel into his arch. It wasn't enough to hurt much, but it did unbalance her attacker. Together, they fell sprawling backwards onto the hard, root-encrusted earth.

"Fucking bitch!" he hissed, as Grace tried to squirm her way out of his grasp.

As he spoke, she knew him. And bit him.

"Fucking hell!" he said but did not release her. "Squirm and bite all you want. You're coming with me."

"I don't think so." Adam had appeared from nowhere, and now towered over Grace and her attacker, gun drawn.

"Let her go. Right now." He saw the flash of a knife, against Grace's throat in an instant.

"Put it down, or I cut her," the man growled.

"Get up, asshole. Let her go."

"No. Back off."

The knife pricked. Grace arched and cried out; thick blood rushed to Adam's head. In the thin light cast by a yard lamp, Adam saw the glint of teeth and knife. The bastard was smiling, and for a split second, he pointed the weapon at Adam as if in victory.

Grace seized the chance and twisted violently to her right, away from the knife. The attacker was left-handed, and for a breath, surprised by his victim's action.

Adam saw his advantage, but Grace still covered most of the attacker's body, and both of them were writhing in the dirt. He couldn't shoot for fear of hitting Grace, so Adam dropped the gun and launched himself at the two-person pile in front of him, reaching for the knife, not caring if he took the blade or the handle. It sliced into his palm, but he grabbed it as he pulled Grace out of the man's grasp and off his body.

Bigger and more powerful than the assailant, Adam won his prize but lost the perpetrator. The man rolled over, leaped to his feet and ran. Temporarily weaponless, clasping Grace on top of him, Adam could do nothing but watch him go.

He lifted Grace's head to inspect her face and neck but could see little.

"Grace, how badly are you hurt? Are you bleeding?"

"Yes. No. A bit. God, Adam. Are you all right?"

"I am now."

Grace began to sob into Adam's chest, as he held her.

"What the hell is going on?" he asked. "Why would someone want to hurt you?"

"I don't know, Adam. I don't know." Grace felt something sticky on her side, and reared back, forgetting her own trauma. "You're bleeding. How badly are you cut? Let me see."

"It's nothing. You're safe, that's all that matters."

"Your hand matters, Adam. What if you've cut a tendon or something, saving me? Come on, let's get into the light. Hurry."

Grace scrambled to her feet and extended her hand to help Adam up; he grasped it with his own uninjured hand. Once on his feet, he looked around for his borrowed weapon, found it, and said, "I have to call Ellard."

"You have to let me look at your hand first," Grace said, dragging him toward the cabin.

Adam, aware he was bleeding copiously, relented and let Grace lead him. Once inside, she gently pushed him into a dining room chair and turned on the overhead light. The cut was clean, deep and long, making Grace gasp in horror; but Adam wiggled his fingers and pronounced his tendons intact.

"You still need stitches."

"I know. But I really do have to call Ellard," Adam said, already dialling with his good hand.

Grace left the table to gather bandages from the first aid kit, a basin with water and an old, clean towel. She had to get him to Meadow Lake Hospital — or, if she was lucky, back over to Tillie's. She had been a nurse; Grace hoped she had surgical needles and thread in her cabin.

Grace overheard Adam explaining to Ellard what had happened, asking him to get over to the Allbrights'. The RCMP officer apparently hadn't heard the fracas, nor seen the assailant disappearing; but he would head over right away.

Adam signed off and grimaced as Grace bathed the wound and bound it tightly.

"I'm sorry, Adam. It must hurt a lot."

"It's not great," he admitted.

"We should really head for the hospital now. Or, we could ask Tillie if she can sew it up for you. Hospital would be better."

"Tillie would be better." Adam hated hospitals, Grace knew. His choice didn't surprise her.

"Are you sure?"

"Well, as long as she has antiseptic, yeah. What's the difference? I gather she was a nurse?" Grace nodded. "She's not going to try anything unsanitary."

"True."

Grace thought about that for a minute, staring at his bandaged hand.

"What about anaesthetic, though, Adam? You think it hurts now. Wait until she starts stitching."

"I'll be fine. I'll take the scotch. Come to think of it, that would work as antiseptic, too, in a pinch. Grace, it beats hell out of driving to Meadow Lake and back. And it's a bad cut, but nothing is damaged."

"Are you sure?"

"Pretty sure, yes. Tillie would be able to say, don't you think?"

"Yes. Okay. Let's go, then."

It was dark, but not yet terribly late. Grace, dazed from the night's bizarre events, was amazed to see that the clock on the wall had not yet ticked nine-thirty. She wouldn't let her body give in to the shock of being attacked, yet again. Only Adam mattered right now.

Back they went to the Allbrights', Adam on high alert, pain driving his jaws together; Grace could see the muscles tauten. No one leaped from the bushes, and they made their destination in two minutes.

She knocked. Tillie answered immediately.

"Tillie, Adam has been injured," Grace said without preamble. "Can you help? His hand has been slashed. And I have to tell you something. Can we come in?"

"Of course. Come in, come in. What happened?" Tillie asked.

"First, could you look at Adam's hand? I was wondering if you could sew up the gash."

Tillie, uncharacteristically, simply nodded and gestured for them to sit down at the kitchen table. She turned on the light, left the room briefly and returned with a medical bag.

"Okay. Let me see."

Adam laid his hand on the table, and let the retired nurse gently unwrap the bandage.

"Were you butchering a pig, for God's sake? That looks like a wound from a big, sharp knife."

"I guess it is," said Adam. He pulled the liquor bottle from his jacket pocket. "Give me a minute."

He shuddered slightly as he attempted to open the bottle with one hand; Grace dove in to do it for him.

"Here, love. Swig it back."

Two ounces of fiery alcohol disappeared down his long throat. "Okay. Ready."

"Doesn't look like anything has been sliced through. I'll be able to sew him up. Hold his arm," Tillie said.

Grace almost lost her nerve. Tillie's request drove the reality of the small operation, and the pain it would cause, into her brain like a splinter. It had to be done. She nodded to

Adam, smiled sympathetically, and took his arm between both hands.

"Hold on, Baby," she said.

"This is going to sting," Tillie said.

Adam clenched his jaw as Tillie poured antiseptic liberally over the wound, spilling it over into a large bowl. He flinched, but Grace held on hard, making small comforting noises. The needle and surgical thread came out; Tillie bent to her task without apology and pierced the skin.

"Uh," Adam grunted.

"Are you sure about this?"

"Yes," he said, between gritted teeth.

The long wound took eleven stitches, black and neat, to close. When it was over, Grace led Adam to the couch and handed him the scotch. "More," she said. He didn't argue.

Tillie cleaned up the small mess on the table, packed up her bag, and returned.

"Now. Tell me. All of it."

Grace sighed. But Tillie had to know.

"I was attacked on your porch. Earlier, I saw someone in the greenway. Adam didn't want me to roam around with him, looking for someone dangerous in the dark, and asked me to come to you. Before I could knock, a man came out of nowhere, put his hand over my mouth and dragged me away.

"I was able to trip him, and we both fell to the ground. While I was wrestling with him, Adam came back. The man drew a knife; Adam got it away from him, but you see what happened to his hand. Then Adam pulled me off the guy, but he got away."

Tillie's terrified eyes said it all. She regained her voice, cleared her throat.

"What is going on? This is so . . ."

"I know. So scary. But Tillie. I have to tell you this. I didn't see his face, because he was behind me; but I think I recognized his voice."

Adam, who had been lounging rather limply on the couch, sat up straight. His head snapped around.

"You didn't tell me that, Grace."

"I didn't have time, Adam . . ."

A sharp rap interrupted Grace. Tillie's eyes widened further, until the visitor announced himself through the thin door.

"It's Constable Ellard. Sergeant Davis, are you there?"

Tillie sucked in a sharp, relieved breath, rose to her feet and hurried to let him in. Standing on her deck was a filthy man wearing a baseball cap, his arms held tight behind him, the constable looming over his shoulder.

"Tom," she gasped.

"Yes. Tom," Grace said. "I was just going to tell you. It was your son who attacked me."

# Chapter Twelve

Grace flinched at the sight of her childhood friend. She had not seen Tom for years — not since she was nineteen, and Tom twenty-three. Confronted with him now, shock at his dissipated, dirty appearance overcame her fear and disgust at their violent encounter.

Tom's brown hair fell lank and greasy from under the Blue Jays ball cap, once white and blue, now grey and black. His once-clear emerald eyes, glazed and red, rolled slightly; his skin was a disconcerting shade of yellow. And his clothes: torn, filthy, hanging on his skinny frame. He twitched and struggled in the constable's grip.

"My God," Grace breathed.

Tillie lurched forward and took her son in her arms, even as Ellard held him in a powerful grip.

"Tom, where have you been? What is going on?"

He shook her off, with an ugly laugh.

"Where did you find him?" Adam asked Ellard.

"Up the loop, hiding in the bushes about ten cabins away."

"What the hell is the matter with you?" Adam asked Tom, his anger boiling over. "Why did you attack Grace?"

"I'm not sayin' nothin," Tom growled back. "Not to you, not to anyone."

"Tom . . ." Tillie started.

"Not to you, either. Like I just said."

Stung, Tillie stepped away from him, eyes filling with tears. She sat down, hard, on a kitchen chair and was silent.

Adam and Ellard shared a look over Tom Allbright's head. Adam shrugged and turned up his palms in a what-can-you-do gesture.

"Tom Allbright," Constable Ellard said, "I'm arresting you for the assault of Grace Rampling, and on suspicion of murder. Let's go."

"Do you need my help?" Adam asked.

"No. I'll call Al and let him know I'm bringing him in. Take care of your hand," Ellard said, inclining his head toward Adam's bandages.

"Tom," Grace said. "Why would you do that to me? Why would you want to hurt me? I don't understand."

Tom said nothing, but the twitching was becoming noticeably worse.

"Get me out of here," he said, finally.

Ellard grabbed him securely, turned him around and pushed him out the door. Grace moved to the kitchen table, sat across from Tillie and reached for her hands.

"Oh, Tillie, I'm so sorry. Can I get you something? Tea, maybe?"

"Some of Adam's scotch might help."

Adam took a glass from the drainboard at the sink and poured her a stiff, neat two fingers. Tillie downed half of it, and carefully set the glass down.

"He was high, Tillie, wasn't he?" Adam asked, as gently as he could. He'd seen it thousands of times. Tom Allbright was a junkie.

"Yes."

"Do you know what he's on?"

"No."

"If I had to guess, maybe methamphetamine?"

"What's that?"

"Meth, for short, is a drug that increases the release of dopamine. It's easy to get hooked very quickly, because users love the fast high. But it also decreases hunger, so people who have been using for a long time can lose a lot of weight. He looked pretty skinny, Tillie. Was he bigger, once?"

"Much bigger. Very muscular. But why did he attack Grace? Oh, Grace . . . I'm so goddamn sorry. You're sure it was him?"

"Yes. I recognized his voice. Earlier, when he was on our deck looking in at me, I thought I'd seen him before, but wasn't sure. He looks so different, Tillie."

"Shit." Tillie wiped her eyes. "Why would he do that, Adam?"

"Meth users get paranoid, irritable and aggressive. Do you know how long he's been on drugs?"

"A while now. He joined the Canadian Forces, maybe ten years ago, but he was discharged. That didn't help him find another job. He got pretty depressed and hooked up with the wrong people."

"Why was he discharged?"

"They said he wasn't mentally fit for the job. He did have problems with depression when he was younger. I thought he'd, you know, grown out of that. I guess not. He never told me what exactly happened, what he did or said to piss off the army. I think he was too embarrassed."

"How does he manage, with no job? Does he have a pension or something? Is he on assistance?"

"No. No pension. He's been on welfare, as far as I know, for a while, and of course we give him a little something, too."

That "little something" was feeding his habit for sure, Grace thought.

"Meth isn't cheap, not when people are using a lot," she said. "Does Tom have any other means of support?"

"No. Well, not that I know of."

"But you haven't seen him for a while, I take it," Adam said. "When he came through the door, you asked, 'where have you been.' How long has it been?"

"God, I don't even know. Months, at least. We send a cheque to a postal box every couple of months. He doesn't come to pick up the money personally. That being said, he lives in Saskatoon, and of course we're out on the farm Kindersley-way, so I don't think about it too much, although I miss him."

"Where's Gord?" Grace asked, out of the blue. She just realized he was nowhere about.

"Fishing. He should be back soon. He went up to Flotten Lake with George and Skip. I'm sure they didn't come off the water before eight-thirty, and it's a forty, fifty-minute drive. Plus, they'd have to bring in the boat."

Grace didn't want to leave Tillie alone. She peeked at the clock and saw it was after ten; Gord should be home soon. Beyond exhausted, dirty from rolling on the ground with her attacker, she craved a bath and bed — and to spend quiet time with Adam, to make sure he and his hand were all right.

As if wishing made it so, the thump of a boot resonated on the deck, and the bulky figures of Gord, George and Skip came through the door.

"Well, hi there, Grace, Adam, and my honey," Gord said, coming to Tillie and kissing her cheek, cold with misery.

He detected it immediately.

"What's wrong?" he asked, abruptly.

"Better sit down, dear."

He did, dropping into the fourth chair, face flushed with worry.

"Tell me. Something to do with the fire? Elias?"

"We don't know," Adam put in quickly. "This might be news for your ears only," he added carefully, glancing at the other two men.

"Yeah. George, Skip, do you mind?" Tillie said.

The two men looked perplexed but nodded. Grace could see a gleam of curiosity in George's eyes.

"Okay, I guess we'll have to have that drink another time," he grumbled. "See you tomorrow."

"'Bye, Gord, Tillie. I hope everything is okay," Skip said, his forehead furrowed with concern. He walked out, giving George a little push ahead of him.

"Now tell me," Gord said.

"Unfortunately, there has been an incident with your son," Adam said.

"Tom?" Gord's brow furrowed. "What the hell?"

"Gord, Tom was here," Tillie said. "He attacked Grace tonight. Right here, behind the cabin. Can you believe it?"

"No, I can't. Are you sure?" Then he noticed Adam's hand; he jerked his head toward Grace and saw the nick in her throat. His head fell into his massive, gnarled hands. "Oh, no."

Grace placed her hand on his back. "I'm so sorry, Gord. He's been sick for some time, hasn't he?"

"Yes. I guess I should've known something bad would happen someday. He's not a bad kid, honestly. Just very messed up. Where is he?"

"The RCMP have arrested him and taken him in to Meadow Lake. They'll probably let you see him sometime tomorrow," Adam said. "We'll leave you two alone. Tillie can tell you the rest, and you need some time."

"We'll drop over tomorrow before we go," Grace added. "See how you're doing, okay?"

"Are you two all right?" Gord asked, as they scraped back the chairs. "I — feel terrible."

"Don't. It's not your fault, Gord. We're going to be just fine. See you tomorrow."

Grace tucked her arm into Adam's, and they walked back through the dark, their way barely lit by the occasional cabin light or star peeking through thin clouds.

"How is your hand?"

"Hurts like hell."

"Anything a painkiller might help? How much scotch have you had?"

"Not enough. Grace, how much can the Allbrights afford to give Tom? How much is 'a little something,' do you think?"

"Good question. They're retired, but Tillie was a nurse and should have a good pension — and their farm did very well. They still live there, but they rent out the land and help a bit with the harvest. I would think they're late fifties, early sixties, so they were able to retire early.

But how much they decided to give him . . . we'd have to ask, if it's important."

"Even if they're coughing up, say, a grand a month, that's not going to go far with, what, eight hundred in social assistance?"

They'd reached their cabin and walked up the steps. Grace shivered; she wasn't wearing a jacket, and she didn't like where this was going.

"What are you saying, Adam?"

He stopped and turned to look at Grace. "If he's on meth and using as much as I think he is, that's going to eat up a hell of a lot of cash. Of which he has very little to begin with."

"He's finding the money somewhere else, of course."

"Yeah."

"And you think that's somehow related to what happened out there."

"Definitely. I just can't figure out the somehow, yet."

"You will."

*****

Warm and submerged in the bathtub, Grace tried to put the pieces together, but failed utterly. She couldn't fathom why Tom might attack her. Was he angry with her, for some reason? Had he been hallucinating? Had he seen her as a monster come to attack his mother — or himself?

They had been friends. Not close friends, because four years loomed between them, along with the gender difference, and that matters when you're young. Plus, they'd only seen one another during summers at the lake. No, not close, but friends just the same.

Growing into their teens, there had been no sexual pull between them; at least, not for Grace. Tom was nice-enough looking, kind and fun to horse around with, but Grace craved a stronger personality, keen intelligence and a powerful sense of purpose. Always had. Once she had discovered those traits in Adam, whose beauty had already overwhelmed her senses, she knew with certainty that he was the one.

But Tom had changed. Or had he? Physically, he had; but he had always worn a cloak of sadness, of distance, especially as he grew older. Grace wondered if he had bipolar disorder, or if something had happened to him in the forces.

As with Elias.

The last thought drove her splashing out of the tub and into a towel. She dried off quickly, pulled on a thick robe and rushed into the living room.

"Adam," she said. "Tom is thirty-three, thirty-four. I don't know Elias's age, but I'll bet he would be — was, I guess — mid-thirties. I wonder if they joined the military at about the same time, when they were nineteen and twenty-one or twenty-two? Maybe they knew each other, and not just because Elias lived across the lake. Would they? I don't know how it works

101

when you join the army. Would soldiers from Saskatchewan necessarily go through basic training together?"

Adam, arm cradled in the crook of his opposite elbow, looked up from his book. He couldn't join Grace in the tub because of his hand, a source of considerable disappointment to her.

"I'm not sure," he said, and thought a moment. "Maybe, if they joined at the same time. What are you thinking?"

"Can it be a coincidence that Elias and Tom were both in the forces, are not too far apart in age, and that Elias was killed at the same lake Tom grew up on?"

"Well, it could be, but I'd say the odds are against it. Unfortunately, it's possible that Tom is capable of murder. Look at what he did to you."

Adam paused, and Grace could see, from the intense expression in his narrowed eyes, there was a dialectic coming.

"But was Tom capable of planning this murder?" Adam wondered aloud. "Tracking Elias, setting fire to his shack, shooting him, returning to move him and dig ammunition out of his brain? I don't know. He's very stoned, very sick and very skinny. Would he be strong enough, or be able to muster the brainpower, to do all that?"

"Good point. Seeing him today, I doubt it, when you put it that way."

"But I think you're right. It's not a coincidence, either. My gut says Tom's involved, but the murderer is still out there."

Grace shuddered.

"Not out there," Adam added quickly, pointing to the lake. "He's long gone. He's a smart bastard. Once the job was done, he got the hell away from the murder scene."

"You said something very different when we found Elias, at his main cabin."

"Yes, because nothing is certain. We didn't know if we'd scared him away from dealing with Elias, or if he'd been gone a

102

while. No way he's still here now. That would be stupid, and stupid, he is not."

"Why did he move Elias, Adam?"

"He couldn't risk being found when we returned with the RCMP. It would have taken a while to hide him and then dig out the ammo — in the dark. And the island is small. It wouldn't have taken long for a bunch of officers to find him, or Elias. He needed a safe, secluded place. So, he dragged Elias, or carried him, back to his cabin. Why he wanted that bullet so badly, I do not know."

Grace had been standing, hands laced tightly together, all this time. Now her shoulders came down, and she sank onto the sectional couch next to Adam.

"So you're saying we're safe here, now."

"With Tom in custody, safe as houses. In my, ah, expert opinion, of course."

"Expert as they come."

"Don't say come."

"Sorry." Grace chuckled, and sobered. "I'm so sorry about your hand."

"Me too. But you're okay, love, and that's not just the main thing. It's the only thing."

"I can't believe you grabbed that knife. Was there no other way?"

"No."

"Thank God it was the left hand, at least."

"Yeah, I'd thought of that."

Grace thrust her face into Adam's neck and threw her arms around him.

"Thank you," she whispered.

# Chapter Thirteen

Exhaustion sent them into sleep minutes after hitting the bed. Grace persuaded Adam to take a painkiller; he hadn't had all that much scotch, and it did help. No nightmares — well, no serious ones — awakened him, which surprised Adam. He put it down to the depressive effects of the painkiller and scotch. And no men with guns, knives or red eyes appeared out of the dark to attack Grace.

Up at seven-thirty, they had the cabin cleaned, winterized and ready to shut down by ten. Adam's lacerated hand prevented him from being quite as much help with closing up as he had hoped. But he could open valves — there certainly were spiders and animal feces under the cabin — carry his share of the canoe's weight and vacuum the floor, while Grace dealt with everything requiring water.

Once the truck was loaded, they made their way once again to the Allbright cabin. Tillie and Gord's ashen faces told them what kind of a night they'd had.

"Come in," Tillie said, weariness thickening her voice.

"How are you, Tillie? Are you okay?" Grace asked.

"Yes . . . well, no, not really. Would you like some coffee?"

"No, thanks. We're ready to head back to Saskatoon. I don't think we thanked you for sewing up Adam's hand, though, and I wanted to tell you how much we appreciate it."

"Yes, Tillie, God, I'm so grateful," Adam added, with feeling.

"Turned out it was the least I could do."

Silence, for a moment, followed that remark.

"I hate to ask you this," Adam said, breaking the quiet. "I don't want to upset you further. But it would help if we knew how much money you were giving Tom."

"How's that?" Gord asked.

"It might give us some indication of how much he's using. His addiction will definitely come into his defence, and how he's treated by the police and the courts."

Tillie nodded, and tilted her head at Gord, who nodded back.

"Yes, okay. We're giving him about nine hundred a month. He only gets around eight hundred from the government. That's not even enough for rent and food."

"I know. It's a tough go on social assistance. Thank you for telling me."

"We really should get going," Grace said. "I'm not sure I have your home phone number. Would you mind?"

Tillie scribbled it on a scrap of paper and handed it to Grace, who reciprocated with her own number.

"Stay in touch, okay? Take care. I know this must be so hard."

"We will. I'm sorry about all of this, Grace. We had no idea he'd become so . . . so wild, or violent, I guess. It had been a long time since he'd been in touch. And we couldn't get hold of him. Or find him. I don't think he stays for long at any one address. We had no idea he was up here, either. Where was he staying?" Tillie shook her head in bafflement.

"I don't know. But it's not your fault, Tillie. None of it is. And we will be okay. Don't worry."

Grace hugged Tillie and Gord; Adam shook their hands, and after a few tears were shed by the women, they left.

Grace drove. Adam wanted to call the Meadow Lake RCMP and check in on Tom but didn't see any point in stopping at the station.

Ellard answered the main line.

"Hey, Sergeant Davis. How's the hand?" he asked, after Adam identified himself.

"Not too bad. I was wondering how Tom Allbright is doing."

"Not good. He's in major withdrawal, sweating, twitching, yelling. We have a doctor coming in to look at him again this morning. He came last night and gave the poor bugger a shot, just to calm him down. He was going crazy. Doc figures he's on meth."

"He sure looks like a meth addict, and acted like one last night, too. Listen, we learned a couple of things from his folks I thought I should pass along. He's on assistance, and they send him nine hundred a month to help him out. It'd be helpful to know if that covers what he's using."

"Right. I'll see if we can get that out of him, or maybe the doc will have some idea."

"Also, is he making it or buying it? That would help, too. His folks send the money to a post office box, not to a street address; he lives in Saskatoon, and they're on a farm near Kindersley. We don't know where he's actually living. I can check with the Sally Ann and the Friendship Inn when I get back, if you want, to see if he's bunking or eating there."

"That would help, yeah, sure. Thanks."

"And his folks didn't know he was up at the lake, nor where he was staying. Might be worth poking around the sheds to see if he was shacking there."

106

"Will do. Good idea."

"Can you send me his booking photo? Here's my email." Adam rattled it off. "And call me Adam."

"Nathan. Or Nate. Thanks, Sarge."

Adam laughed. "Whatever works. Stay in touch. Oh, by the way, is Al in today?"

"No, he took the day off. Been working pretty hard lately."

"Okay. I'll call back in a day or two. Did Elias Crow's body get to Saskatoon?

"Yep, went by air ambulance. Your forensics guy called us; he was pretty adamant we get him to Saskatoon pronto."

"Good for Jack. Thanks for the update. Cheers, Nathan."

"Cheers, Sarge."

Adam hung up and turned to Grace. "Sorry about that."

"It's fine, Adam. I take it they sent Elias to Saskatoon?"

"Yeah. First thing, when we get home, I'll call Jack."

"Can you drive for a while? I really have to call Dad. I sent him an email yesterday, but he's going to want to talk as soon as possible. I guess that's now."

Grace pulled over, Adam took the wheel, and she dialled Wallace Rampling.

"My girl," he said immediately. "Are you all right?"

"Yes, Dad, I'm fine. Adam's been hurt, but it's not serious. I just wanted to call and see if you had any questions. The cabin is fine, by the way."

Wallace chuckled, briefly. "Just like you to reassure me about the damn cabin. I'm just glad you're okay." A small catch had crept into his voice. "I love you, kid, you know."

"Aw, Dad, I love you too. I'm sorry, but I have to ask you something. Has Uncle Howard tried to buy that island again?"

"Not that I know of. But I'll poke him, see what I can find out." Wallace paused. "What are you thinking?"

"Nothing at all, Dad," Grace said, carefully. "Just wondering if the government's been rethinking that policy. If Uncle Howard was interested, maybe someone else is, too."

*****

Back in Saskatoon by two-thirty, Grace dropped Adam at the police station. He vibrated, wanting to get at a case that wasn't really his. In a way, it was hers.

"See you tonight, Babe."

"Should I come pick you up?"

"I'll get James to drop me off on his way home. Not to worry. Sorry to leave you with all the crap in the back of the truck. You could let some of it wait for me?"

"I'll be fine. What would you like for dinner?"

"Pork tenderloin?"

"I can do that. Please take care of that hand."

"I will, Babe." He kissed her, touched her face, missed her already and jumped out of the truck. "See you at seven, I hope."

Once in the station, Adam took the stairs two at a time and was almost at his office when Detective Constable James Weatherall stepped out to stop his sergeant.

"Yo, Adam," he said. "What are you doing here? You're supposed to have the day off . . . hey, what the hell happened to your hand?"

"Long story. I took a gun to a knife fight but didn't get the chance to use it."

"So you used your hand instead."

"Something like that."

"Sarge, I'm sorry to switch gears, but your timing is impeccable."

"Why is that?"

"We have a dead man. He was found an hour ago."

"I can't actually ever leave town," Adam said, "especially with Grace. All hell breaks loose. What's going on? Come into my office. I have to print something off from my email."

"A man, maybe thirties or early forties, was found dead on an acreage by a neighbour," James told him, as they strode together down the hall. "Turns out it's in our jurisdiction, not the Mounties', since the municipality's police don't do homicides. He was shot."

"Shot where? Could it be a suicide?"

"Nope. In the back, chest level."

By now Adam was in his chair and opening his email as they spoke, with James standing across from him.

"Are you going to sit down?" Adam asked.

"No. You have to stand up. We have to get out there."

"Why? Who's there?"

"Lorne and Joan," James said, referring to enormous Constable Lorne Fisher and Sergeant Joan Karpinski, of a more average size.

"Crime scene?"

"Either there or almost. I haven't seen the body, but Adam, what Joan told me over the phone is pretty weird. I think we have to get out there right away."

Adam's eyebrows went up.

"Okay. You can drive. I have to call Jack McDougall."

The two officers strode out of the office, down the back stairs and into the parking lot where they jumped into an unmarked car. James turned the key as Adam pulled his cellphone out of a pocket and dialled.

"Jack McDougall, please," he said when a receptionist answered the pathologist's direct line. "It's Detective Sergeant Davis."

"One moment, sir. I'm afraid he's in the middle of an autopsy, so I'll ask him if I can set you up on speaker phone. Please hold on."

The line switched to terrible elevator music for a minute or two, then crackled back into live voice mode.

"Adam," Jack said. "I have your man on the table."

Adam punched the wrong fist in the air, then flinched. That hurt, but the more important thing was that Jack was on the job.

"How's he doing?"

"He's very dead, Adam, for fuck's sake. What do you want to know? I'm not finished yet."

"I want to know about ballistics. Can you tell anything from that mess in his head?"

"Mess is right. No, not much. He was certainly shot, but with what? Your killer did an excellent job of smashing the skull, macerating the brain and extracting the bullet. Nice work, if you're an asshole."

"Great." Adam sighed. "What can you tell me?"

"Probably a medium-calibre pistol, close range. No exit wounds, as you said, so one bullet to the brain, which he felt motivated to remove. In other news, your corpse did inhale some smoke but not enough to kill him. You know that, though. And some deep cuts and bruises."

"Consistent with throwing himself out a window? Or inflicted?"

"Consistent, although I could go both ways. But there are shards of glass in his arms."

"Thanks, Jack. I'll be in touch. Can you send me a copy of the autopsy report when you send it to the RCMP?"

"A mere flick of the send button. Will do, Adam."

"As always, Jack, you're my hero."

"In writing, please." And Jack's assistant hung up.

"What the hell happened up at the lake?" James asked immediately, having heard the entire conversation.

"Like I said, long story."

"We have time."

"How far out is our dead guy?"

"Fifteen, twenty minutes."

Adam gave James a quick rundown on Elias Crow's death, the strange little burning shack and Tom Allbright's attack on Grace. He was rewarded by a "holy crap" expression on his constable's face.

"You really shouldn't go away," James said.

"Right."

The city now behind them, James drove down a two-lane highway and turned right into a pastoral area dotted with acreages, both posh and aging. Some were five acres, some forty; the homes were generally some distance from the others. A few kilometres further, James slowed to peer at the numbers painted or stuck on mailboxes.

"Here we go," he said, slipping the vehicle down a rutted path that barely resembled a road. It let out into a wide and weedy yard, already populated with police vehicles. Standing beyond was a small two-storey home in dire need of paint, and several outbuildings.

"He's in the house," James said, as they stepped out of the car, boots crunching on the gravelled drive.

Adam opened the trunk and both men pulled on white coveralls, gloves and masks before heading for the house. Joan apparently had seen them approach and met them at the door.

"Hey Sarge, James. He's in the living area. This way."

The sunny room, crammed with old, bulky furniture, crawled with cops and crime scene investigators constantly excusing themselves as they tripped over each other. They drew aside as Adam walked in, nodded to the crew, and knelt by the body splayed in the middle of the floor.

111

"Jesus Christ," he swore, with a mighty exhale.

The man's back had been opened in four strips of skin, neatly folded away from the primary wound — a huge, gory opening through which Adam could see organs and broken ribs.

"James said he was shot. Got ballistics?" he asked, looking up at one of the crime scene people, name of Taylor. He could hope, but he knew the answer.

"No, sir," said Taylor. "Looks like the bullet's been removed."

"But you know he's been shot."

"Yes, sir. See here?" He pointed to the middle of the wound. "That damage to the rib is from a bullet, not a knife."

"How long has he been here?"

"About a day, I'd say. Maybe not quite. He's still in rigor mortis."

Adam got to his feet. "Thanks, Taylor."

He gestured to Joan, James and Lorne and led the way into the kitchen.

"Any ID?"

"No. He looks like he might have been living on the streets, judging by his clothes, but hard to say. Killer could've taken it, too," Lorne said.

"Okay. So right now, there's a dead man on Jack McDougall's table with a big hole in the back of his head. No exit wound. No ammunition inside. Someone dug it out."

"Like this corpse. What the hell, Adam?" James asked.

"We have a killer with too much time on his hands. Someone who doesn't want us to find his bullets. That someone was in Meadow Lake Provincial Park thirty-six hours ago, and here in the last twenty-four."

"Got to be the same guy," Lorne said.

"Got to be. Job one is to get an ID on this victim. Kind of hard to make connections without knowing who he is. We do know the identity of the victim from Ferguson Lake. I have a photo of him, and of the guy who attacked Grace . . . "

"Someone attacked Grace, too?" Joan interrupted Adam. "What happened up there?"

Adam realized he had told James about Grace, Tom and Elias, but not the others.

"I'll get you up to speed at the station, but the attacker, name of Tom Allbright, is in RCMP custody in Meadow Lake on charges of assault and suspicion of murder. I don't think he's the killer, but he might be.

"As I was saying, I have his photo waiting in my email. We'll print it out and hit the shelters.

"Allbright's a junkie, no fixed address. Do we know who owns this property? Could it be the victim?"

"No. It's a Mrs. Margaret Robertson, Sarge."

"Who is she? Does she live here? Was anyone home when this happened? Is her body in the house somewhere, too?"

"No, no one else in the house. Don't know yet where she lives. Got the name from Charlotte only about fifteen minutes ago," Lorne said.

"Get as clean a shot of the victim's face as you can, then meet me at the station. I'll have the photos printed out for canvass.

"And tomorrow, we're going to have a meeting, oh-eight-hundred. We need to talk about what makes these bullets so damn special."

# Chapter Fourteen

Adam handed every available Saskatoon police officer a photo of Tom Allbright's gaunt, grey-yellow face, no longer topped by a filthy Blue Jays ball cap. He also gave them a horrifying picture of their new victim, temporarily dubbed John Doe, who was very obviously very dead. Blue lips. White face. Still and grim.

A hastily-called meeting in the incident room produced the attendance of fifteen cops, ready to hit the streets, bars and shelters on the west side.

"We'll start there," Adam told them. "By end of day, we need to cover the Salvation Army, the Friendship Inn, the Coronation and Ellis bars, the Twentieth Street liquor store, the bandshell in Kiwanis Park and the stroll. You never know what the sex trade workers might come up with; they see more than we'll ever know. And get your vests if you're not wearing.

"Where is this killer? If we seriously think he snagged our victim from the street, is he back out there? If he's connected at all to the stroll or the shelters, or looking for another vic, he'll see us coming, so stay safe. Anything else?"

There wasn't. Adam didn't have to point out the murderer was packing.

"Okay. Let's go. You get anything, anything at all, call me immediately. James, you're with me."

Once Adam had assigned locations and the officers had streamed out, he asked James and Charlotte Warkentin to hold up.

"Have we found Mrs. Robertson yet?"

"Not yet, Sarge," Charlotte said. "We have at least five Margaret Robertsons. Some of the M. Robertsons might make it more. We're working on it."

"Okay. Char, can you stay here and keep looking for her? It's crucial."

Adam knew Charlotte Warkentin, with her remarkable head for detail and dogged, determined methods of investigation, would find the owner of the house before anyone else would.

"Yes, of course, Adam," she said. "Good luck out there."

"Thanks, Char. Let's get out there, James."

"Where do you want to start, Adam?"

"The crisis centre on Twentieth. Let's see if Tom Allbright or our new victim showed their faces there, or if any of the patients recognize them from the street."

Adam knew the homeless shelter well. He was a perpetual visitor to the dingy little house, tucked between pawn shops and down-at-heel businesses. It was a haven, where street people could drop in any time — if they weren't too high — to find a few hours of peace and solace from Father Adrian Cey. Unfunded by any government, Harbour House scraped by on donations; but Father Cey was undaunted. A former addict himself, despite the clerical collar, he was determined to help Saskatoon's lost souls get off drugs or, at the very least, keep them from freezing or starving to death. Adam kept it quiet, but he signed an annual cheque to the house. In his opinion, Father Cey was truly a gift from God to people Adam couldn't personally help otherwise.

Adam rang the doorbell — the premises were locked from the inside — and waited. Seconds later, Cey himself opened the door.

"Hello, Father," Adam greeted him. "How are things going? Do you have a couple of minutes?"

"For you, Sergeant, I have all the time in the world. Come in, come in. Hello, Constable."

The tall, slightly stooped, but fit-looking priest led them to a tiny former bedroom that served as his office and counselling area and gestured for the officers to take a seat.

"What can I do for you? Has someone been involved in a crime?"

"Yes, but not just the way you mean," Adam said. "I'm sorry, Father, but I have to ask you to look at a couple of unsettling photos. One of these men, as you will see, is dead. The other is in jail, in Meadow Lake."

"Oh, no. What can you tell me?"

"The man in jail is a meth head, we're pretty sure. He attacked my partner, Grace, while we were up north this weekend, and he's also a suspect in a murder."

"I think I saw a story on that in the StarPhoenix this morning — a man who was killed on an island?"

"Yes. That's the one. Here's the suspect's photo."

Adam presented the picture of Tom Allbright, and waited, but not for long. Father Cey nodded.

"Yes, I've seen him around. He has never come to seek help here, but I have certainly seen him."

"What do you know about him?"

"Not much. A few members of my flock have run into him on the street with unpleasant results. I've asked him to come in, once or twice, and he refused."

"How unpleasant?"

"A few scrapes, bruises, cuts from altercations. The poor man has little control left. He's very agitated, very angry."

"His name is Tom Allbright. Do you know if he has a street name?"

Father Cey shook his head. "Can you leave me the photo? I can ask around."

"I'd appreciate that. This is the second photo, of a recent victim. Are you ready?"

"Yes, of course. I've seen my share of unpleasantness, Sergeant," said the father, only a slight admonishment in his voice.

There was that word, again — unpleasant. Adam smiled. The father was a master of understatement.

"Of course. I'm sorry. Here he is."

Father Cey looked closely at the picture, and slowly shook his head.

"I don't think I know him. Is he — was he — on our streets?"

"We don't know. He may or may not be a street person; we have no idea as to his identity. His clothing and general appearance suggest he wasn't in good shape, so we're starting with that premise."

"Sadly, many of them look so much the same. If I'd just seen him on the street, I likely wouldn't recognize him."

"May I leave this photo with you, as well?" Adam asked, rather tentatively. Showing pictures of dead people to addicts might not be the best possible thing for the father to do.

"Of course. I can see you're worried, but these people are, in some ways — many ways — tougher than you think."

"Right. As always, Father. Thank you very much, and please stay in touch, even if you have no news. I'd like to know, either way."

"I'll do that, Sergeant."

The father ushered them to the door, and Adam and James were back on the street.

"A bit early for the stroll," James said.

"Yeah. Let's hit the Barry."

The infamous Barry Hotel with its reeking bar stood shabby, scarred and shifting on a corner not far from Harbour House. Rumours swirled that a local businessman planned to buy and demolish the building, and Adam couldn't help but hope they were true. For now, though, men and women down on their luck, but with a few panhandled or prostituted coins to spend, still drank their afternoons away into stuporous, staggering states, or broke into boisterous brawls.

Adam had been shot in a bar similar to the Barry. To this day, he had to force himself to enter the premises, drawing himself up to his full height and deliberately pulling the mantle of authority about him. The vest he wore would not have saved him from the arterial wound to his leg six years ago, but it still gave him a measure of comfort. Adam sucked in a lungful of air, knowing he wouldn't take another pristine breath for some time, and strode through the door, wondering how many patrons would be inside. It was Monday, not Friday; and mid-afternoon, not midnight, but one never knew.

The bartender recognized and nodded at the two officers as they walked in, but his expression suggested he was not particularly pleased to see them. Adam approached him to put him at ease.

"Hi, Burt," said Adam. "How's it going today?"

"Not too bad, not too bad, Sarge. You?"

"I've been better. I've got a dead guy, Burt, and I need to find out who he is. I'm hoping you can help me."

"Got a picture?"

"Right here. Brace yourself."

"Yep. No problem."

Adam produced the photo, and Burt leaned over it, peering through the dust and dim light. He shook his head.

"Nope. Dunno him."

"How about this guy?" Adam brought out the likeness of Tom Allbright.

"Yeah, I've seen him a few times. Not a regular, but he's been in. Had to kick him out a couple times. Likes to pick fights."

"Know his name? Street name?

"N-no . . . can't recall a name."

"Okay if we ask around?"

"Help yourself."

James and Adam split the copies of the photos and prepared to canvass the patrons.

"How drunk do you have to be before you don't recognize someone?" James said, sotto voce, to Adam.

"I don't know. I was just asking myself the same question."

Adam, coughing a little in the thick atmosphere, approached a table of three men to the left, and James chose a nearby group of women to the right. Saskatoon had banned smoking indoors three years earlier, but somehow the denizens of the bar managed to sneak in a few butts by hanging in the bathrooms, back lobby and God knew where else. The place reeked from years of chain smoking, spilled beer, sweaty bodies, vomit and greasy food.

Good riddance if the place does get torn down, Adam thought, fighting the urge to hold his breath.

"Excuse me," he said. "I'm a cop. Detective Sergeant Adam Davis. I'm not here to roust you. I'm just looking for a little help."

"Heeey, Sarrge," one of them slurred. "I seen you around. What's happening?"

"I have a dead guy I'm trying to ID. I need to know if you recognize him. It's not a nice photo, though. You up for it?"

"Yeah, shurrr, no problem," said the man.

He leaned to one side, rocking slightly, and took the photo with an unsteady hand, forehead furrowed in concentration.

119

"Nope," he said, shaking his head slowly. "I dunno him. You guys?" he asked, passing the glossy to his companions. They simply shook their heads. No.

Adam decided not to bother with Tom Allbright's photo. If they didn't recognize John Doe, it didn't matter all that much whether they recognized Allbright since Burt already had. Adam mostly wanted to know if they'd been seen together. Were they friends, former colleagues, drinkers in arms? So far, it didn't look that way.

James was having similar bad luck with the ladies, although they were all over him, touching his shoulder and back, rubbing their breasts on his arms. They didn't seem to care that he was a cop yet chose their words wisely.

"You're lovely," purred one of them, named Misty. "Maybe I could make you happy."

"I'm better," said Nikki, her companion. "What I could do to you, pretty boy."

James, accustomed to such attention, laughed, protested he was very busy, and suggested they answer his questions. He wasn't there to pop prostitutes, and no mention of payment had crossed their lips.

Pouting, the two women dragged their eyes away from James and to the photos.

"Seen him," said Misty, pointing to Tom Allbright.

"Ever spend time with him?"

"Nope. Too fucked up, likes to fight too much. Kinda scary."

"Not the other one, though?"

"No. Never seen him. Hey, is that your friend?" she asked, spying Adam. "Maybe he's not as busy as you are. Mmmm. Nice."

"He's even busier. That's my sergeant. Okay, ladies, thank you very much. Have a nice evening."

"Boo," said Nikki. "Well, drop by for a drink sometime. We could have some fun."

James simply waved, smiled, and moved on to the next table.

Twenty minutes later, he and Adam were back outside, breathing deeply.

"That wasn't much help," James said, snorting from the stink that stuck in his sinuses.

"Well, we didn't get an ID, but so far it looks like Tom Allbright and John Doe didn't know each other. Allbright had been in that bar. Doe hadn't. And Father Cey recognized Allbright, but not our Saskatoon vic. It's unlikely they knew each other, at least from the street."

"Early days," James warned.

"Yeah, but it's also an indication. If it bears out, Allbright is not as likely to have been involved in John Doe's death. He couldn't have done it himself; he was either at Ferguson Lake or in the Meadow Lake jail. If he didn't have John Doe killed, he didn't kill Elias Crow. This was the same murderer."

"But he could still be involved."

"He's definitely involved with Elias Crow's death. But he knew Crow. I don't know how well, or even how, but he knew him and where he lived. I'm starting to doubt that he knew our other vic."

"Where are you going with this?"

"Elias Crow knew John Doe. That's our link. But who the hell is he?"

\*\*\*\*\*

Further canvassing brought the same results. Some of the street people they approached were too out of it to respond; others recognized Tom Allbright; none had seen John Doe.

121

Adam and James returned to the station, where they sent out the unidentified dead man's photo to the RCMP, Regina Police and the forces in smaller Saskatchewan cities. Adam called in the officers on shift for a debriefing.

"We didn't find anyone who recognized John Doe, but did find a few who knew Tom Allbright," Adam told the assembled officers. "Anyone get anything different?"

"No," said Lorne. "Same thing." The other officers nodded in agreement.

"Okay. I'll keep the canvass going on the night shift until the bars close. Thanks, everyone. Keep it front of mind until we figure this out. Ask everyone you catch up to on the streets. See you tomorrow."

Returning to his office, Adam sat down heavily in his chair, exhaling sharply. His hand stung and ached, and the dead men's faces swam before his tired eyes.

"Sarge?" Charlotte's head poked in through the half-open door as she knocked. "I have an update on our property owner."

"Come in, Char. Tell me."

"Are you all right, Adam? You're a little pale. Is it your hand?"

"Yeah," he admitted. "I hope the pain means it's starting to heal."

"You need to take care of it, and of you. Don't dwell on the past, but don't forget it, either, okay?"

Adam gave Charlotte a lopsided, affectionate grin. She had dragged his butt through the worst of the early days after he'd been shot, and likely saved his career to boot. Adam had descended into heavy drinking after he was released from the hospital, until Charlotte confronted him and forced him to seek help. Eternal gratitude and deep fondness didn't begin to cover how he felt about Char.

"You're right, I know. Thanks, Char, for the reminder. I think Grace will be all over it when I get home."

"How's it going? It's been all of a couple of weeks since you moved in, yes?"

"Not even. But so far . . ." he stopped, stuck for the right word.

"So wonderful?"

"That's pretty close." So domestic, so amazing, so erotic . . . Adam could have added several more descriptors.

"I'm so happy for you. Both of you."

"Thanks, Char. So am I. So what have you found?"

"Mrs. Margaret Muriel Robertson, age 72, lives in Sherbrooke Nursing Home. She's been there for about two years with encroaching dementia. Not too far along, but she couldn't live at home anymore considering she has a few other issues, including peripheral neuropathy. The numbness in her feet affects her balance and she'd fallen a few times. Living alone on an acreage didn't improve matters, not to mention the lack of proximity to health services. Her husband passed away a few years ago; he was older than she."

"Well done, Char. Any kids?"

"The home thinks she has two kids."

"Thinks she has?"

"Two they know of."

"Any other relatives they think they know of?"

"A sister."

"Okay. When can we meet Mrs. Robertson? Please say tonight or tomorrow."

"Tomorrow. Two-thirty. Too late for her tonight; it's almost seven, and she goes to bed early. She has therapy in the morning, and I'm told she'll be brighter after her post-lunch nap."

"I'll want you with me, Char. Can you do it?"

"Of course, Adam. Now, can you please go home to Grace and take care of that hand?"

"I should stay, see if anyone identifies our guy."

"Not happening, in my opinion. And I'll tell the staff sergeant to call you if it does."

"Why do you say not happening?"

"You're right, I think. James told me what you said outside the Barry. If no one had a sniff today, he's not from here, or at least he wasn't on the streets."

Adam nodded. Charlotte's validation meant a lot to him.

"Okay. Thanks, Char. I'll head home, but make sure they call me if anyone recognizes him, name or no name."

As Adam turned off his computer, he dragged his brain for answers.

If John Doe was not from Saskatoon, how did he end up dead in a vacant home near the city?

If he was not a street person, why did he look so very much like one?

And how was he connected to Mrs. Margaret Muriel Robertson?

# Chapter Fifteen

Grace roamed around her little house, images of the past few days flashing through her mind. Rarely so twitchy, the bizarre events at the lake had her rattled, she had to admit. Not unlike the day Adam had moved in, she couldn't help checking her watch every few minutes.

At seven-thirty, he finally walked through the door, and she flung herself at him.

"Hey, Grace, are you doing okay?" he asked.

"Better now that you're home. I can't seem to settle in. How did the day go?"

"Brace yourself. We have another dead man."

Bloody hell, thought Grace, as he told her about the second victim found dead on a nearby acreage. She would have wanted to write the story, but had decided to stay home and get organized, damn it. And all she managed was a perpetual pacing from room to room.

"I should have gone to work," she said. "I considered it, but I thought, what could possibly happen after everything went down at the lake? Next time, please call me."

Adam's set face betrayed his exhaustion and pain, and Grace relented.

"Oh, Adam. I'm sorry. I know you were busy."

"I thought about calling you," he said. "It all happened so damn fast. Before I knew it, we were in a car and out at the crime scene, then back in town looking for someone to identify the body. Won't they let you work on the story anyway?"

"They might. Well, probably, since I filed the Elias Crow piece. But you're not telling the media you suspect a connection between the two murders yet, are you?"

"No." He sat down abruptly, wincing.

"Let me see your hand," Grace said, story forgotten in her worry over his pallor and obvious discomfort.

Gently, she unwrapped the bandage to view the angry, stitched crimson skin, crinkling at the edges of the slash. She felt Adam's forehead; he was damp, but not feverish.

"It looks mean, but it doesn't look infected," she declared, deeply relieved. "It's not puffy or an ugly colour. And I don't think you have a fever. You must be reacting to the pain. When did you last take a painkiller?"

"Last night, I think."

"You went all day without any pain meds, for God's sake?"

"I don't like the damn things. I don't feel sharp when I'm on them."

"Well, you don't have to be sharp now. Dinner's almost ready, but maybe you could lie down for a few minutes? I'll bring you some dope."

By the time Grace returned with pills and water, Adam was out cold, breathing deeply. She drew the TV-watching blanket over him, put the meds on the coffee table, and retreated into the kitchen.

First thing tomorrow, she thought as she opened a bottle of red wine, she would start a deep dive into Elias Crow's past — even if she had to file Freedom of Information paperwork, a task she hated. She didn't know for certain that he had served in Somalia; it was her best guess, though, and she would start there.

Twenty minutes later, after planning her attack, she gently awakened Adam, fed him and led him off to bed. He fell asleep immediately, but Grace lay awake for a long while, wondering what the night would hold.

*****

She started awake at three in the morning. She felt Adam twitching first; then heard a low moan, more of a growl, emanating from his throat. Was it pain, or a nightmare? Both?

*No fear,* she told herself. *No fear. Give him a minute.*

She turned and regarded him, lying naked, partly uncovered and sweating, head thrust back. It was all she could do not to touch him, cover him with her body. An abrupt toss and a cry sent her into action.

"Adam," she said, quietly and firmly. "Adam, it's all right. You're safe. You're safe, love, here with me. It's just Grace, here in bed with you, in our home. Sh, now, you're all right."

That didn't work. He continued to moan and thrash. Grace breathed in sharply and tried again more loudly, the words catching.

"You're safe, Adam. It's only a dream. You're here with me, Babe, here with me, Grace. You're asleep and dreaming."

He gradually stilled. *Did he hear me?* she wondered. She mentally went back over her words. The second time, she had told him he was just dreaming. Did that break through?

Adam's eyes, directed at the ceiling, snapped open; a moment later, he turned his head to stare at her. *Is he awake? Please, let him be awake . . .*

"Grace?" he said, voice thick and low.

"Yes, Adam, it's me. Are you all right?"

"I . . . think so. Was I thrashing?"

"Yes. Can I comfort you now?"

"Oh, God, Grace. Make love to me. I can only touch you with one hand, but I want you so much. I need . . . I need to feel alive, awake, whole. I hate this . . ." he held up the injured hand.

Grace reached for it, kissed it, knew it reminded him of being shot.

"It doesn't matter, Adam. And it will heal; you will be all right, very soon. You hurt it to save me . . . oh my God."

"It wasn't your fault . . . "

"If we hadn't been at the lake . . . "

"It's not your fault."

Tears were now pouring down Grace's cheeks. She curled up at Adam's side, hand roving over his chest in a passion of arousal and guilt. He was damp from the nightmare, muscles still rigid. *Pull it together,* she told herself.

"Just a minute, Adam. Just one minute."

"Don't leave me."

"I'm going to get a warm cloth. Don't move."

She slipped out of bed, hurried to the bathroom, soaked a small towel in warm water and wrung it out. Returning, she removed the sheet half-covering Adam's body and gently patted the towel over his forehead, cheeks, throat and chest.

"Is that all right? Does it feel good?" she asked.

"Yes. Please, don't stop."

Grace continued, rubbing down his arms, moving to his abdomen and finally his legs. Ducking her head, she found the healed blue wound on the muscular left thigh with her lips and kissed it, drawing a groan and a small, tight buck of the hips from her aching man. The towel moved higher, softly bathing Adam's groin.

Hard as steel. Grace moved in.

Tongue and lips met Adam at the base and slid upwards, delicately licking and sucking.

"No!" he said. "No, Grace. I want to be inside you. Stop, please, come here."

She'd heard that before, from her own lips. But she craved him, and couldn't help herself from sliding up his body, straddling his thighs and slipping him inside, taking his entire length in one smooth motion.

"Don't move," he gasped. "For God's sake don't move, for a minute."

Grace felt his muscles tighten, stretching for control, even as he raised his head, pulled her to him with one powerful hand and latched his mouth roughly to her nipple.

"God Almighty, woman," he muttered, releasing her and seeking the other breast with his lips. "You are so fucking beautiful."

He had never said that before, using the expletive. The intense language had a strange effect, sending Grace over the edge of arousal. Her body responded, clenched, rocked; she couldn't stop. Adam's hand went to her hip, in an effort to still her movements, but it was far too late. Grace was beside herself, grinding into him, gasping, clutching his shoulders and finally crying out; and Adam came to her uncontrollably, thrusting upward and shouting her name.

For a moment, Grace stared at Adam's face, gulping air, her breasts heaving; then she collapsed on him, arms tight around his neck. His good arm came up around her back, the hand sliding under her mane of curls.

"One day," Grace muttered into his throat, "someone is going to get hurt."

"I have no control with you, most of the time. I'm trying, though, Grace. I'm so sorry."

"Sorry for making me lose my mind, do you mean? There are two of us here, you know. Did you . . . awaken aroused, Adam? I assume you remember your dream."

"It wasn't erotic. Line of fire sort of dream. It still gets the juices flowing, so to speak. The body rises to the danger."

"Do you want to tell me?" Grace asked, straightening so she could see him.

"No." Adam paused. "But Grace, I didn't want to make love because I awakened with an erection. I wanted you, to be with you. Admittedly, I needed to feel normal, and it had also been a while."

"Two days, I think."

"Well, it felt like longer."

Still inside her, Adam reached for a breast, then her face, and drew her down to kiss her.

"You are all I want. Always."

"You are all I want, Adam. More than I could ever have imagined."

"Oh, Babe . . ."

Grace burrowed into him, emotion overtaking her. The thought crossed her mind, even so, that she had dragged him out of the dark dream and into the bright flame of her love. *It worked, Anne Blake, my brilliant friend. Thank you.*

\*\*\*\*\*

What was it about Adam, Grace wondered, that made every lovemaking episode unique, intense, mind-altering? Yes, the man was beautiful. But that wasn't the whole explanation. Intelligence helped; so did his ferocity. He was imaginative, reactive, engaged, expert.

As Grace gazed at her sleeping lover, knowing she had to awaken him soon, it came to her in a burst of amazement that speared her heart: he was vulnerable to her. He allowed himself to be vulnerable to her. My God, she thought, moved all over again. Why me? How did that happen?

"Adam," she whispered. "Adam. I love you."

His eyes opened at her words.

"Grace. I love you. So much, Babe. Good morning. Do we have to get up? What time is it?"

"Six-thirty."

"Hell."

"Can you hold me for just a moment?"

"Hell, yeah."

Adam's shift started at seven, but he tucked Grace against his heart, closely enough that she could feel its strong, regular beat under her breast. Finally, she reached up, kissed his mouth and smiled, a little sadly.

"I'll make you a quick breakfast. You can hit the shower."

"Thank you. For now, for last night, for everything."

"Don't thank me, Adam. We're in this together."

"Together. I still can't believe it."

"Believe it, beautiful man."

Grace scrambled into a robe, hit the kitchen and put the coffee on. Half an hour later, Adam was out the door, hair still wet, late for work.

An hour afterward, Grace was in her car and on her way to the newspaper's offices, thinking only of Adam and the night.

Switch gears, brain, she pleaded with herself as she parked in the south lot at the StarPhoenix. It was time to dive in, to uncover the life of Elias Crow, and why he met his death at Ferguson Lake.

\*\*\*\*\*

Grace headed for Claire's desk after plunking down her bag and turning on her computer. Informal protocol demanded pulling up the arts editor's chair, if he wasn't in it, across from the city editor and settling in for a chat.

Claire started right in.

"Are you all right, Grace?"

"I think so. It's been a wild few days, and Adam was rather badly hurt, but I seem to be coping."

"How was he hurt?" Claire frowned. "You didn't tell me that."

"It happened after I called you." Grace quickly gave Claire a précis of the Tom Allbright episode.

"Oh, my God." Claire peered at Grace's neck and found the poke-wound from the attacker's knife. "That's quite the souvenir. I gather Adam's is worse."

"Much worse. He can't really use his left hand for much and has to cover it with a plastic bag to shower. He's tough, though. So," Grace said, changing the subject, "I saw the story about the local murder yesterday. You've got Lacey on it."

"Yeah. She's becoming our surrogate Grace, since you're always getting yourself involved in these crimes."

"I'd like to investigate the death of the man killed at the lake, Claire. There's a big story there. I'm sure of it."

Grace couldn't tell Claire that the two murders were connected; she had promised Adam. It was part of their pact, since their jobs crossed over at so many points. What Adam told her in private was off-limits, but that didn't mean she couldn't work the angle. She just couldn't make it public. Yet.

"What are you thinking?"

"I'm going to start searching for his army record, see what comes up, if anything. I'll also look for courts martial from the mid-1990s, especially stemming from peacekeeping efforts in Somalia and Rwanda. I use the term loosely, in the former case."

"Okay. I'll have to send you to court if something comes up but carry on for now. And maybe you could help McPhail, if she needs it, on this John Doe."

"Of course. Thanks, Claire."

"You're sure you're all right."

"Yes. Thanks. I appreciate that, Claire, but I'm fine."

Back at her desk, Grace checked her emails and phone messages, and fired up her search engine.

"Okay, Mr. Google. Be good to me," she instructed.

But searching for courts martial transcripts proved to be no easy thing. Grace, accustomed to requesting and easily accessing documents at the Court of Queen's Bench, was unfamiliar with the military system and surprised at the dearth of information.

She found aged, almost-unreadable photographed documents dating back to the Second World War years. The Court Martial Appeal Court of Canada site contained, of course, appeals — which might have helped if the case she was seeking was appealed. Searching for Elias Crow produced no results, so if he had been involved in a court martial, he had neither appealed nor appeared as a witness.

For a second, Grace thought she'd struck gold at The Office of the Chief Military Judge, until she read the first sentence on the site: "The Office of the CMJ retains judicial decisions rendered since its creation in September 1997."

*Damn it to hell*, she swore under her breath. Where, then, were the trial transcripts for between 1945 and 1997? Including the case she sought, if it existed?

Now what? Grace leaned back, thunked her head against the top of her chair and stared sightlessly at the television. The newsroom TV was perpetually on one news channel or another. At the moment, the Canadian Broadcasting Corporation was airing the federal government's cabinet shuffle. Minister of Justice, Alain Bourgault. Good choice, thought Grace. Minister of Finance, Helen Martin. Was she related to the former prime minister, Grace wondered? Minister of Defence, Richard Phillips. Minister of Canadian Heritage, Eleanor Collins-Booth.

Heritage. Ha, thought Grace.

She spun back to her computer and went to the website of Library and Archives Canada, part of the Heritage department, with a flicker of hope; but her suspicion was quickly confirmed that access to military records for living soldiers, and those who had died in the last twenty years, was restricted. They fell under privacy legislation. So much for that, she thought. Still, she would be able to file a request under their regulations, although it would take forever to get a response.

She gave up her search, for now. This was getting her nowhere. Instead, Grace started a search for Canadian Armed Forces in Somalia.

Apart from the Shidane Arone murder, and the shooting of the thief at Belet Huen, there was nothing else.

# Chapter Sixteen

W hy," Adam asked the assembled police officers at oh-eight hundred, "would someone dig ammunition out of a dead man? Give me some reasons."

"The obvious thing," said James, "is that the killer didn't want it found."

"If he's a whacked-out freak, maybe he wanted to keep the bullets," Lorne suggested. "Keepsake of some kind."

"Or he likes gore," Charlotte added. "Just killing the victims wasn't enough, maybe? He wanted to mess with them, too? But he could have done that without going for the bullets. Still, maybe that gave him a sick thrill."

"If James is right, why didn't the killer want the ammo found? How special could these bullets be?" Adam wondered aloud. "Are they silver-tipped or some damn thing? Let's assume there's something unique about them. Maybe they're not common in Canada, or home-made?"

He shook his head to clear it.

"I assume we've had no luck on John Doe, since I didn't get a call last night or this morning."

"No. Nothing. I'm hoping we'll hear from another police force today," James said.

"Me too. Okay, let's break it up. Keep me posted."

Adam's cellphone vibrated as he left the meeting room and headed for his office.

"Grace," he answered. "How are you? What's up?"

"I'm very frustrated. I'm having a terrible time finding military records online. But first, how's your hand feeling?"

"Not too bad. Tell me what you're up to."

"I've been trying to figure out where Elias served and what might have happened to cause his PTSD. I've been looking for courts martial transcripts and service records, but having no luck. But I had a thought. The military apparently holds summary trials for most disciplinary issues; there are hundreds of them every year, right up to disgraceful conduct. But get this. No proceedings are recorded.

"What if someone in the military wanted to keep an event out of the public eye? Let's say an event didn't hit the news and no one blew the whistle. They could just hold a summary trial to discipline a soldier. No one would ever know, outside the hearing room."

"Or they could do nothing, using the same logic."

"True. Damn. Okay, but what if they were worried that the soldier would do something that would jeopardize the military's reputation again — I mean, look at the Arone killing — and had to get him out of active service? What do you think?"

"It's possible. I didn't know summary trials had no transcripts."

"Neither did I. I've never covered military trials. So, because there's no paperwork, I wouldn't be able to find witnesses. Like Elias."

"Assuming he was a witness, and not a perpetrator."

Grace sighed. "Yes, assuming." She thought for a moment. "Have the RCMP found Elias's family yet?"

"Not that I know of. They haven't called me, but then it is their case. I'll contact Al this morning and let him know about our progress, or lack thereof, on John Doe. I'll ask him then."

"I've always assumed Elias was from the Meadow Lake area, or at least Northern Saskatchewan. Nothing else makes sense. How else would he have known where to build his shacks? It can't be too hard to ask the reserves nearby, can it?"

"No, it shouldn't be. I'll let you know, officially, if they've found the family. That's what's holding them back from releasing some of the details, including his name."

"Thank you, Adam."

"See you later, love."

Spurred by Grace's call, Adam's next move was to call the Meadow Lake RCMP. Ellard answered.

"Hey, Nathan. It's Adam Davis. How's it going today?"

"Not too bad, Sarge. You? How's the hand?"

"Also not too bad, thanks. Is Al around today? Or should I ask you my questions?"

"He's in. I'll find him for you. Give me a sec."

Adam spent the moment waiting for the RCMP sergeant mulling over what Grace had said about summary trials. Only the armed forces, he thought, would get away with that in this century.

"Hi, Adam. Sorry for the wait. How are you doing? What's going on?"

"I'm fine, thanks. Just wanted to check in with you about a couple of things. I sent a note up late yesterday about a man who was killed in Saskatoon, along with his picture. We have no ID on him yet, so I wondered if anyone in your detachment recognized him?"

"No. We all took a look and I'm afraid he's still a John Doe."

"Damn. I'm positive his death is related to Crow's."

Adam launched into a detailed description of the dead man's body and explained his reasoning. How many killers removed ammunition from bodies? Adam had certainly heard of such a thing, but it was extremely rare. Most killers wouldn't hang around waiting to get caught.

"True," said Al, after that comment. "Doesn't look like anything else is connecting them, though."

"Can you show his picture to Tom Allbright? What kind of shape is he in?"

"Rotten. When he's sleeping, he's rolling around and moaning. When he's awake, he's shrieking his head off. I don't know what kind of sense we'll get out of him. I'll try, though. Anything else you need?"

"Yeah, also wondering whether you've found Crow's family yet."

"Not yet."

Adam's brow furrowed, and he pressed his lips together. Grace had made a good point: it couldn't be all that difficult to check with the neighbouring reserves, although there were several of them, if Elias had First Nations status. Were people not admitting to knowing Elias? If not, why?

"Okay, well, keep me posted," was what he said. "Thanks, Al."

Adam sat, frustrated, at his computer for several minutes, willing his email to ping with a missive from the Regina Police, or the RCMP from southern detachments, identifying his victim. Come on, come on. I need to know who this guy is, he thought. Then he picked up the phone.

"Adam," answered the chief of police. "Want to come to my office?"

"Yes, if you have a few minutes."

"I do. Bring coffee."

Adam grinned. "Are you sure? Should I make a Starbucks detour?"

"Mighty tempting, Sergeant. But no, I'll stick to the station dreck, thanks. Black."

Five minutes later, Adam stood at Chief Dan McIvor's door clutching the handles of two mugs, filled with very bad coffee, in his right hand and knocking lightly with his left.

"Come on in, Adam," said the chief cheerfully, turning from his computer and immediately noticing the bandage. "What the fuck happened to your hand?"

"A little altercation with a suspect," Adam said, and explained, again, what had happened at Ferguson Lake with Tom Allbright.

"Shit," McIvor said. "How's Grace? Is she, at least, okay?"

"A small puncture wound in her neck, but she seems fine otherwise. Thanks for asking."

"Well, at least the, ah, altercation was not for nothing since you caught the guy. Should you be here?"

"Yes. I'm fine, Chief. Well, not great, but functioning."

"Look after yourself, dammit. I do not need you in the hospital again. Now tell me about your victim."

"Not much to tell. He's still John Doe. We've done a street canvass with his picture, sent it to police forces across the province and to the hospitals. This afternoon, though, I'm going to interview the elderly lady who owns the house he was found in. I sure hope she knows who he is, but I gather there's some encroaching dementia there. She may not recognize him."

"Terrific," said McIvor, after a sip of his bitter brew.

"Have you been briefed on the man who was killed near Meadow Lake, Chief?"

"I know he's dead, there was a fire, he was shot, you were there, and it's the Mounties' case. I haven't seen the autopsy."

"I haven't either, but I've seen both victims. Whoever killed John Doe also killed the guy at the lake — Elias Crow, by

139

name. He was an army vet, possibly served with the so-called peacekeeping tour in Somalia, according to Grace."

McIvor's eyebrows shot up. "According to Grace?"

"She knew him."

"What?"

"Yeah. He had PTSD from serving in the forces. He lived alone in a shack south of the lake and had a fishing hut near the water. Dropped off the Earth after serving, apparently. Grace says the timing lines up with Somalia or Rwanda."

"Wow. So why do you think it's the same killer?"

"Both men were shot from behind, and in both cases, the killer removed the ammunition from the wounds. Crow was shot in the head, the other vic in the middle of the back.

"And they were killed within, say, twenty-four hours of each other, in different locations but just four hours apart by car. It's the same guy."

"Holy crap. Why the hell would he do that? It would take some time. You'd think he'd scram after the job was done. And so much for ballistics. Have you ever heard of that before?"

"A couple of times, but not around here."

"Weird. So, you're talking to this older lady, the homeowner. What's up after that?"

"If the homeowner — a Mrs. Robertson — can't identify John Doe, we're going to have to get creative. We've been working on the assumption, which could be erroneous, that he's a street person, based on his appearance. No ID, of course. So far, that hasn't worked. If you have any ideas, I'm listening."

"Maybe it's time to send the photo of our victim to the Canadian Armed Forces."

Adam chewed his lip. It was the obvious next step, and he knew it; but somehow, it didn't feel right to go there. Not just yet.

"I'd thought of that, but can you give me a few more hours? They may not want to play. If not, we don't want them to know what we're up to. Or they may want to play, but all by themselves. And this is my case, Chief."

It was McIvor's turn to chew on the problem.

"Okay," he said at last. "Let me know what happens with this homeowner. But somehow, we have to ID this guy. Very, very soon."

"And we have to figure out why the killer dug out the ammo. As James said, it's probably because he didn't want it found . . . "

Adam stopped talking and stared at his chief.

"Holy hell," he whispered. He couldn't believe it hadn't occurred to him before.

"What, Adam?"

"Full metal jacket. It's got to be."

McIvor's eyes widened. "The bastard's using military ordnance. Bullets that don't fragment as easily. Bullets that are easier to identify. And he doesn't want us to know that."

# Chapter Seventeen

Mrs. Margaret Muriel Robertson perched primly in her wheelchair, grey hair curled into a soft halo, a dab of lipstick and a puff of rouge adorning her still-pretty face. A blanket of many colours draped her lap and legs, allowing patent leather shoes to peek out from underneath.

"Not, strictly speaking, that I have to be in this thing," she said, indicating the chair, and sighed. "But sometimes my feet go all funny. They don't want me to fall, you know."

"No, it's best to be safe," Adam agreed.

The older woman awaited them in a sunny common room when Adam and Charlotte arrived at the seniors' home. Adam introduced himself and his colleague, and inquired about her health, as politely as possible while skirting the senility issue. Interviewing a frail or sick person was not his favourite thing; it felt vaguely unfair, adding stress and sometimes misery to a life already etched with pain or confusion.

Adam had asked Charlotte to send the photo of John Doe to the nursing home staff, but none of the nurses or aides recognized him. Angie, the nurse attending Mrs. Robertson, had told Charlotte earlier that the dead man was not Margaret's son; she had seen the latter, a few times.

Adam asked the nurse if she could stay, in case her charge became agitated or emotional. She nodded, smiling warmly at Adam with her eyes as well as her mouth.

"Mrs. Robertson," Adam said, finally, ending the pleasantries. "I'm afraid I have something upsetting to tell you."

"Margaret," she said. "Call me Margaret, please, Sergeant."

"Margaret, then. Thank you. I have to tell you this, and I'm very sorry. Do you feel ready?"

"Yes, of course. What it is, Sergeant?"

Adam cleared his throat, giving himself another moment to find the right words. He sighed, then, knowing there were none.

"Margaret, we have found a person dead in your house. The person is male, but we know he is not your son."

Predictably, she paled.

"Oh no, oh no," she whispered. "It's not my son, is it? Or my daughter?"

"No." *Shit*, thought Adam. She understood someone was dead, apparently, but had completely missed — or already forgotten — the second part of his statement. How bad was her dementia? he wondered. He cast a quick glance at the nurse, who shrugged slightly.

"No, Margaret. It's not your son. But the person is male."

"Who is it, then?"

"That is partly why we're here. We need to know if you recognize the person. Do you think you could look at a photograph of him? It's not a very nice picture, I must warn you."

He looked again at the nurse, pleading with his eyes, and she came over to put her arms around Mrs. Robertson.

143

"I'm right here, Margaret. We will get through this together, okay?"

The older woman nodded. "Okay."

Adam slowly drew out the print and placed it on the table. "Take your time."

Margaret leaned forward and peered for several breath-stopping moments at the man before her, grey and blue and closed in death, as Adam and Charlotte silently prayed for recognition.

But no. Margaret pulled away, shaking her head.

"I don't recognize him. No. I'm sorry."

A stream of curses flowed through Adam's brain.

"You're quite sure, Margaret?" Charlotte asked.

A very definite nod. "Yes. I'm sure."

"When is the last time you were home, ma'am?"

"Ages ago. I don't really remember. Angie?" she asked the nurse. "Do you know?"

Angie pursed her lips in thought.

"I don't know if she's been to her former home since she came here," she said. "That was about two years ago. But of course, I wouldn't know for sure. You may want to ask her children. We don't necessarily know where they take her, when she goes out on visits."

"No, of course," Adam said. "Who takes care of your house, now, Mrs. Robertson? Um, Margaret? Is it rented? Does someone usually live there?" Adam had wondered more than once if the dead man was a tenant.

"I leave all of that up to the kids, Sergeant," she said. "I think they've let it a few times, but I really don't keep up with all that."

"Tell me about them, Margaret. Your kids. Do they live here? Do you see them often?"

144

"My daughter, Elaine, lives in Calgary with her family," she said, sadness weighing on every word. "I don't see her all that often, of course. They're very busy."

"How often do they come to Saskatoon?"

"I'm not sure. Twice a year, or so."

"And your son?"

"Alan is a police officer, like you two are. I'm very proud of him."

Adam cocked his head and looked at Charlotte. Alan Robertson. He didn't know an officer of that name on the Saskatoon police force. Charlotte shook her head back at Adam.

"He's not in Saskatoon, then?" Adam prompted.

"No, he serves up north. I just can't remember the town. But he does come to the city every month or so, I think. It's always so nice to see him."

Adam raised his brows at the nurse, who nodded in confirmation. Yes, the son did come to visit every month or so. The monthly regularity would fit with managing a tenant and collecting rent, he thought.

"And would he be able to help us with . . . identification? Or would it be your daughter?" he asked.

"Oh, it would be Alan. He takes more responsibility for the house, since Elaine is so far away. Come to my room. I'll show you pictures of my family. You can see my grandbabies."

"What a nice idea, Margaret," he said. "Let's do that."

Perfect, he thought. I don't have to ask.

Angie snapped back the brake levers on the wheelchair, backed Margaret away from the table, and wheeled her out to the hallway.

"Just follow me, Sergeant, Constable," she said.

The room was a good distance away, and Adam had trouble slowing his long, impatient stride to match the wheelchair's progress. Finally, Angie stopped in front of a wide door, and Adam pushed it open, allowing the nurse to take Margaret in first.

"Just over there, Angie," the older woman said. The nurse stopped the wheelchair in front of the wide windowsill, crowded with snapshots in tiny frames. Margaret picked one up and, with a gentle finger, touched the dusty faces before handing it to Adam.

"That's my Elaine, and her children Jordan and Ashley," she said. "Her husband isn't in this one though . . . do you want to see him? He's very handsome, just like you."

She chose a wedding photo, from at least twenty years ago, of Elaine and her groom.

"There, now. That's our Bob."

Margaret turned back to the window, and reached to her left, selecting a slightly larger photograph of a man and his family.

"And this," she said, "is my Alan, his wife Gillian, and their children."

Adam's jaw, quite literally, dropped. He snapped it shut quickly, and nodded, but not before Charlotte caught his momentary lapse of control. She shot him a questioning look, but he shook his head, once. Later, the gesture said.

"What a lovely family, Margaret," Adam said, as warmly as he could manage. "And thank you so much for seeing us today. Again, I'm so sorry we had to show you that photograph, and for the — ah, other circumstances."

"No trouble, young man. No trouble at all. It's nice to have visitors."

"And thank you, too, nurse. We'll see ourselves out."

Adam and Charlotte left the room, and this time, Adam did stride down the hallway, toward the nearest exit.

"What is going on, Adam?" Charlotte asked, as evenly as possible, watching her sergeant vibrating with some powerful emotion as she hurried to keep up.

146

"I'd like to wait," he said sotto voce, "until we are outside. Please."

"Of course, Adam."

They made it to Adam's unmarked car before he exhaled and leaned against the hood with a thump. He crossed his arms, threw his head back and took a breath.

"Cough it up, Adam. What the hell?"

"I recognized Margaret's son. Alan."

"Alan Robertson. But he doesn't work around here, she said."

"No. He's in Meadow Lake. The man we assumed would be named Alan Robertson is RCMP Sergeant Al Simpson, for fuck's sake."

\*\*\*\*\*

The moment they returned to the station, Adam and Charlotte made a beeline for the chief's office. Adam called McIvor en route to warn him that he needed to speak to him immediately.

"Back already? Didn't we just chat this morning?" McIvor asked. "Did you get your ID from Mrs. Robertson?"

"No. But we have a problem. The lady's son, name of Alan, takes care of her house. She told us he was a cop, too, and showed us a picture of him. Chief, her son is Sergeant Al Simpson of the Meadow Lake RCMP."

McIvor blinked at Adam.

"You've got to be kidding."

"Wish I was."

"What the fuck does that mean? Why does he have a different name? Lay it out for me."

"I assume she was married twice, but it really doesn't matter. She has two kids, verified by the nurse, and Al is one of

147

them, whether he shares her last name or not. My first thought is that he rented her house out, to cover its expenses, and either John Doe or the killer was, or is, the tenant. We're going to have to ask him."

"Yes, we are."

"So, what's the protocol, here, Chief, police force to police force? Can I just barge in and ask him what he knows?"

"I think so, since the John Doe murder is your case." McIvor paused, and narrowed his eyes. "You're thinking something else. I can see it. Out with it."

"What if he's directly involved in this somehow?"

"Like how?"

"Hell, I don't know. But it seems like too much of a coincidence. I just talked to him this morning. He claimed not to recognize the victim, and that was an end to it. That was all he said. In retrospect, it seems strange. They haven't found Elias Crow's family yet, either. That could be legit, but come on; how long could that take?"

McIvor's lips thinned into a grim line.

"God damn it. I hope you're wrong, Adam."

"I do too. Chief, I think I have to head back out there. Doing this on the phone, when I can't see him, or even in video conference, isn't going to work. Plus, there's the element of respect. I have to see him in person."

"I agree. How soon can you go?"

"Tomorrow, I hope."

"Okay. Let's plan for that. Let me dig into the protocol, see what I have to say to his superior officer."

"It would be better if he wasn't warned, Chief."

"Yeah, I know. Timing is everything, as they say in comedy. Although this really isn't funny. Let me know when you leave, and I'll do my best to call in the nick of time."

"Here's the other thing," Adam said. "I'd really rather know who our victim is before I talk to Simpson. Since we've had zero luck on that, I'm going to expand the search outside the canvass and law enforcement. How far can I go? Can I, for example, put his face out in the media? Have we ever done that with a murder vic?"

"How much would that suck if you're a family member?" Charlotte put in.

"I know," Adam said. "I know. Good point. Okay, let's hold off. I'll brainstorm another way before we do that."

"Where are we at with the autopsy on John Doe?" McIvor asked.

"Not done yet. But I don't think it'll tell us much, frankly," Adam said. "In this case, it's less important to know how he died, since he was mutilated afterward, like Crow."

"Right. Okay, Adam. Let me know if you're taking someone with you. I would strongly advise it. I don't need you to come back with another fucking knife wound, or worse."

*****

Adam found Grace standing and stewing in her tiny backyard, a hand curled around a glass of wine and staring over the garden, still populated with a few late tomato plants.

"Hey, Babe," he greeted her, adding a warm and thorough kiss. "You could sit down, maybe, and enjoy your wine."

"Grrr," said Grace, baring her teeth. "I'm too wound up. That had to be one of the most frustrating days not just of my life, but anybody's life, ever."

Adam grinned at Grace's exaggeration. "No progress, then, on Elias."

"Nope. Damned military and stupid Internet. Have the RCMP found his family yet?" she asked hopefully, brightening a bit.

"No. Grace, I have to tell you a whole lot of shit, but it has to be off the record. All of it."

Grace nodded. "I'll get you some wine, first."

"I'll get it. Be right back."

She was still standing when he returned, but finally sank into a lawn chair.

"Let me have it. What's happening?"

Adam told her about his suspicion about the ammunition; then he told her about Al Simpson.

"I have to go back to Meadow Lake," he said.

"I'm coming with you."

"That'd be nice, Grace, but why?"

"I'm going to look for Elias's family."

"Okay . . . but why would you have better luck than, say, the RCMP? Or even me?"

"They're not looking for him hard enough, obviously. And maybe people aren't telling the police what they know. I, on the other hand, have contacts."

"We're going to need two cars, then."

"Too true. Are you bringing James or Charlotte?"

"James. Okay, that would work. You can have the truck while we're up there; James can follow us in a police car, and we'll use that."

"When are we leaving?"

"Tomorrow. I'm hoping we'll identify our John Doe first. I'd rather go in knowing, when I confront Al."

"Let me see the picture of this guy."

"Are you sure?" Adam had a powerful desire to protect Grace from, well, everything, although obviously that wasn't working. Still.

"Come on, Adam. Of course, I'm sure. You know I've seen worse, in person. Let me see it."

Adam got up, went inside and returned with the photo he now carried everywhere. Grace took it and looked at the man closely.

"God, he looks awful," she said. Adam grinned, and she smiled back. "I don't mean awful as in dead. I mean rough. Reminds me of Tom. I see why you think he lived on the street."

"But as far as we can tell, he didn't. At least, not in Saskatoon or Regina or the other major centres. We've done, with help from the other police forces, a serious canvass in both big cities, not to mention Moose Jaw, Prince Albert . . . no one recognizes him, or can ID him. That doesn't mean he wasn't living rough, but it's starting to look unlikely."

"Other cities and towns, too?" Grace asked.

"Everywhere with a police department or an RCMP detachment, which is a lot of everywhere."

Grace mulled that over.

"Okay, so he looks like crap, but let's say he's not homeless. Where else could he have been staying?"

"Well, he could have been staying in that house. He could have been Mrs. Robertson's tenant. Or, I suppose, Al's tenant."

"And he wasn't recently in prison or in jail, somewhere."

"No."

"Well, if he wasn't in the psychiatric centre —"

"No, he wasn't."

"There's one more place you could try."

"Where, Grace?"

"Saskatchewan Hospital. In North Battleford."

Adam breathed. "Of course. The mental hospital."

He leaned over, took away Grace's glass, lifted her to her feet and enclosed her in his arms.

"You're not just fucking beautiful," he said, with a sly smile. "You're a fucking genius, too."

# Chapter Eighteen

I f it's okay with you, I think I should go back up north," Grace told Claire Davidson the next morning. "I'm never going to get to the bottom of this if I don't find Elias's family, or at least a friend."

"No luck online, I take it."

"Nothing. It's like Elias didn't exist, which of course is what he was trying to achieve; but still. And how long is it going to take for me to wrest information from the military? Weeks? Months?"

"Years?" Claire added. "I know. When are you leaving?"

"As soon as I can get organized."

"Stay in touch, and for God's sake, don't find any more bodies."

"I'll do my best. Thanks, Claire."

"Is Adam coming with you?"

Grace hesitated. She couldn't tell Claire what was going on with the RCMP sergeant, nor what Adam was thinking about the ammunition's origins. But Grace also hated lying and sucked at it besides.

"He is. He's as anxious to find out more about Elias as I am, but he also wants to compare notes with the Mounties."

"This is very good. I won't worry about you quite so much. Okay. Keep me posted."

Grace gathered her digital recorder, extra batteries, work computer and several notebooks and headed home to pack for the lake . . . again.

Adam was already loading up the truck when she arrived; James was helping.

"Hi, love. Just need your clothes," Adam said when she came into the yard. "We're almost ready to go."

"Okay. Give me ten. Here — can you put this stuff in the back seat? It's my work gear."

Not knowing how long they'd be staying made packing a little tricky. How much food? How many pairs of socks and underwear? Grace decided to be ready for three days, and if it ended up being longer, they'd just have to do some shopping and laundry.

She threw clothes and toiletries into her suitcase, locked the door and jumped into the truck with Adam. James was already behind the wheel of an SUV, ready to follow them back to Ferguson Lake.

They had discussed where to stay. It made more sense for Adam to get a hotel room in Meadow Lake, but Grace wanted to talk to her fellow cabin owners — those who were still there in late September, and those who more or less lived at the lake. Adam didn't want Grace to be alone; and if Grace was honest with herself, she didn't want to be, either.

"We'll have to reopen and close the cabin again," Grace had warned him the night before.

"It takes two hours, Grace. No big deal."

"What about James?" As much as she loved James, Grace wasn't sure she could get through three days without making love. Having someone else in the cabin might cramp her style.

"He's already booked a cabin rental."

153

"Perfect."

The trip was uneventful until they reached North Battleford, where they turned down a winding, tree-lined road leading to the stately red-stone hospital. It had housed patients with various mental disabilities since 1914, and while it was beautiful on the outside, it was starting to rot on the inside.

Adam hadn't sent the administrator a photo; he had simply called to book an appointment. He wanted to see her reaction, in person, to the photograph of John Doe.

Adam and Grace pulled up in the parking lot with James right behind them. They climbed the concrete steps to the double doors, set under a wide and deep overhang, to find the administrator, Kate Deverell, awaiting them.

"Welcome," she said, a slightly uncertain smile on her lips. "Please, come in. You are Sergeant Davis?

"Yes. Nice to meet you, Ms. Deverell. This is Constable James Weatherall, and Grace Rampling."

Adam glanced at Grace with a strange expression, and she realized that Adam was in an uncomfortable position. How should he identify her? As his partner or a reporter?

Grace offered her hand, and quickly intervened to reassure the administrator.

"I'm a reporter with the StarPhoenix, working on this story," she said. "But I'm only here on background, for now. If you are able to identify this man, I won't report anything without your permission."

Deverell tilted her blonde head for a moment, then nodded.

"Come into my office," she said, and they followed her down the long, green and grey hallway.

Once settled in her space, she folded her hands on the desk and said, "Okay. Let me see."

"Are you in fact missing a patient?" Adam asked. "You seem resigned."

She inhaled sharply, then exhaled slowly. "Yes. Please, let me see the photo."

"This won't be pleasant."

"I've seen much worse than unpleasant, Sergeant," she said, much like Father Cey.

"Of course."

Adam drew the photo out of his shoulder bag, put it down carefully and pushed it across the desk. Deverell closed her eyes, inhaled again, then opened them and looked down.

She didn't move, for a moment, nor did she speak. Neither did Adam.

"Yes," she finally said. "This man was our patient."

Grace's stomach tightened, and she could see a flicker of triumph in Adam's eyes. Even so, he gave the woman some time and waited for her to continue.

"Damn," said the administrator, under her breath. "I'd hoped he would return."

"Who was he?" Adam asked.

"He was Martin Best. Martin Joseph Best, age thirty-six. He came to us about three years ago, I think. He had tried, very hard, to manage on his own; to fight his disorder. But he had little support, and finally, he came here."

"We thought he might have been living on the street," Adam said, and by his flat tone, Grace could tell he was trying not to sound accusatory.

"Many of our patients are very, very sick," Deverell replied. "They don't look very healthy, no. And Martin was . . . in bad shape."

"When did he go missing?"

"He didn't *go* missing," she said, colour rising in her face. "We don't normally lose patients, Sergeant."

"I'm sorry. I didn't mean to imply you did. What happened, then?"

Deverell's eyebrows came together in an expression of contrition.

"No, I'm sorry. He is missing, after all. A man claiming to be his cousin, with a substantial amount of evidence for that claim, came to take him on an outing two days ago. He did not return. We've been worried. Rightly so, apparently."

"Not worried enough to call the police?"

"We did call the police," she retorted. "But as you know, they don't start looking for twenty-four hours, and in theory, Martin was with a relative."

"What was this man's name?"

"Charles Best. Or so he, and his identification, said."

"Describe him for me, please."

She thought for a moment.

"He was tall, but not quite as tall as you are. Brown hair; not as dark as yours. Slim, but reasonably fit-looking. Stood very erect, shoulders back. I noticed it particularly. Remarkable posture."

Grace's head, which had been bent over her notebook, snapped up. She looked at Adam with wondering eyes but didn't want to intervene in the interview without permission.

"What are you thinking, Grace?" he encouraged her.

"Did you see a tattoo?" she asked the administrator.

"I don't recall seeing one."

"Did he wear a hat?"

"Yes, he did. I remember thinking it was odd at the time."

"But you could still see his hair."

"Yes. His cap didn't cover all of his hair."

"Ball cap?"

"Yes."

Grace cast Adam a sidelong glance and nodded. Charles Best, or whoever the hell had picked up the victim at the hospital, fit the description of the satellite salesman as provided by Tillie Allbright, minus the tattoo.

156

"Was he wearing long sleeves, do you recall?"

"Um. I think he was." Kate Deverell squeezed her eyes shut, in an obvious effort to see the man better in her mind's eye. "He wore a shirt, yes, a button-down white shirt, rolled up just over his wrists."

Bingo, thought Grace. That would have covered the tattoo. With another nod, she turned the interview back over to Adam.

"What can you tell us about Martin Best?" he asked.

"We do have privacy regulations, Sergeant."

"I'm aware of that. Will I have to get a warrant?"

"Probably."

"The man is dead."

"Yes, but his health information remains protected."

"I realize that, but in this case, other people's lives may be in danger. I believe there are other regulations surrounding such circumstances?"

"Oh." Deverell paused. "I see. Let me speak to his psychiatrist and I'll renew my understanding of the regulations. Give me your card, Sergeant Davis. I'll be in touch."

"I'll start working on the court order, as well. It's important, Ms. Deverell. We don't know if there may be another potential victim."

"I'll do my best, Sergeant."

Adam rose and offered his hand again. "Thank you. You've been very helpful."

Kate Deverell gave a short laugh. "Perhaps not very."

\*\*\*\*\*

On the way north, they discussed Martin Best's apparent abductor, agreeing that he was almost certainly Tillie's satellite salesman. Grace drove, allowing Adam to call and ask Charlotte to procure a court order for the victim's history, and to seek a man named Charles Best.

Two and a half hours later, they were back at Ferguson Lake. James had turned off to his cabin nearby, and Adam and Grace opened the Rampling cottage, mere days after having closed it.

The weather was not quite as warm as it had been a few days ago, and the aspen leaves were falling in a golden shimmer all around them. A few of the remaining late-season cottagers had apparently gone south after the weekend, leaving boarded-up and locked cabins behind.

Immediately after unloading the truck and going down to the water — business trip or no, Grace had to follow the ritual — she and Adam slipped over to the Allbright cabin, to ensure they were still there. Grace stood uncertainly at the end of the path, chewing her lower lip, for a moment.

"Maybe I'd better make sure they're not leaving tomorrow," she said.

"Good idea."

But while their vehicle was in the driveway at the back, sheltered by the towering pines, the Allbrights themselves were not there. Probably visiting friends at another cabin. Grace couldn't decide if she was relieved, since she and Adam could spend the evening doing whatever they wanted, or frustrated at not finding them at home.

"Want to go for a wander?" she asked Adam.

"Yeah. Let's walk and talk. What's your plan tomorrow, then?"

"First thing I'll go see Tillie, see what she has to say. I hope she knows more about Elias than I do; it just never really came up. She's up here much more often than I am. And if she doesn't, she might know someone who does."

"You've never discussed his family?"

"We've never really discussed him. It's always been a quiet sort of understanding, that we — the cottagers who knew a bit about him — would protect him, but none of us really knew him. I think I probably knew him best, which isn't saying much. So, there wasn't much to gossip about, except when Uncle Howard tried his land grab. And the less said, the better, to preserve his privacy. And maybe his sanity, or what was left of it."

She sighed. "Obviously, I should have asked her when we were here. I never thought the RCMP wouldn't find his family. What will you do tomorrow?"

"I'll head into Meadow Lake in the morning," Adam said, with a small sigh he couldn't repress.

"You're not looking forward to this."

"No. It's hard. I don't want to confront a fellow officer."

"I don't blame you."

"What if he's involved in the murders, and not just the landlord of Mrs. Robertson's house? Can you remember if he said or did anything strange after we found Elias?"

"No. Nothing. He seemed to react normally, although you'd know better if he was following protocol."

"He was, as far as I can recall. But he'd have to. Especially since I was there."

Grace thought for a moment. "The RCMP did get here remarkably quickly that night."

"Maybe he was in the neighbourhood."

"Maybe he was."

"Let's go start on dinner. James will be by soon."

\*\*\*\*\*

Adam and James left for Meadow Lake at eight in the morning, and Grace was ready for a visit with Tillie Allbright soon after. Too anxious to wait in the cabin, Grace went for a walk in the thin morning light, trying to wait until nine before she knocked on the neighbours' door. Was even that too early? she wondered.

She decided to roam around the greenway and along the path, in the hope that Tillie would see her and invite her in. That didn't work, so Grace, beside herself with impatience, gave up her grasp on self-control and approached the cottage.

Tillie answered her tentative knock right away.

"Grace. I didn't expect to see you again so soon. Come in."

"Thanks, Tillie. Sorry if I'm disturbing you. It is a bit early."

"No, no. When you're a farmer all your life, you're up at first light, or earlier. Coffee?"

"Sure, thanks."

"How's Adam's hand?" the older woman asked as she poured.

"Healing well, thanks to you. I'm ever so grateful, Tillie."

"Least I could do, as it turned out." Tillie sighed heavily. "Do you know what's happening with Tom? I haven't heard from him, nor the RCMP."

"I'm sorry, I don't. Adam is in Meadow Lake today; hopefully he'll have some news when he gets back."

Tillie looked confused. "Why is Adam in Meadow Lake?"

"I can't say; I'm sorry. Something to do with the case. Nothing to do with Tom, specifically, though." Grace sipped her coffee. "Tillie, I have to ask you about Elias."

"What about him?"

"What do you know about him? And his family? I barely knew him. He never told me anything about his background, just that he had served with the forces. But you're up here more often, and I've been wondering if you know more about him than I do. It just never came up. But now, it's important. What do you know?"

"I don't know a lot. I don't know much about his time in the forces. But I do know a bit about his family. He's from a

160

reserve further south, but he was adopted by his uncle over at Raven River when he was pretty young. Maybe eight or nine."

"Do you know the uncle's name?"

"Elijah Starblanket."

Grace found it hard to conceal her excitement.

"How do you know him? Let's face it, Tillie, we cottagers don't mingle much with the local people, which you could say is pretty awful of us. But we don't. How do you know Elias's uncle?"

"Do you remember that night — you must have been only what, five or six? — when Tommy went missing? Everyone gathered at your cabin to organize a search party. Remember?"

"I couldn't ever forget that night. It was so scary."

"No kidding. We didn't know if Tom had drowned or was lost in the bush or mauled by a bear. It was awful." Tillie paused. "Elijah Starblanket was the man who found Tom in the forest. He'd been out fishing or trapping or something and heard the little bugger thrashing about and crying. You may recall he marched Tom back here and disappeared. But eventually, I found him. I needed to thank him for finding my kid. It took a few years."

"How did you manage that?"

"It took a while. I went to the reserves around here whenever I could, which wasn't often, and just kept asking questions until someone finally told me it had been Elijah. I barely saw him in the dark, that night; but I did get a peek at him. And it had to be someone who knew the forest and the lakes, and that meant, more than likely, an Indigenous man.

"That's when I met Elias, too. He would have been about thirteen or so. Sweet kid. Elijah doted on him, although he was also very strict; I could tell by how he spoke to him. Kind, but strict."

"Please tell me Elijah is alive. And at Raven River."

"Oh, yes. Well, as far as I know. I haven't seen him for a while, but I've tried to stay in touch a bit. He was certainly fine and still around a year or so ago."

"Tillie," said Grace, slowly. "You must be very upset about Elias. You are obviously very fond of his uncle. You haven't contacted him, then?"

Tillie's mouth worked; her eyes filled with tears, and with a sob she broke down completely. Grace moved her chair beside Tillie's an put an arm around her shoulders.

"No. Oh God, what a terrible thing. What an awful, disgusting, terrible thing," Tillie gasped, a few moments later, between heaving breaths. "I just couldn't contact him. What if Tom had something to do with his death? I can't stand it. Especially since Elijah saved his life. Please, Grace. Get Adam to find out. I have to know."

Grace leaned in further and hugged Tillie tightly.

"He'll find out. I promise. He's brilliant, and he never gives up. If anyone can figure it out, Adam can."

Tillie nodded, and wiped her eyes on a sleeve.

"What will you do now?" she asked.

"Go to Raven River. Want to come?"

# Chapter Nineteen

The truck bumped and lurched over the dirt road into the Raven River reserve. Despite the vehicle's considerable size, Grace was forced to fight the steering wheel to keep from bouncing out of the ruts. Shitty roads were ubiquitous on Saskatchewan reserves, which Grace always thought was a result of very bad government policy and jurisdictional confusion. This road, little more than a trail, was exceptionally dreadful.

She glanced at Tillie. "How are you doing?"

"Okay. I'm a bit nervous about seeing Elijah, considering Tom, but it's really time I expressed my sympathies, too. I assume he knows about Elias. Pretty tight grapevine around here, on the reserves."

"How's your back? This can't be helping it."

"I'm fine, Grace. Thanks, but don't worry about me. Must be done. And I will be glad to see him again."

"Any idea which house is his?"

"Oh, yes. Keep going up to that turnoff, head right. We're almost there."

Three minutes later, Grace pulled up in a tidy yard in front of a small, white house nestled among pine trees. The road sucked, but Raven River was one of the prettiest reserves she had ever seen, tucked as it was into the forest with a river flowing along its western boundary.

Would they find him at home? Grace's shoulders tightened as she wondered if their trip had been for nothing, and what their reception might be. She climbed out of the truck and helped Tillie clamber down from its high running board.

The two women approached the door, took deep breaths together, and Grace knocked. No answer.

"He might be around the back," Tillie said. "He has a shop out there."

"Let's go see."

They walked around the south side of the little house, and Grace soon saw a large garage at the back.

"Hello!" Tillie called. "Elijah! It's me, Tillie. Are you there?"

The door opened, and an incredibly tall, lean man with long, thick black-and-grey hair appeared, holding a wrench.

"Tillie," was all he said, before he walked over and embraced her. The look on his face told both women he knew Elias was dead. Tillie hugged him back and wept.

"I'm so sorry, Elijah," she said. "I'm so sorry about Elias."

They stood like that for a while, until Tillie collected herself, stepped out of the hug and said, "I've brought you a visitor."

"I see," said Elijah. "You're Miss Grace."

Grace's eyes widened. "Just Grace. Sir, nice to meet you. But how do you know me?"

"I know Elias found you in the forest. He described you perfectly, and I'm sure you haven't changed that much. You were very frightened. He told me."

"It's something you shared, then. Saving us stupid children when we got lost."

The big man just smiled, sadly, down at her.

164

"Come to the house," he said. "I think you have something to ask me."

"Yes, sir. If you don't mind."

Elijah led the way to the house, and once inside, put a kettle on to boil.

The kitchen and living room were small, but quite comfortably furnished and very tidy. Tillie and Grace took chairs at the dining table, waiting for their host to prepare tea. It was a fascinating procedure. Elijah Starblanket didn't simply pull out a teabag but tossed rosehips and a variety of leaves into a pot, along with dried blueberries, as far as Grace could tell. When he poured the boiling water over the tiny cornucopia, the aroma was spicy, rich and complex. Grace couldn't wait to taste it.

Finally, he bore three cups, the steaming pot and a plate of bannock spread with crushed cranberries to the table. Briefly, he closed his eyes as if in blessing, and Grace suddenly knew how to address him.

"Elder Starblanket," she began. "You may already know this, but I'm a reporter for the Saskatoon newspaper. We are covering Elias's murder, as well as a second murder that occurred very shortly afterward in the city. As I understand it, you have not yet been officially informed of his death. Is that right?"

"Yes. I called the RCMP; we must have Elias's body returned to us. But no one has responded."

"I'm so sorry, sir. And sorry to have to ask you about this. Please tell me if it's too upsetting."

The Elder shook his head.

"It is time for the truth to come out. It is too late, for Elias. I will answer any questions you have."

Grace's stomach knotted. In a flash of realization, she understood that Elijah Starblanket's life might also be in danger.

165

"Is it safe for you to speak to me?" she asked, voice low.

"Possibly not. But I will. I must."

"If you're sure, sir."

"I am sure."

Grace inhaled deeply and took a sip of the fragrant liquid in front of her. It tasted of sun and pure water, berries and pungent herbs. It awakened her senses and calmed her nerves. What on Earth was in this? she wondered. Her eyes betrayed her.

"Don't worry," said the Elder, with a small smile. "There's nothing mind-altering in my tea. It is simply nature's medicine. Now I will tell you a story."

Elijah Starblanket closed his eyes, folded his hands, and began to speak. He told them how he had adopted Elias: Elijah's sister had married a man of the surname Crow, moved south, had a child and died a few years later. The father was clearly uninterested in the boy, so Elijah took Elias in and raised him, along with his own four children.

Elias joined his uncle on the trap lines, on fishing excursions, and learned the ways of the Nation and of the forest. But he also wanted to follow Elijah into the Canadian Army.

"I tried to talk him out of it," said Elijah, a small choking noise escaping from his throat. "I loved my son; I wanted him to stay here with us. But I had gone overseas and served as a peacekeeper in Cyprus, and Elias thought it was a noble thing to do. So, he signed up. It turned out he was right; it was a noble thing to do. At least, for himself."

Early in his army days, Elijah continued, Elias made a name for himself. He was tall, strong, agile and kept his mouth shut. He did well in basic training, and ultimately ended up with the Canadian Airborne Regiment in Petawawa, Ontario. An elite soldier.

His company was shipped to Somalia, ostensibly for peacekeeping during the country's civil war in 1993.

"One night, when Elias was on patrol, he came upon a small group of children trying to sneak into the supply tent," Elijah said softly, in his measured speech. "He was very worried about it, because there were some sick men in his unit; he wasn't sure what they might do to the kids. Elias grabbed the oldest of the group by his shirt collar and told him to run away and not come back."

"Much like you did with Tom," Tillie said, "when you brought him home that night."

"Yes. I had done it to Elias, too, when he needed a little march toward home," he said.

"The boy did run away. The others, of course, were scared out of their wits and had already vanished. But a couple of the soldiers saw Elias letting the little ones go. They reported him to the brass."

Elijah swallowed. Grace could see he was struggling for control.

"What happened then, sir?" she prompted, gently.

"They followed the children into the village, and unleashed hell," Elijah said. A single tear tracked down his left cheek, but he did not wipe it away. "They set fires to the homes, shot their weapons into the air, beat some of the people and demanded that the boys be brought forward.

"Of course, the villagers wouldn't hand over their little boys, so the night went on and on. Finally, the boy Elias had spoken with stepped forward and took responsibility. They beat the hell out of him, dragged him away. Elias saw the beating, but he never found out what happened to the boy. Whether he lived or died.

"Elias witnessed some of that night of terror but was taken back to camp before it was over. Some of the soldiers felt he couldn't be trusted, and of course, from their perspective, that

167

was true. Afterward, he was ostracized. And you know the rest. He came back a different man. A broken one."

"Were any of the soldiers disciplined for the attack on the village?" Grace asked.

"I heard that one of the men went to trial a couple of years later and was sentenced to a few years. I'm not sure how many. Army proceedings are not always made public."

"I know. I've been searching for information about something, anything, that happened in Somalia or Rwanda, apart from the two incidents that were covered by the foreign press. I couldn't find anything on this. How did you know there was a trial?"

"Army grapevine. But very little information came out. They were trying to keep it quiet."

"And Elias never found out what happened to the boy?"

"No."

"It didn't come up at the trial?"

"It may have. But I don't know. I assume they dealt with it through a summary, since no details have ever come to light."

"Is that legal?"

"Might be, if barely so. If no deaths among the Somalis were proven, they might have wiggled it through a summary as disgraceful behaviour."

"And Elias, not knowing if anyone died, couldn't have done anything else about it."

"No. He was too far gone in the first few years, anyway. No one would have believed him, and maybe rightly so. It's hard to say how accurate his memory was."

"Just from the PTSD?" Grace asked, frowning. "I don't know much about it, really. Can PTSD cause memory blackout?"

"It can," said Elijah, slowly, "but that wasn't the only problem."

"What do you mean?"

168

"The Airborne soldiers all had to take an anti-malarial drug before they shipped out. Mefloquine. Nastiest dope on the planet. It makes you see things you never thought could exist. Because they don't."

"They saw monsters," Grace said. "Elias told me, 'they followed them. They saw monsters.' Is that what you mean, sir?"

The Elder nodded.

"Just like Clayton Matchee. Why didn't I think of that sooner?" Grace asked aloud, more of herself than of the Elder.

"That wasn't all," Elijah said. "They were also chugging cough medicine. Codeine. It kept the patrols from coughing in the dry air, to avoid giving their positions away. They must have been severely strung out. I don't know if there were any other drugs in the camp; there may have been. But mefloquine and codeine? That would be enough to scramble anyone's brain. And it did a number on Elias. He just didn't have it in him, I guess, to hurt little children."

No, he didn't, Grace thought. She remembered how gentle Elias had been when he found her in the dark forest. How kind.

"How did he get home?" she asked.

"His tour was almost over, thank God. I wonder what would have happened to him if he'd stayed. As soon as he hit the ground at the air force base, he went AWOL. A month later, he showed up here; took him a long time to figure out his way back.

"Once I dragged the story out of him, and it took a while, I knew we had to hide him. But where? If anyone was looking for him, he'd be a sitting duck on the reserve, or in Meadow Lake, or anywhere else in a nearby community.

"So, I took him to my shack south of Ferguson. I'd built it after I got back from overseas. I needed a place to rest and recover, too, and it was peaceful there — especially then. I roamed around the area, fished and hunted, and finally built that hut, too. That's why I found Tom that night. I was often around your lake. Still am, although less so."

"Who killed Elias, sir?" Grace breathed. "Do you know?"

"A cabal," said the Elder. "It was mefloquine. It was codeine. It was the commanding officer. It was the soldiers. It was the Armed Forces. And the government, which allowed it all to happen and turned the other way."

# Chapter Twenty

Adam inhaled deeply before walking through the doors of the long, low brick building that housed the Meadow Lake RCMP detachment. He liked Al Simpson. As far as Adam knew, he was a hell of a cop, or at least had been.

The only other police officer Adam had ever been forced to confront was his direct superior, Inspector Terry Pearson; but Adam loathed the man, and knew the feeling was returned. Getting into Pearson's face was not a problem. Asking Al if he had something to do with the death of a human being was another thing altogether.

James felt more than heard Adam's intake of breath. "Sucks," he said.

"Yeah," Adam agreed, exhaling. "Let's get this over with."

Swinging the door open, they approached the desk, announced themselves, and Adam asked for Sergeant Al Simpson. He had called during the forty-minute trip from Ferguson to make sure the man was in.

"One moment, please, Sergeant," said the woman at reception, giving both men a surreptitious and approving once-over with her big hazel eyes. Adam, head down, didn't notice, but James gave her a smile. The occasional ego boost wasn't such a bad thing.

There was a delay. Adam wondered if Al smelled something amiss and was preparing himself either with lies or truth. Too many little things were adding up in Adam's brain. He didn't like the sums.

Finally, Al emerged through a set of doors to the right of the lobby.

"Detective Sergeant Adam Davis," he said, with a little smirk. "Didn't expect you back on my turf so soon. How the hell are you?"

"I'm fine, thanks," Adam replied, wondering if Al was trying to make a point about the Saskatoon police trampling on his territory. "Al, this is Detective Constable James Weatherall."

"Nice to meet you," Al said, offering his hand.

"And you," James said, shaking it.

"So, what brings you back to the north?"

"As you know, Al, we've had a second death in Saskatoon that I think might be related to Elias Crow's murder. Is there somewhere private we could go?"

Was that a shadow passing over Al Simpson's face? Certainly, his expression changed.

"Come to my office. Just down here. Coffee?"

"Sure, I could use a cup. James?"

"That'd be great."

They paused at a tiny kitchen set up with a microwave, coffee pot and small refrigerator, poured mugs of black coffee, and proceeded to Al's office; but not before a few drops of hot liquid met Al's shirt and brogans.

"Shit," he said, wiping at his stomach. "Sit down, sit down. How can I help?"

Adam cleared his throat. His brain screamed to give Al fair warning, but he couldn't do it. He did give him another chance.

"We're working on identifying the victim in Saskatoon," Adam began. "Do you have the photo handy?"

"Uh, no. It's on my computer . . . do you want me to bring it up?"

"No. I have it right here." Adam pulled out his constant companion and placed it in front of Al, watching the other man's face intently.

Al's brow furrowed and his eyes narrowed, as anyone's would when taking a careful look. Then his cheek twitched, and he looked up.

"Right. And so?"

"No one around here recognized him, you said, the last time we talked. Anyone weigh in since then?"

"No."

Damn it, thought Adam, running a hand through his hair. Come on, Al.

One more time.

"You're sure."

"What the hell is this about, Adam?" Al's voice betrayed anger and impatience. Did it also betray fear? Adam wasn't sure, but he felt James tense beside him.

"I think you know this man, Al. Want to give him another look?"

"What d'you mean, I know him?"

"He was found dead in your mother's house." Adam let that sink in for a moment.

"Oh, my God." Al paused, and a second later, realization sparked in his eyes. "How the fuck?"

"Come on, Al. We're not complete idiots. We searched for and found the owner of the house, and it was a Mrs. Margaret Muriel Robertson. She was kind enough to host us in her room, and to show us the picture of the son she's so proud of. You."

Adam could see the blood rising in Al's face from throat to forehead. The RCMP officer took a deep and clearly difficult swallow and wrestled visibly with his self-control as he shifted in his chair and gripped the desk.

"Who was he, Al? Why did he die on your mother's property?" Adam kept his voice low and level.

"I . . . don't know him."

"You mean you don't know his name?"

"I mean I don't know him."

"Do you know why he died?"

"I'm not saying anything more."

"Come on, Al. This could go badly."

"It will go badly anyway."

Before Adam could respond, Al violently shoved his chair back from his desk, lurched to his feet and lunged for the door, pulling it open and dashing out before James, who was closer, could react.

But James sprung to his feet in a flash, darting after Al on legs that Adam thought, for the thousandth time, seemed spring-loaded. He was right behind his constable a second later, running at top speed down the narrow hallway.

"Fuck, Al, stop!" Adam yelled. But he didn't.

James caught up to Al first, launching himself at the heavier, less-fit sergeant and knocking him to the floor. RCMP officers emerged from office doors to see what the commotion was about and threw themselves at James, who was wrestling with the by-now screaming Al, punching his fists in all directions. One punch landed on James's cheek, eliciting a loud "oof" as an RCMP constable reached down and grabbed him by the shoulders.

"Stop!" Adam bellowed. His big baritone froze the officers in a strange tableau of lifted arms, clenched fists and bemused faces.

"Al Simpson," he continued, still yelling. "I'm arresting you on suspicion of conspiracy to commit murder. Now quit fighting. Everyone else, please back away. Right now."

"On whose authority?" one of the officers asked.

"Mine. And by now, your superiors." Adam, flashing his badge, hoped Chief McIvor had fulfilled his promise of split-second timing, and had reached the RCMP commander.

"I'm not saying anything!" Al yelled.

"Shut up, Al," James told him. "Just be quiet for now and calm the hell down. Okay?"

Stunned, the RCMP officers backed off. James and Adam rolled Al Simpson over and cuffed him. What else can we do? Adam thought. He's obviously not coming quietly.

Dragged to his feet, Al stood swaying slightly, his face a mask of shock and fear. Adam and James each took an arm, pulled him out to the Saskatoon Police SUV, and drove him to the correctional centre for booking. James drove, and Adam called the chief.

"We have him in the car, sir," he said, when McIvor answered. "He's not talking."

"Okay, Adam. I've informed the commanding officer. Call me later."

An appalled expression on the face of the booking sergeant told Adam that he had been informed of Simpson's imminent arrival.

"We'll be back to talk to him later," Adam said, giving up custody. "Can we talk to Tom Allbright, please, while we're here?"

"Uh, ah, yeah, sure, Sergeant," said the desk man. "I'll just get someone to take you into the interview room. One sec."

"Take care, Al," Adam said, as two burly constables drew him into the back for processing.

"I'll see you later."

Al didn't answer.

*****

A few minutes later, Adam and James found themselves across a table from Tom Allbright, who, to Adam's eyes, looked very slightly better than on the night he had attacked Grace. Adam looked down at his still-bandaged hand, remembering.

"Hello, Tom."

"Why are you here, again?" Tom asked, sounding more puzzled than anything.

"First of all, how are you feeling?"

"Like shit. But they give me something to help me sleep."

"We have to ask you some questions. I know you've been asked before, but as far as I can tell by these reports, you haven't answered them."

"I have nothing to say. I told you that at the lake."

"We're going to try again," Adam said. "I highly recommend co-operating. We have two dead men, Tom. And you are involved."

Tom's hooded eyes flew open. "Two?"

"Yes. Two. Elias Crow and a second man who was found dead in Saskatoon. These two deaths are related and . . . are you all right?"

Tom had gone paper-white, his red eyes huge, his mouth open in a horrified circle. He stared at Adam, unseeing and saying nothing.

"Tom, do you need something? Water?"

"I need some fucking dope, man," he finally said.

"Not happening."

The prisoner's head went down in abject misery. "Come on, just a little bit. I'll feel better."

"We can't go out and score you some meth, Tom, for God's sake. If you're hurting that much, we'll check with the doctor. But first, questions." And the photo came out, again. "Do you know this man?"

Tom looked and shook his head. "He looks more like shit than I do."

"That's because he's dead. Are you sure you don't know him?"

"I — I'm pretty sure. Maybe he looks a little bit familiar, but I don't think I know him."

"A little bit familiar. How?"

"Like maybe I'd seen him a long, long time ago. But I don't know."

"What do you know about Elias Crow's death, Tom?"

"Nothing. I don't know nothing."

"Tom. If you know nothing, why were you hiding at the lake when he died?"

"Just happened to be in the wrong place, that's all."

"That's bullshit. You hadn't been up there in years. Why, then, on that weekend? And why the hell were you carrying a knife, if you were just up for a happy little holiday? Why did you attack Grace? And why didn't you tell your folks you were there? You know something. I know it. You know it. You're going to tell me, right now."

Something Adam said seemed to click with the junkie before him. Maybe Tom Allbright, now off meth for several days, caught his logic — that it was obvious he was connected to at least one murder.

"I can't talk to you," he whispered. "I can't. Please, leave me alone. I didn't shoot Elias. You have to believe me."

A chink. Adam jumped through.

"How did you know he was shot?"

The police had carefully and purposely left the details of Elias's death out of all correspondence with the media, and everyone else. Adam now knew for certain that Tom had played a role in the veteran's death. But Tom was silent.

"Tom. How did you know?"

"Please, Sergeant. I can't say anything. Even if I have to stay in here. It's safer."

177

"What the hell are you talking about? Tom, fucking talk to me."

"I can't. They'll kill me. Not that that would be much of a loss to anyone."

"Who will kill you?"

"I can't tell you. They'll kill me. They might even kill me if they know you've been here. Please. Can you leave now?"

\*\*\*\*\*

Now what was he going to do? Tom Allbright was in a jail shared by Al Simpson, scared to death for his life. Neither of them would point a finger, nor take any responsibility for two deaths. Did Tom need protection? Did Al?

And would moving them to a different jail make any damn difference?

Adam pondered and worried as he and James left the centre.

"I can't just leave him there, in general population," Adam said, once they were outside. "He's messed up on drugs, but obviously he's scared to death and equally obviously, he's connected to Elias's murder."

"Solitary seems like a bad idea for a guy that fucked up," James observed.

"Yeah. That's another problem. And what about Al? How's he involved in all this, and if we can believe Tom, is he in danger, too?"

Adam shook his head to clear his thoughts. "I want to go back in there and tell the desk sergeant to keep an eye on them. But shit, James, if Al is a suspect, who else might be involved? And could that person, or those people, be here, or in Saskatoon?"

Adam's phone pinged. He looked down to see a message from Grace.

*Found Elias's uncle*, it read. *He thinks army involved.*

*Why?* Adam texted back.

*Told me what happened to Elias. Much news. When can we talk?*

*Soon. Have to deal with a problem first. Four?*

*OK. See you at the cabin.*

Adam showed James the conversation.

"We have to get them out of here."

# Chapter Twenty-One

Adam and James stood firmly before the desk of the Ford dealership in Meadow Lake, pulling rank.

"I need to rent a vehicle," said Adam, showing the salesman his badge.

"We don't rent cars here, sir," he said.

"You do now."

Meadow Lake, population approximately five thousand, was devoid of car rental companies, to Adam's considerable chagrin. Hence, the dealership.

The salesman still looked dubious.

"Let's pretend we're taking it for an extended test drive," Adam suggested.

The man sighed.

"Let me call my manager."

An hour later, having signed copious amounts of paperwork and putting the Saskatoon Police's insurance policy on the line, James had his own slightly-used SUV. Adam called Chief McIvor and insisted that Tom Allbright and Al Simpson be moved to Saskatoon, there to be held temporarily in police cells under constant supervision.

"Until I know they're safe, Chief. We can't just leave them here. Allbright's testimony and Al Simpson's body language were pretty convincing. They're also our witnesses — well, hopefully — as well as suspects."

"This better not be a fucking tempest in a goddamned teapot."

"I know, Chief." Adam held back a burst of laughter at the chief's language, peppering the old saying with his usual expletives. "Could you please call the correctional centre, and tell them James will be hanging out there until the wagon comes to pick them up?"

"Will do. The wagon should be there in about four hours. When the hell are you coming back?"

"Tomorrow, I think. Unless some other crazy thing happens."

James got behind the wheel of the newly-rented vehicle, and Adam hopped into the police SUV.

"Come by the cabin when you're finished here," Adam said, through the windows. "We'll feed you and catch you up."

"Okay. Will there be beer?"

"Beer there will be."

Adam saluted his constable, rolled up the window and started the drive north to Ferguson Lake, ready to let the forty minutes of solitude clear his mind — and more than ready to see Grace. What the RCMP couldn't, or wouldn't, accomplish in a few days she had managed in less than one.

The thought brought another. Adam pulled over onto a farmer's grid road, hauled out his phone and called Nathan Ellard.

"Hey, Sarge," he answered, sounding sorrowful. "That was some crazy shit."

"Yeah, I know. Sorry, Nathan. I should have stuck around to talk, but we had to get Al out of there. So, I'm calling. I need to know what efforts were made to find Elias Crow's family."

"Well, we sent out an email to the reserves in the area, to the chiefs. Al did some calling around."

"Did you actually hear or see him do so?"

Ellard paused, then quietly said, "No. He said he would handle it."

"It looks like he didn't. And no response to the emails?"

"I've only seen a couple, but no one so far has admitted to knowing Elias. He had been off the grid for quite some time, Sarge. I don't know if he was originally from around here."

"He was. I'm going to find out more in about half an hour. Okay, thanks, Nathan. I'll be in touch."

Adam turned back to the highway, wondering how Al Simpson thought he would get away with not making every effort to find the dead man's family. Did he have an exit strategy in place? Did he think he'd be long gone before his detachment realized something was wrong? If so . . . where was he planning to go?

Suddenly, Adam was anxious to return to the cabin. There were two men dead, two men in jail, Grace had been attacked and someone out there was ultimately responsible. Who was it, and where was he?

Or, where were they?

He pushed down the accelerator and pulled into the cabin driveway thirty minutes later. Jumping out of the SUV, he felt his heart tick faster as he walked up to the cabin and opened the door, calling out for Grace.

No answer. She wasn't there. His heart thumped a little harder, as he headed down the path to the beach.

There she was, sitting on the last dock remaining in the water. Her arms encircled her knees, and her hair flew behind her in a stiffening breeze, as she looked out over the shining blue water.

"Hey, Babe," Adam said as he came up behind her, his shoulders dropping in relief. He crouched down and hugged her, nuzzling. "Are you all right?"

Grace turned in his arms, rising onto her knees, and threw her own arms around him in a clutch of passion.

"Is that a no, then?" Adam asked, trying to look into her face, but it was buried in his neck. "Honey?"

"I'm better now," she mumbled into him. "Hold me. Kiss me," she added, removing her face from his body and offering her lips.

Adam touched her mouth with his, gently, but Grace placed her hand on the back of his head and kissed him hard.

"Right here in front of God and everyone?" Adam said lightly, and a touch breathlessly, after the kiss had finally ended. Then he looked into her eyes and saw her distress. He helped Grace to her feet and led her to the little bench at the end of the dock.

"Talk to me," he said, pulling her down.

"As I told you, I found Elias's uncle," Grace said. "Elijah Starblanket is his name. He's an Elder on the Raven River Reserve."

She told Adam the entire conversation, from Elias's adoption through to the Elder's final words.

"It was a cabal, he said. He also blamed the army for giving the soldiers a really nasty anti-malarial drug as well as codeine. He said it messed them up horribly, including Elias."

"Mefloquine?"

Grace nodded.

"I looked it up. Mefloquine was brought into use as a prophylaxis against malaria in 1989 in the United States — four years before our soldiers were dosed with it before being shipping out to Somalia. It was still very new to the military, but the drug came with a "discontinue" warning if someone experienced psychiatric symptoms, vivid dreams or even insomnia."

Grace paused and looked down, shaking her head.

"If they didn't know the side effects, that's one thing. But even back then, there were indications that this drug could cause extreme symptoms. One study's authors recommended that pilots not use it, and that was in 1982. No wonder so many soldiers came back with PTSD."

"There are other anti-malarials, aren't there?" Adam asked.

"Yes, at least two that were — and still are — commonly used for people travelling to Africa or other places where malaria is a problem."

"So how many armed forces members are out there with long-term mefloquine side effects?" Adam mused.

"Too many," Grace said, bitterly.

"Including our killer, possibly. And definitely at least one of our victims."

"Yes."

"Okay. Well, we can release Elias's name now; or at least, we can as soon as I talk to his uncle. But should we?"

"What are you thinking, Adam?"

"Is there a benefit to withholding his identity? You've already reported that someone was murdered at Ferguson Lake. If the killer is following the news, he knows we found him; but he knew that anyway, right? He was on the island when we arrived. But he doesn't know we've identified him, unless he heard you calling Elias's name. That might buy us some time. We know something he doesn't know."

Adam paused for a moment and ran a hand through his hair.

"And it might protect Elijah Starblanket. If they don't know we've talked to him, then theoretically, we don't know what Elijah knows. But if we release Elias's name, they'll know we've informed the family, and probably interviewed him."

Grace nodded.

"When you say 'they?'" she prompted.

"We already have Al Simpson, Tom Allbright and at least one other person involved in this — whoever picked up Martin Best at the psychiatric hospital. That qualifies as 'they.' If Elijah is right, there are more."

Grace shivered. It was after five by now, and the September sun was slipping toward the west, taking the day's warmth with it.

"This sucks," she said, turning her face toward the water.

"Yes, it does." Adam checked his watch. "We have three hours, more or less, before James returns."

"Late dinner, then."

"Yes. Want to, ah, build up an appetite?"

Grace smirked. That's better, Adam thought.

"Do you want to go for a walk?" she teased him.

"I had a little indoor exercise in mind. It's getting chilly out here."

"So it is."

\*\*\*\*\*

Adam lay on his side, touching the tips of Grace's breasts, one after the other, back and forth in a steady rhythm, like a musician with two tiny drums.

"Feeling any better?" he asked her.

"Much. Amazing what making love will do. All those endorphins block out everything else. If you keep that up, though, mister . . . "

"Then what, Grace?" Adam increased the pressure of his touch.

"Oh!" she cried, her hips coming up. "Damn it, man."

"Do you want me to stop?"

185

"No. That depends. Do we have time to . . . ahhh . . ."

"More, then."

"Yes. Oh, God."

Afterward, Grace held Adam tightly, stroking his hair and back.

"My beautiful man," she finally murmured.

Loath to leave his warm home, Adam stayed inside her for a while as she crooned, but finally eased himself up and over onto the bed. He pulled her into him, and they fell asleep in a cocoon of remembered pleasure and peace.

*****

"Adam! Adam!"

He awakened with a start. Someone was shouting. Damn. Who?

"Adam!"

"I'm coming!" Adam shouted, recognizing James's voice. In the same moment, he smelled smoke. "Grace! Wake up. Something's wrong," he said, pulling on jeans.

Adam dashed out the bedroom door and toward the back of the cabin; James's calls had come from that direction. In the darkness, all he could see was the bright flare of an orange flame.

"Holy God," Adam whispered, and lunged outside.

James was already at the side of the cottage, rummaging in the fire-thrown shadows for the garden hose. Adam saw that the shed immediately behind the cabin was alight, and knew they had seconds to tame it. Gasoline for boats, propane for cooking, all the explosive fuel an arsonist could possibly want was in that little hut.

James obviously knew it too. Every cabin owner or guest in Saskatchewan would have.

"Grace! Get out of the cabin! Now!" Adam yelled, grabbing a shovel and vaguely thanking himself for forgetting to put it away. As fast as his arms would allow, he began throwing loamy dirt at the flames, as James turned on the faucet and aimed the hose's icy flow at the shed.

Seconds later, Gordon Allbright appeared, panting and on the run with a second shovel in his hands.

"Skip's getting the water truck," he gasped. The subdivision had its own small fire-fighting trailer, always filled with water. It required several strong people to move it, but it was nearby in the clearing that served as community meeting space.

Adam could hear more shouting, then, the calls among the late-season cottagers raised in hectic, organized chaos. He and Gordon continued to fling dirt, as James kept the water focused on the flames.

The little shed, old and worn from years of weathering, burned hot and fast; and with a snap, the sixty-foot pine tree looming inches away ignited. Adam feared it would burn and fall.

And where was Grace?

Not ceasing to dig and throw, he screamed her name. "Grace! Where are you?"

"Adam! I'm all right. I'm here," she said, struggling with the other cottagers as they dragged and pushed the heavy water reservoir into the driveway.

How the hell had she slipped by him? Adam wondered with half his brain, amazed.

"Get the tree!" he shouted, and another stream of water instantly shot into the air, dousing the pine and falling in a heavy, needle-spiked rain over the by-now filthy Adam and Gordon.

187

They fought like mad men and women, Tillie and Grace joining other cottagers, including the reliable Skip, behind the big hose as Adam and Gordon and James battled closer in.

Finally, the fire relented. The shed crumpled and hissed under the weight of the sodden, scorched wooden walls and shingled roof. Adam moved in, shovel poised, to dig for the gasoline can, always stored just inside the door.

"Adam!" Grace shouted. "Be careful! Anything in there will be blazing hot!"

Good point, he thought. Hacking through the rubble, he located the jerry can, drove the shovel's shaft through its handle and dragged it out of the ruined shack. More dirt showered over the container, courtesy of Gordon.

"Anything else flammable, Grace?" he asked. She was by now right behind the men.

"One propane container. Thank God the barbecue is on the deck."

Adam went in and dug for the tank, dragged it out and sat heavily on the back step, which was blackened but otherwise more or less unscathed. James drew the back of one hand across his sweaty, dirty forehead, while Gordon and Skip just gazed at the destruction.

"James," Adam said. "Thank you. You have excellent timing."

"Not quite good enough, apparently," answered the constable, with a shaky grin. "If I'd been here two minutes earlier, or even less, I would have caught him in the act."

"I'm personally good with you saving our lives," Grace said, going over to hug James. "Not to mention the cabin. I can't think what to say, to thank you properly."

"Hugs are good, Grace," James said, returning the favour.

"What the hell is going on?" Gordon asked as he neared the trio.

"I don't know, Gordon, but thank God for you," Adam said, wearily. "Thanks for coming so quickly."

"I appreciate that, but damn, what the hell?"

"Someone knew we were here — me, or Grace, or both of us. He didn't count on James. One of us knows something the killer doesn't want us to know."

# Chapter Twenty-Two

For two more hours, Adam, James and the cottagers covered the steaming rubble with dirt, sprayed hot spots with cold well water, and checked the vicinity for errant sparks. The park's fire department came, checked, sprayed again and left. By then, night had fully fallen; it was after ten, pitch dark apart from a scatter of stars. To a person, everyone was dirty, stinking of smoke and very hungry.

Grace finally went inside, followed by Tillie, washed her face and hands, and started to rummage through cupboards and the fridge for food and drink. She handed bottles of cold beer to Tillie and brought out some white wine.

"Well, I have hot dogs, anyway," Grace said, wearily opening packages. "How many people do you think are out there?"

"Maybe ten or twelve?" Tillie said, pulling buns out of bags.

"Okay. At least I can do a small meal. First, I really want to beer Adam and James."

She grabbed two of the bottles and went back outside, where she handed the beer to the men. When Adam took his, he looked down at her with a tired but slightly reverential expression.

"You were amazing," he said, hugging her with one arm. Grace flung her own arms around him.

"No! You were. And James. And Gord. And Skip. Oh, God, Adam," she added, as the possible outcomes of the fire washed over her. "We could be . . . if the shed exploded . . . "

"But we aren't. We're here, love. We're all right. But we will have to change how we do things, immediately. He's hunting us."

"I know. This isn't over yet." A small sob escaped her throat.

"No. But we will take care. It'll be okay."

"Why is it that every time we make love, something awful happens afterward?"

"Every time?"

"Okay, I'm exaggerating. But the night of the first fire, then in the greenway with Tom after, ah, being in the lake, and now . . ."

"It's coincidence."

"I don't think so. Not entirely. I mean, it's not that this awful person — or Tom, for that matter — knows we're having sex, but . . ."

"Shit happens when we're not paying attention. Well, when we're paying attention to each other." Adam paused. "Do we know if Tom saw us in the lake?"

"No. I didn't exactly chat with him that night."

Adam's brow creased.

"What are you thinking?" Grace asked.

"Never mind. Nothing. Let's get this night over with. We can talk later, love."

"Okay," Grace said, dragging out the word. She wondered what thought had occurred to Adam, but also had to get people watered and fed.

"Oh," she added. "How's your poor hand?"

Adam looked down at the ruined bandage ruefully.

191

"I'd forgotten about it. Adrenaline surge, I guess, when I saw the fire."

"Let me see." Grace peeked at the wound. "Looks a bit ravaged. Tillie's in the kitchen, Adam. Please get her to check it out."

Adam followed her in, and Grace continued through the front door to start the barbecue as Tillie clucked over the raw-looking palm.

"Needs a little cleaning up, Adam," she said.

"After we eat, maybe, Tillie. I better call the RCMP first."

Hot dogs were cooked and eaten, and the beer flowed, but it was far from a party atmosphere in the Rampling cabin. The mood didn't improve when Constable Nathan Ellard appeared, looking as ashen as the demolished shed.

"What happened?" he asked Adam, after turning down a beer and accepting a hot dog.

"Someone set fire to the shed," Adam said briefly. "James returned just in time, and with the help of all these people, we put it out."

"Why the shed?" Ellard asked.

"Probably because it contained fuel. It would have made a nice little explosion and set fire to the cabin as well, if it didn't blow out the back wall entirely. It's possible James scared away the fire-starter. He must have arrived just after it was set; it went up like dry leaves. And the shed was much easier to ignite than the cabin. But maybe the guy intended to set fire to the cabin, too, but was scared off by James."

"I'll talk to James, see if he remembers seeing anything now that the excitement is over. But holy crap, Sarge. That could have been really bad."

"I know."

"I've got a few people roaming around the crescent. Again. We'll see if we can find anyone hiding in the bushes, like we found Tom Allbright."

192

Ellard went to speak with James, and another constable canvassed the small crowd of cottagers still lingering in the cabin, perhaps afraid to return to their own places. No one had seen anything, until the flames became visible. Still, it was dark, and with any luck evidence lurked outside in the form of footprints or detritus.

Finally, the crowd dispersed. Tillie cleaned up and re-bandaged Adam's hand, as Adam asked James to remain at the cabin; they would take turns sleeping and keeping watch. Ellard assured Adam and Grace that he and the other constables would prowl the perimeter until morning.

Tillie and Gord approached Grace as they prepared to leave, the last of the firefighting cottagers to go.

"Did you see George?" Gord asked. "I thought he was still up. Maybe not, though."

"No, I didn't. I thought they were going back last weekend."

"They ended up staying, but maybe they've left in the last couple of days. I thought maybe I'd get one last fish in with the boys."

"Well, Skip is still here," Tillie said, comfortingly. "I'm sure you'll get out tomorrow. Unless this bastard burns us all in our beds."

"Now, Tillie," Gord said. "Let's go home. I'm sure the RCMP will look out for us."

"I'll walk you back," Adam said.

"No, no, we'll be fine . . ." Gord started, but Adam cut him off.

"No, Gord. We have to be careful, okay?"

The older man just nodded.

"Be back in a minute, Grace," Adam said.

She sat down abruptly on the sectional couch, straight-backed as if it were a pew, and white as a sheet.

"Something up?" Adam asked.

"N-no. Just hurry back."

James also noticed Grace's sudden change of body language. After the door closed behind Adam, he came to sit beside her.

"Hey, what's up?"

"I'll wait for Adam, if that's okay, James. Might as well just say it once, to both of you."

"Something is up. I mean, more than just the fire."

"I think so, yes."

"Can I get you a glass of wine, or something? You look pretty spooked, Grace."

"Whisky. I can get it, though."

"No. Let me."

James was already on his feet. He chose a glass from the cupboard, poured two fat fingers of scotch into it, and handed it to Grace.

"Am I going to need one, too?"

"Maybe. You should have one anyway."

Grace swallowed half her drink in one go, tipping her head back to let the burning liquid slide down her throat, just as Adam returned.

"Whisky, Grace?" he said, seeing the amber liquid in her glass. "Not wine? Wait, let me get one and join the party."

Adam poured his own and sat down heavily beside Grace. She sensed his exhaustion.

"Okay. What are you thinking?"

"It's what Gord said. He didn't see George around while everyone was fighting the fire. I didn't see him, either; he wasn't here. He may have left to go home, but either way . . . that's not my main point."

She shuddered.

"I could be wrong," she added, slowly. "It could be a coincidence."

Adam and James waited patiently as Grace mulled for a moment, turning her glass around in her hands.

"But how could it be?" she asked aloud, more of herself than anyone. She shook her curls.

"George. His last name is Best." She let that sink in for a moment, eyes trained on Adam's face. "As in Martin Best and Charles Best."

"The Saskatoon victim and his abductor," said Adam, exhaling. "What the hell does that mean? Is one of them his kid?"

"I don't know his kids. He hasn't been here at Ferguson as long as we have, or the Allbrights. I didn't grow up with them, like I did with Tom."

"You're right, though. That would be a hell of a coincidence if they weren't related. If, in fact, Charles Best is Charles Best. But Martin is definitely a Best." Adam paused for a moment. "So, what's going on here? Any ideas?"

"Not really. But we should go and see if George and Delores are here."

"We have to talk to Charlotte. I don't know if she's found any of Martin's family members yet. But it's too late to call her." He looked at his watch. "It's nearly eleven. But yes, let's go see if they're here."

They put their drinks down and set off. George Best's cabin was well down the loop to the east, tucked in off the crescent and into the trees. No lights shone in the windows, but a lone truck sat in the driveway.

"Can we barge along and awaken them, if they're in there?" Adam wondered aloud. "We don't know anything about how he, or they, might be involved. Maybe he's just a grieving father, if he knows what's happened. And if, of course, you're right. James, what do you think?"

195

"What are we going to say, if they answer the door? If we knew Martin was his kid, or his brother or whatever, it would help."

"Good point about Martin possibly being a brother or cousin, and not a son. How old is George, Grace?"

"I'm not really sure, but I'd say late fifties?"

"Martin could be his son, then, but also a nephew or a much-younger brother."

Adam dragged a hand through his hair; Grace could see he wanted to knock on the door and ask questions.

"I think we have to try. I'll fake it; I'll mention the fire, ask if they're all right, and go from there."

He marched up to the door and knocked. No answer. He tried again, knocking louder, and calling, "Mr. Best. It's the police."

After the third, even more insistent knock brought no response, Adam turned reluctantly away.

"So much for that. They're either not there, fast asleep, or not answering. Let's head back and try to get some sleep. We'll check again in the morning. I'll call Nathan and get him to patrol by here tonight."

They wandered back to the cabin, and Adam told James and Grace to hit the hay. He would take the first shift on watch, call the RCMP constable and send an email to Charlotte.

But sleep was elusive for Grace; she tossed restlessly without Adam beside her, thoughts churning. Was George Best behind all of this, some of this, or none of this? What was his relationship to Martin, and would Tillie maybe know?

She finally drifted off into a doze, dreaming of bright fires and dead Elias, until Adam crawled in beside her some hours later.

"Adam?" she said, groggily.

"Go back to sleep, Babe," he said, cuddling her into his body. "James is on it. Don't worry, just sleep."

Adam's breathing became regular within minutes, soothing her, and she finally felt safe enough to turn off her brain.

It felt like seconds later when a quiet knock came at their bedroom door. Adam was instantly awake.

"James?"

"Yeah, Sarge. You'd better get up. The Bests' truck. It's gone."

# Chapter Twenty-Three

*Somalia, 1993*

**W**here's the body?"

"Don't worry, Major. I've taken care of it."

"I am worried, soldier. I want to know where the body is."

"Buried."

"Deeply? This is the desert, you know. Sand goes away in the wind."

"Yes, sir. Deeply, sir."

"No one must know about this. It's bad enough that Crow saw the beating. That was sloppy of you."

"Yes, sir."

"The OC would be very unhappy if this came to light, Lieutenant."

"I know, sir."

The major glared at his junior officer. This goddamn mess was going to land him in a whole lot of shit if anyone found out about the destruction of the village, not to mention the kid's death. *Fuck.*

There was also the drug problem. The Colonel had assured him that it would be perfectly fine; the Americans had been using mefloquine for a few years already. It made them a little more aggressive, but how bad could that be in theatre? They'd talked him into giving it a trial, on men trained for war, not peacekeeping, for God's sake. And there was the codeine, on top of it.

Well, he was in the commanding officer's pocket now, and if all of this became public knowledge, he'd be taking the fall. Maybe not alone, but he would definitely be court-martialed. These men were under his command. He'd be screwed. How many years would he get? It didn't bear thinking about.

They were just supposed to scare the villagers, maybe teach a few of them sharp lessons. He hadn't counted on another dead kid.

"Okay, Lieutenant. Get out of my sight. That kid better be deep in the ground."

Al Simpson saluted his major and slipped away.

# Chapter Twenty-Four

I f fire man is still up here," Grace said, "is Elijah in danger? And if so, what are we going to do about it?" The question had been rolling through her thoughts all morning, as they closed the cabin for the second time and packed the truck.

"Would he be willing to leave his home, do you think?" Adam asked.

"I doubt it. He is very attached to his community, and I don't think he's afraid."

"We could call him, lay it out for him, see what he says?" James suggested.

"Should I call him?" Grace asked. "Or does it have to be official?"

"You've met him," Adam said. "He seems to trust you. Why not? I'll call Charlotte while you're doing that."

Grace nodded and went out to the deck to make her call, leaving Adam in relative quiet indoors. Elijah answered on the third ring, and Grace offered a small mental prayer in thanks.

"Elder Starblanket, it's Grace Rampling. How are you?"

"I'm fine, Grace. And you?"

"I'm all right, sir, but I have to tell you something. Our shed, behind the cabin, was set on fire last night. Accelerant was used, and it could have blown up. I'm worried that whoever started it may try to hurt you, too."

He didn't ask why. Whoever had killed Elias would probably realize that Elijah knew what his nephew knew.

"Thank you for letting me know, Grace. I'll be sure to keep an eye out."

"We were wondering if you'd consider coming to Saskatoon, or at least go into Meadow Lake. It may not be safe for you at home. You can't even go to your cabin in the woods, here at Ferguson. They know that place, too, now."

Elijah emitted a sharp laugh.

"I'm a sitting duck, then," he said. "Don't worry, Grace. What will happen will happen. Who's to say I'd be safer somewhere else? Didn't this second man meet his end in Saskatoon?"

It was a good point, but Grace was thinking something more like a safe house or hotel room than visiting relatives or friends. She put the idea to Elijah.

"No, thank you. It's very kind of you, but I am not in the habit of running away. I can be bait for the angler. Or fuel for the fire. If the bastard shows up, we'll know who he is. And the people of the Nation will be on alert."

"Promise me you'll take precautions and let everyone know you might be in danger."

"I've been in danger for years, Grace."

"But something has changed. Something new has come to light. Otherwise, why would this be happening more than a decade later?"

That brought a rare sigh from the older man.

"Yes. I know. I will see what I can find out. I still have a few contacts, here and there."

"Will you call me? Please? I want to know if you're okay."

"I will. I will call when I know something. Take care, Grace."

201

"You too, sir. Please, take good care."

Grace walked back into the cabin as Adam hung up with Charlotte.

"What did he say?" he asked.

"He won't leave. Says he'd be good as bait, and if fire man appears, he'll see him and case closed. What can we do, Adam?"

"Not much. We can't force him to come to Saskatoon."

"What did Charlotte say?"

"She's filed papers to the court asking for the release of Martin Best's health information, but they haven't been signed by a judge yet. And she's still looking for his family."

"Damn it." Grace scowled and ran both hands through her hair until it stood up in a wild red halo around her face. "What on Earth could have happened, you two brilliant police officers, that has brought this carnage on now?"

"I've been thinking about that," Adam said. "And what I think is, I don't know."

James nodded in agreement.

"Fine," she groused. "Have they found the Bests yet?

"Not yet."

The Bests lived most of the year in the Saskatoon area, as far as Grace knew. At least, that was what Tillie thought. Grace had run over to say goodbye to the Allbrights earlier in the morning, and asked about the Bests' home, family and vehicles. Gordon fished with George, for God's sake; he should know all about him. But he actually knew very little. The Bests had three children, two sons and a daughter, well into adulthood; they lived somewhere near Saskatoon; they owned a truck and a sedan; they were business owners. And that was about it.

Grace begged them to take care of themselves, suggested they leave Ferguson Lake and go home to the farm, and returned to the cottage.

An hour later, the cabin had been re-winterized. She hopped into the truck, Adam drove the police SUV, and James led the way to Meadow Lake in his rented Ford. The vehicle returned to the dealership, they headed back to Saskatoon.

"Adam," Grace asked again, after a long quiet stretch. "Why is this happening now? Do you have any ideas?"

"A few. None of them seem quite right to me. One thought, which we won't be able to prove unless we can see those summary trial proceedings — or courts martial — is that someone was sentenced for the attack on the village and has recently been released. But the timing doesn't work very well, does it? It was fourteen years ago, and if the matter was dealt with at a summary, there's no way the soldier has been in jail that long. No way."

"That's true. In the Shidane Arone case, one person went away for five years. That hardly seemed enough. I thought it seemed a terribly short time for such a horrific act. But then again, the men responsible were not entirely at fault. They were on mefloquine, too."

"Maybe it took him, or them, that long to find Elias. But it seems a very long hunt, and extreme violence, to find someone with such bad PTSD — who also didn't know very much about that night. Or at least didn't know the whole story."

"I'd thought of that one. It doesn't make sense, I agree." She paused, squinting her eyes in the effort to solve the puzzle. "Is it possible the killer has PTSD as well, or is otherwise messed up on mefloquine, and he just exploded into a rage, or out of fear, after all these years?"

"I really don't know, but I'd say it's unlikely. Just based on my own experience, though."

By the time they reached Saskatoon, it was late enough that Grace decided to go home instead of into the office; but Adam wanted to check in with his chief and catch up with Charlotte.

"I won't be long, Babe," he said, climbing out of the truck in front of the station.

"Good. We need some sleep tonight, Adam. How will you get home? Should I pick you up?"

"No, no. You just relax. I'll get the unmarked or get James to drop me off."

"See you soon."

"See you soon, love."

Grace was relieved to be going home. Exhausted from the events at the lake and lack of sleep, she craved a shower and a nap like she rarely had before. The trip from the police station to her bungalow took only a few minutes, and she pulled the truck into its parking spot off the alley with a deep sigh of gratitude.

She hopped out of the truck, grabbed her suitcase and headed for the back door, key at the ready. Grace stepped inside, closed the door, dropped the luggage and let her thirst lead her to the kitchen.

"Hello, beautiful."

Grace jumped and gasped, shock forcing her eyes into a wide stare. She took several quick steps backward, hands thrust defensively out in front of her body, until she realized who the interloper was.

Mick Shaw.

Grace swallowed hard.

"Mick. You scared the hell out of me. What are you doing here? How did you get in?"

"Hey," said Mick, rising from his chair. "What kind of a greeting is that? I'm back in Canada, and wanted to see you, Gracie."

"Don't call me that. How did you get in?" she asked again.

"I," he said, fishing in his pocket and producing a small item with a flourish, "have a key. Remember?"

No, she hadn't remembered. It had been so long ago that she had given him access to her home, and they had later moved together to Australia. She had left him there. Retrieving the key did not occur to her.

"Give it back."

"Now, come on, Grace. I've missed you, hun. Still don't really understand why you left. We were having a good time, weren't we?"

"No, we weren't. At least, I wasn't. What are you doing back in Canada?"

"I was getting bored. Time to mix things up, go travelling again. And I wanted to see you."

"I don't want to see you, Mick. Please leave. After you return my key."

"Grace, come on," he said, advancing. "Let's try again."

"No, Mick. I've moved on. Don't touch me," she added, as he came nearer.

But he did. He put his hands on Grace's waist, pushed her against the kitchen wall and leaned in to kiss her. Grace snapped her head to the side and shoved back, but Mick just laughed.

"I always liked it when you played hard to get, my girl."

"I am not playing hard to get, Mick, and I am not your girl. I moved out for a reason, and I have, as I said, moved on. Take your hands off me."

A thunderous roar, more like a lion's than a man's, interrupted Mick's response. Adam stormed into the kitchen like a hurricane, fury and determination etched into every feature. Before he uttered a word, he grabbed Mick by the shoulders, whirled him around and threw him against the opposite wall.

"Who the fuck are you?" Adam spat, one hand circling Mick's throat, the other fisted and poised to strike.

Adam had three inches in height on Mick Shaw, as well as a bigger frame; but Mick was still fit and strong. He wriggled powerfully in Adam's grasp.

"Who the fuck are you?" he croaked back.

Grace, momentarily astounded by Adam's ferocious response, finally found her voice.

"Adam," she said, going to him, "this is Mick Shaw. He was just leaving."

"Was he. Didn't look like that to me."

"I was not just leaving," Mick confirmed, still struggling. "I was getting reacquainted, actually. Let me fucking go."

"Grace?" Adam asked. "Do you want to be reacquainted with this asshole?"

"No. Mick, please leave. After you give me my key."

But Mick swung wildly at Adam's face, fist glancing off the cheekbone. Adam flinched and reacted by pinning Mick's arms to the wall. Mick was angry, but Adam was furious.

"You are going to leave, and not ever come back," he hissed in Mick's face.

"Who the fuck are you to tell me what to do?" Mick snorted back.

Adam breathed heavily but for a moment did not reply. Grace knew him well enough to realize he didn't want to say, "she's mine" or something equally possessive. She loved him for it. Mick had used her key, walked into her house uninvited and made physical contact without asking permission or even any questions about her life. The difference between the two men amazed her.

"Mick, Adam is my partner. You and I are over, and we have been for more than two years. Don't make this messy."

Adam still stared Mick down, waiting for acquiescence, but ego seemed to overcome common sense; Mick bared his teeth and reared back. Adam instinctively knew what was coming, and just dodged a violent head butt.

Adam spun Mick around and planted him into the wall, grabbing his hands and twisting them together.

"I am Detective Sergeant Adam Davis, you fucking asshole," Adam said into Mick's ear. "And you are under arrest."

Mick gaped. He clearly had not had time to register the existence of Adam's duty belt, clear evidence of his profession. Adam yanked handcuffs off the belt and had Mick, finally chastened, in a chair seconds later. Then he called the station.

"It's Davis," he said. "Get a patrol car to my house immediately. I have an intruder here, under arrest."

"What? Holy shit, Sarge. Okay, we're on our way," said the staff sergeant on the line. "Are you all right?

"Yes. I've cuffed him and he's unarmed. Thanks."

Adam hung up and turned back to Mick.

"The key. Where is it?"

"In my pocket, asshole."

"Shut up, Shaw. Which pocket?"

"Back left."

Adam dragged Mick to his feet again, extracted the key, and shoved him back into the chair.

"Do not speak," he said. "Do not give me an excuse to beat the shit out of you. Because I really, really want to."

Grace watched the scene from her place by the kitchen sink, shaking and shivering, yet still impressed by Adam's prowess. He was so fast, so dexterous. And so angry.

Adam stood silently, looming over his prisoner, until they all heard the siren. Moments later, two officers banged on the door and then plunged into the house, grabbed Mick by each arm and started to drag him out.

"What's the charge, Sergeant Davis?" asked one.

"Home invasion, sexual assault and assaulting a police officer."

"Okay. See you later, Sarge."

From the doorway, Mick said, "Goodbye, Grace. I wish you luck with this madman."

"Goodbye, Mick. Get the hell out."

The officers walked him out the door, slamming it behind them. Adam slumped on a kitchen chair and dropped his head in his hands.

"Grace," he said, still looking down. "Tell me I did the right thing."

"Oh, Adam, of course you did." She dropped to her knees next to him and touched his face. "Adam. Look at me. What are you thinking?"

"Do you want him back? What was he doing here?"

"How can you ask me that? Of course I don't want him back. I walked through the garden door and there he was, sitting in the kitchen. I had no idea he was coming, or even that he was in Canada. It never occurred to me that he might use the key. I completely forgot he even had it. He was in Australia, for heaven's sake."

"Oh, God. I'm sorry, Grace. I saw green before I saw red. I never thought I could feel like that. Jealousy is a new experience for me. I'm so sorry. I didn't mean to accuse you of anything. I saw him touching you, and I lost it."

Grace forced herself into his clenched arms and put her own around his neck.

"Babe. I only want you to touch me," she whispered. "Ever."

At her words, Adam turned his head and plumbed her mouth with a passionate kiss, pulling her forcefully against his chest. She could feel him tremble as he tugged her in.

"Thank God," he finally said, against her lips. "I still needed to hear it."

"As did I, when I saw you with Jilly."

Jilly had nearly run her over after learning of her existence a few weeks ago. Grace and Adam were at his parents' place for harvest, when the woman who had been chasing him since teenage days appeared and kissed him soundly in the farmyard. Devastated and misunderstanding the scene, Grace had run out of the house and down the grid road. Adam had come after her, but not in time. Jilly had turned her car around, sped toward Grace and swerved toward her, resulting in a leap into the ditch, a concussion and some nasty scrapes and cuts. The scenario was different; Adam and Jilly had never had a relationship, as Grace and Mick had, but Grace hadn't known that and needed Adam's reassurance more than the country doctor's medical treatment.

Remembering that day, Adam shuddered, and produced a crooked smile.

"We're even, then?"

"Yes. We're even. But how did you get back so quickly? I wasn't home for fifteen minutes when you arrived."

"The chief was out, and so I talked to Charlotte and beat feet." He stopped. "I have a piece of news, by the way. Charlotte found Charles Best."

"What?"

Adam nodded.

"Charles Best, son of George and Delores Best, has been dead for thirty years."

# Chapter Twenty-five

Charles Best, Adam had realized at the Saskatchewan Mental Hospital, was almost certainly a pseudonym. The man who had likely killed Elias Crow and unearthed Martin Best to murder him would not use his own name.

Yet Adam had been both surprised at and excited by the news Charlotte had given him the day before. Somehow, Charles Best, the dead child, had passed his identity on to a killer. Progress.

In the office by seven, Adam arranged to interview Tom Allbright and Al Simpson again. Would they talk this time? One of them, Adam thought, personally knew the impostor, or at least his identity.

The sergeant in charge of cells assured Adam the two prisoners would be available by mid-morning, which left Adam to stew about the case and mull over yesterday's events at home.

He had allowed his temper to boil over. He knew that if he had found Mick — or anyone — assaulting Grace, he could have killed him. That awareness had brought on a dark nightmare, but he had awakened and slipped out of bed before Grace could detect his shaking. She had been so tired she had fallen asleep like a stone. Damn it, I have to pull myself together, he thought. Love is one thing. Jealousy is quite another, as is violence. Even if the bastard deserved it.

She had loved him sleepily, languidly, easing his doubt and soothing his fear. And still the evil dream came.

That morning, Grace awakened bright and ready to get back to the newsroom, and relief flooded Adam. She had not perceived that he had dreamed, thank God; nor did she agonize over his attack on Mick or his arrest. God, he loved her.

He ran a hand through his hair and wrested his thoughts away from Grace and back to the day's work.

The clock finally clicked to eight-thirty. Adam picked up the phone and called the justice department.

"It's Detective Sergeant Adam Davis calling," he said. "I'm calling about a court order to release the biographical and health information about a Martin Best. He was a patient at the Saskatchewan Hospital. Has there been any progress?"

"Oh, yes, hello Sergeant. Let me just take a look." He heard keys clicking on the other end. "Yes, sir. Justice Mary Sutherland signed the court order late yesterday. You may go ahead and request the documents from the hospital. I'll send you a copy of the order now."

Adam, who was not Catholic, nevertheless resisted an impulse to raise his eyes to heaven and cross himself. Yes, he thought.

"Thank you very much," he said fervently. "That's great. Thank the judge for me."

"Will do, Sergeant."

Adam immediately called the hospital's administrator, but Kate Deverell was not in yet. He left a message and rose to his feet. He could not sit still another moment.

He had an hour to wait before his scheduled interview with Tom Allbright. And so, he left the station and walked the three blocks to the goldsmith's shop. It was open.

211

*****

Tom Allbright sat fidgeting at the interview room's table when Adam strode in, ready for another round of battle, the thrust and parry of questioning a hostile or terrified witness.

"How are you doing, Tom?"

"Shitty. What do you think?"

Great start.

"I have to ask you some more questions, Tom. I really need you to answer them. I know you're scared, but we will keep you safe here."

"Nice. But how are you going to do that when I'm in prison?"

"Are you going to prison?"

"I assume so."

"For what?"

That shut Tom up. He screwed up his face and regarded Adam.

"For attacking Grace, not to mention me?"

"Could happen, right?"

"It could. It might not. Depends what you have to tell me. Do you know a Charles Best?"

"No . . . don't think so. Related to the dude at the lake?"

"Yes. His dead son."

"No shit? I didn't know they had a dead kid."

"Is that the truth, Tom?"

"Yeah. We — me and Grace and the rest of us — didn't grow up with the Best kids. The family wasn't at the lake in those days."

That was true, Adam reflected, remembering that Grace had told him the same thing.

"Let me tell you what I think," Adam said. "I think someone paid you for some information. You weren't getting enough funds from the folks, or social services, to feed your meth habit. You knew where Elias was — more or less — from your mom. Someone guessed that was the case. And you told that someone, in exchange for some heavy money. Am I right?"

Tom Allbright's face told Adam he had hit the mark. A very different thing from getting him to admit it out loud.

"Come on, Tom. Save yourself, here, for Christ's sake. You say you had nothing to do with Elias's death, but you know something. And you're scared shitless of someone. The one who paid you."

Still no verbal response.

"You said yourself you'd be in danger if you went to prison. You're right. This is your stay out of jail free card. Take it. One time offer. And what about your family, your parents? How are they going to feel if you're incarcerated? Do you care at all about them?" Adam stopped himself from suggesting that the Allbrights might pay a price, as well — a terrible price — if the perpetrators were not caught. But he had to admit to himself they might also be in danger if Tom talked.

The junkie chewed his cheek, narrowed his eyes and contemplated Adam. Fear sparked from his pupils.

"Okay. Fuck. Okay. You're right."

"What happened, Tom?"

"Some dude found me on the street. I didn't know him. I still don't. Said he'd pay me for just a little bit of information; that's all he wanted. Half on the spot, half when he contacted Elias.

"So, I took the money, but when it all rolled out and he gave me the second instalment, he told me to keep my mouth shut or he'd kill me, too. And if he couldn't get to me, there were some big boys in Ottawa who'd make sure I'd never be found."

"He was pretty sure you wouldn't talk."

"He was very fucking scary."

"Why didn't he just kill you, too?"

"Maybe he figured no one would listen to a fucked-up meth head like me. Maybe he thought he'd need more information down the road. I dunno."

"So you told him about Elias. Where he lived."

"Yeah. Well, more or less. I didn't know where his cabin was, exactly; but I knew it existed, and I told the guy. It had to be near the shack, and I knew where that was."

"And then Elias was murdered."

"He didn't tell me he was going to kill him." Tom leaned forward. "You gotta believe me. He told me some bullshit about how he had to find him for some important operation. He thought I was stupid. He was right."

"Important operation? What do you mean?"

"I don't know. I didn't ask. I just wanted the money. I assumed it had something to do with the army, but I'm done with the forces. They threw me out. I didn't care. But when he threatened me, I knew something else was up."

Adam regarded Tom for a moment.

"The attack on Grace," Adam said. "It had nothing to do with all this, did it?"

Tom flushed and looked down.

"You weren't trying to scare her, or me, away from investigating the case. You didn't know enough about it to care."

"No. I never thought you'd figure out that I had anything to do with Elias. Why would you?"

"It only occurred to me because you grabbed Grace. That was stupid, Tom, for more than one reason. You didn't mean to actually attack her, did you?"

He shook his head.

"You wanted her."

Tom nodded.

"Always did, right?"

"Yes."

"So in your fucked-up meth brain, you thought that after pulling her off the deck and scaring the hell out of her, you were going to . . . have sex with her."

"Yeah. I heard you guys in the lake from the greenway. I was upset. First time I've seen her with a man."

"You wanted her for yourself. You peered in the window first, when she was alone, and were going to try to persuade her, but she ran out of the cabin. Then you heard us and realized that wasn't going to happen."

"Yes. Fuck. I'm sorry."

"You were jealous."

"Yes. Angry."

Adam's conscience poked him, hard. He had just experienced that himself. He knew how it felt, and he wasn't hooked on some godawful drug; but he, too, was angry. Tom could have seriously hurt Grace. Could he have raped her, too? Adam swallowed, and returned to the first line of questioning.

"Would you recognize this guy?"

"Probably. Wore a hat the three times I saw him, but I think so."

"Tall guy, tattoo, military posture?"

"Yeah."

"By the way, what the hell were you doing at Ferguson?"

"Part of the deal was showing him where the shack was, and where I thought the cabin had to be, considering the marshland. I had to meet him there. I caught the bus up, hitchhiked to the lake and hid in Skip's shed. Stole some food from the folks. Fuck, Sergeant, I didn't expect all of this to happen."

Goddamn drugs, Adam thought. What a mess this witness was.

"Okay. You're going to have to stay here, Tom. And you're still going to trial for the attack on Grace. And me. But you saved your life today."

Adam left the room, feeling that progress had been made to the extent that Tom had been eliminated as the killer — and that the killer was Alias Charles Best. He believed him. He also doubted that Al Simpson, a police officer, would be as easy to crack.

Back in his office, he picked up his phone to retrieve voicemails and found that the hospital administrator had called back.

"Sergeant Davis, it's Kate Deverell from the Saskatchewan Mental Hospital," she had said. "I see you got your court order. I'll email you all the information I have this morning. I — I really hope it helps you catch his killer. Let me know if you need anything further. Thanks, and it was nice meeting you. Goodbye."

He swiveled to his computer to check emails, and there it was — a full biography of Martin Joseph Best, along with a précis of his health problems and conditions.

It took a while to read it all, but when he was finished, he knew what had happened and part of the why. He still had to figure out who the hell was behind these two murders.

Half an hour later, he was back in the interview room, facing a very different man across the small wooden table.

"How are you doing, Al?" he asked.

"Great. Love being on the other side of the bars. Thanks."

"Are you going to talk to me?"

"Nope."

Adam pulled out the photo of Martin Best, one more time.

"This is Martin Joseph Best. But you know that, don't you?"

"Do I?"

"Yes. Because you either killed him in your mother's house, or you allowed someone else to kill him there."

Al continued to stare at Adam with a stony expression, arms crossed over his chest.

"And you know this because?"

"Come on, Al. Your little performance at the precinct told me you're in deep. I'm going to find out how deep. If you're not in over your head, we might be able to keep your sentence short, and you'll be less likely to die in prison. I can't protect you there, you know that better than I do."

Al barely moved, but he did twitch, his lip jerking upward.

"You served in the forces before you became a cop, didn't you?"

No answer.

"I can check. It might take a while, but I can check. You know I can. And if someone finds out that I'm nosing through military files trying to find an Al Simpson, or maybe an Alan Robertson, that might not go so well. For you."

Al's mouth worked. He shut his eyes, tightly, and finally exhaled heavily.

"Fuck, Adam. Don't do that."

"Tell me, then."

"Yes, damn it. I was in the forces."

"Canadian Airborne."

"Yes. For two years."

"And you were in Somalia? Same time as Elias Crow?"

Al nodded.

"Say it out loud," Adam reminded him.

"Fuck. Yes."

"And Martin Joseph Best?"

"Yes."

"Tom Allbright?"

"No."

Adam breathed. It was more validation that Tom had been telling the truth. Not that Adam was surprised; he couldn't see Allbright as an elite soldier, even when he was in good shape.

"How well did you know Martin Best? He wasn't from Saskatchewan, was he?"

Al shook his head.

"No, he was from Manitoba."

"And?"

"Yeah, I knew him pretty well. We were in the same company, got sent over together."

"I assume you were on the ground when a village near Belet Huen was shot up and a kid was beaten. Nothing else makes sense. Were you?"

Al's eyes widened.

"How the hell do you know about that?"

No way Adam was going to tell him. Even with Al in jail, God knew if the information would be traced back to Elijah Starblanket, putting him in even graver danger.

"That doesn't matter," Adam said. "You were there. What the hell happened that night, Al? You might as well tell me. I know most of it, anyway."

The former soldier slumped forward, his forehead almost meeting the table. Adam left him to think in silence, for a moment, and finally Al raised his head.

"Okay, Adam. God damn it. I guess I always knew this would go to shit, anyway.

"One night, Elias was on patrol. He discovered a bunch of little kids trying to sneak into the supply tent. I saw him grab the biggest one, probably the leader, by the collar and speak to him; I couldn't hear what he was saying. But he let the little bugger go, and all the others had already run away. I had to report him to the major. It was strictly against policy to let them go. Stealing was a capital offence."

"They were little kids, for fuck's sake, Al."

Al threw his head back and glared at the ceiling.

"You think I don't know that? I mean, I get it now, but then we were all seriously fucked up on the malaria drug and the codeine. The culture in that place was bizarre. Violent, weird, insomniac. Everyone saw things that weren't there."

"So you guys went to the village to round up the kids, scared hell out of everyone, and fired your weapons? Really? Because children stealing from the tent deserved beatings? Or worse?"

"Short form. Yeah."

Adam glared at Al like he'd never seen him before. Perhaps he hadn't, not really.

"Then what happened?'

Al shut his mouth with a snap, and Adam stood up to roam the tiny room as he fought to swallow his temper.

"Two men are dead, Al. Both of them had PTSD. Both were in Somalia with you. Something beyond scaring the villagers and shooting up the sky happened, and I know you beat the kid." Adam paused. "He died, didn't he? Your buddies, and maybe you, killed him."

Moments passed. Adam waited. His witness sat still as stone. And then . . .

"Yes," he whispered, so quietly Adam had to strain to hear him. "But I did not kill him."

"What was his name? Did you know it?"

"Yes. I knew it, and I'll never forget it. His name was Abukar Dualeh."

"If you didn't kill him, why are you in this mess, Al?"

"Because I buried him."

"You what?"

"I buried him, on the major's orders. With Martin Best. We buried him."

"Holy hell, man. Where?"

"In the desert, not far from the village, near a rare hill to protect the grave."

"Did anyone go to trial for this?"

"Not that I know of, no."

"Why the hell is all this happening, fourteen years later? Why didn't someone just eliminate Elias and Martin long since?"

"Elias didn't know the kid died. He let him go, remember? We weren't going to tell him or let him see. He just thought we'd taught him a sharp lesson. It doesn't do, Adam, to murder your fellow soldiers. People find out about that. Then he went off the grid, but it wasn't all that important back then. The guy was seriously fucked up; no one was going to listen to him, and he didn't know anything much, anyway. And Martin went AWOL."

"Why is this happening now?" Adam repeated.

And then, a bolt of bright light seared his brain, so intense it stunned him, in the moment his prisoner opened his mouth to speak.

"They found him," Al said. "The boy. After all these years, they found his bones. The desert wind blew away our secret, and our future."

# Chapter Twenty-Six

Once Adam fought down the urge to vomit, he returned to his office, pale and shaky, to put the pieces together.

Martin Best had, more than likely, gone AWOL because he couldn't live with what he'd done — nor what his fellow soldiers had done — and the major knew it.

Elias Crow was less of a threat, since he hadn't known Abukar Dualeh, the child he'd tried to save, had died that night. If they had found Abukar's remains, however, he suddenly became a powerful witness, since he'd seen the beating and the attack on the village.

The search was on, then, for both men. Someone wanted them out of the way, permanently, to avoid the kind of scandal and courts martial that had erupted after the Shidane Arone killing. They'd kept it quiet for so long. Now the secret of Abukar's death was out — somewhere — and it was only a matter of time before the news hit Canada.

But, Adam thought, it wasn't just the child's death. There was something else, something to do with the mefloquine. Someone knew the drug was blowing the brains of tough soldiers trained for battle but performing a peacekeeping role they weren't appropriate to serve in.

How high did it go?

Before leaving the interview room, Adam had turned back to Al and asked, "Who was the major, Al?"

"You know who it was."

"Maybe I do. Why don't you tell me, anyway?"

"George. George Best."

Adam nodded.

"And the killer. You don't know his name."

"No."

"You let him kill Martin Best in your mother's home, for God's sake. How do you not know him? And why did you agree?"

"He threatened my mother. Do you know how easy it is to slip into a nursing home, and whack a defenseless old woman?"

"He could pose as a relative, or even just slip in the back door. Yeah, I get it. So how did that work?"

"He called me. He knows who I am and where I am. He knows all of us. Said he needed a quiet, safe place to take Martin. I said, why not in the middle of nowhere? There's plenty of nowhere in Saskatchewan.

"But no. He wanted me to be involved, right? So that I wouldn't talk. And so I would maybe take the fall if and when Martin's body was discovered. I wasn't clear on whether he would bury Martin on the property, or just leave him there in the house, in case the Saskatoon cops made the connection to me. And of course, you did. How did you find him so fast?"

"Nosy neighbour, I gather. He was out in his garden, heard the shot and called the police. I wasn't here, but apparently, we asked if it wasn't just a car backfiring. He got his back up and said he knew a fucking gunshot when he heard one." Adam permitted himself a small grin. That neighbour was quite the guy. "Do you know why Martin would agree to go with him?"

"Not really. He probably did some fast talking, and Martin was so fucking confused, I don't know if he'd object. He'd just take his word that the guy was a relative or a friend."

"Was Martin related to George?"

"Yes. Martin was George's nephew. They're both originally from Manitoba."

"And they allowed them to serve together?"

"George must have made a case for having him there, someone he could easily manage. I'm thinking the top dog bought the argument. Whoever he was."

"Have you ever heard of a Charles Best?"

"No, I don't think so. Who is that?"

"George Best's dead son. Dead infant son."

Adam let that information work its way through Al's brain cells.

"Holy shit," he said, suddenly. "Charles Best, whoever he really is, took Martin out of the hospital, posing as a relative. Didn't he?"

Adam raised his eyebrows. Al's backbone left something to be desired, but there was nothing wrong with his intelligence.

"Did you recognize the man's voice, when he called you about your mother's house?" Adam asked.

"No. It was disguised; he was using an electronic device to speak through. But he did say he was calling on behalf of someone higher up, and I'd better fall in line. Or else."

"Can you think of anyone it might be?

"I can think of lots of anyones it might be."

"You don't have a list, by any chance, of the men you served with in Somalia? And the officers?"

Al gave a hollow laugh.

"No."

"Will you write them down for me?"

"Is there any other way? I'm a sitting duck, Adam. And what about my mother?"

223

"Well, it's that or I try getting a list from the army. I admit that's going to take some time."

"That threat again."

"Yeah, that threat again. But what do you want me to do, Al? I have to find this killer. And his superiors, if possible."

"I'll think it over."

"Think fast."

\*\*\*\*\*

Martin Joseph Best had been born in Winnipeg. His biography did not mention his uncle George. He had joined the military in his late teens, and had scrabbled his way into the Canadian Airborne, due to a remarkable aptitude for anything mathematic. His talent may have partly explained why he was allowed to serve in the same regiment as his uncle.

The hospital's email revealed that Best had indeed suffered from PTSD, severe depression and some psychosis. The resident psychiatrist theorized that Best's experiences overseas, mixed with a brain-bending cocktail of mefloquine and other drugs, had caused his disorders.

Adam had wondered how a Manitoban ended up in the Saskatchewan Mental Hospital, and finally got his answer. After going AWOL, Best eventually landed in a small southern Saskatchewan town. His PTSD, however, became more and more troublesome, and one night, Best had gone apeshit at the local gas station, screaming and toppling shelves of merchandise. Authorities were called, and after spending some time in the psychiatric unit at a Regina hospital, he was transferred to the facility at North Battleford.

He was no longer off the radar.

Although Adam had interviewed Tom and Al alone, Charlotte and James had watched the proceedings from behind the one-way mirror. In Adam's office at the end of the workday, both of his constables noted his pallor.

"Are you okay, Adam?" Charlotte asked. "It can't be easy on you dealing with this." She didn't specify the PTSD problem central to the case, but Adam knew what she meant.

"I'm getting there. I'll be fine. The next two items will be finding George Best, and getting that list of the Airborne soldiers. I'd rather get it from Al, for now. It will take forever to get it from the army, if we get it at all. And as he says, he might be at risk if we ring the wrong bell in Ottawa. We still need him as a witness. We'll get at it tomorrow morning."

"Okay. See you then, Adam."

"Bye, Adam."

Adam had so much to tell Grace, he wasn't sure that the few hours before bed would give him enough time. He also had to ask her a favour. Grace's language skills far outstripped his, as did her Internet abilities. It made him wonder all over again how she could possibly feel less intelligent than he. Or less beautiful, for that matter.

He found Grace bustling in the kitchen, thankfully alone and not fending off an attacker or a former boyfriend.

"Hey, Babe," he greeted her, encircling her waist with his big arms.

"Hey yourself," she said, turning. "And hey, what's up? You look a little tired or something. Is it your hand? Is it infected?"

"No, it's fine. It was just a very long day. Grace, I have a lot to tell you. It's going to take a while."

"Start now," she said. "I can cook and listen."

"I can help and talk. But first, I need to hold you and explain something."

A shadow of wonder crossed Grace's face, but she stilled and nodded.

"Tom Allbright," he began. "It turns out he was peripheral to this case. He's definitely to blame for pointing the killer to Elias, but his motivation appears to have been simply financial. He needed more money to buy drugs. The man who approached him said he needed to find Elias for an important operation, and Tom either bought that line, or just decided to ignore the possibilities, or didn't care."

Adam stopped speaking for a moment, and Grace prodded him.

"Okay . . . so . . . what does that mean?"

"He didn't grab you off his parents' porch to silence you or attempt to silence me."

"Was he just confused, then? Or having some kind of meth-related event?"

"No, Babe. He's . . . well, he's in love with you. Or at least he thinks he is. He certainly was when you two were growing up at the lake."

"Oh," Grace said, in a small, shocked voice.

"He heard us that night we made love in the lake, from the greenway. He didn't see us, but it was obvious to him what was going on. He was jealous and angry, Grace. Like I was yesterday."

"I have to sit down."

She moved to the table and sank into a chair.

"I didn't know," she said. "I didn't even suspect. I thought we were just old friends. He never said anything, and in all these years he's never looked me up."

"He must have thought you wouldn't have him. Would that be true?"

"Oh, yes. I mean, I was very fond of him, but more like a brother. I was never attracted to him, not even back then. I wonder if I ever said anything, though, that made him realize there was nothing between us, and couldn't ever be." She shook her curls, trying to remember.

"It doesn't matter, love. He's very messed up and acting on anger is a classic symptom of meth addiction. He was as angry as he was jealous that night. And then he tried to hide, because by then, he knew he was culpable in Elias's death. He didn't want the police to find him, but not just because he'd attacked you."

"No, right, I see that." Grace did not want to talk about Tom Allbright anymore. "Okay, so what else happened today?"

"I found out why all of this is happening now." Adam leaned over and took Grace's hands in his. "It's because that child's remains have been found. The child Elias found trying to steal from the supply tent and sent away."

"Oh, God." Grace's face furrowed, in an effort not to cry. "So, he was murdered, then," she said, very quietly. "How did you find out?"

"Al Simpson told me in an interview. He was one of two men who buried the child. The other was Martin Best. The killer called Al and threatened him, both with exposure of the crime and with hurting his mother. That's how Al knew the child had been found. His name was Abukar Dualeh."

"That also explains why Martin was murdered. But he wasn't much of a threat, was he? Do you know yet how sick he was?"

"Very sick. PTSD, psychosis, depression, all of it. But the hospital records also said he was improving. Even if the killer didn't know that, he couldn't take the chance Martin wouldn't talk if the police or the military came to interview him."

Adam shook his head. "Either way. The child was found, and somewhere on Earth, someone, somehow has reported that fact. That's why I need a favour from you. I need to know if it's been in the media. Can you attack the Internet, and see what you can find? It's going to come out in Canada, but when? Can you find out if it has been publicly reported in Africa?"

"I don't know. I can certainly give it a go. Can you not just contact the authorities in Somalia?"

"I can, and I will. But I'd like to keep this quiet until I have as much information as possible. I would assume the Somalis have contacted the military, but they still have to prove that our peacekeepers killed the boy. Either way, though, I'd like to know if it's been in the media, and if so, when it came out and what's been said. I need to know how much time I have. When this hits the news, those responsible will be seriously ducking for cover."

"There may be a bit of a language barrier, unless Reuters has been on it. I can't see that, though. Our papers would have picked that up."

"Unless the news agencies haven't connected his death to the Airborne yet."

"True. Okay. Let's have dinner, and I'll get at it, see if there's a paper publishing in a language other than Somali or Arabic."

"How many languages can you speak, Grace?" Adam asked, amazed.

She laughed. "Two and a half. But I can muddle through reading a few others, for the gist, anyway. Pray for German, French or Italian."

After dinner, Grace plunked herself in front of her computer and began searching for Somali newspapers. Never having done so before, as a local reporter, she was stunned to find several online news outlets. Canadian papers had been online for some time, but Grace didn't expect the same coverage in Africa, and castigated herself for being unaware of that and making assumptions that Somalia was a much more backward country than it was.

Searching proved somewhat frustrating. Not all papers published in languages other than Somali or Arabic; but some, indeed, carried content in Italian and even English.

Somalia had a significant Italian population and influence, especially in the south; and English was clearly taking over the world in terms of news dispersal.

And there it was.

"Adam!" she called. "I think this is it."

He flew to her side and looked over her shoulder. Grace pointed to a tiny story on an Italian site.

"As far as I can tell, it says a youth's remains have been found partly uncovered in a sandy grave, several miles outside Belet Huen," she told Adam. "I can put some of this through a translation site, to be sure."

"Not fluent in Italian, then?"

"Nope. Not hardly."

"When was it published?" Adam asked, peering at the screen.

"Twelve days ago. This won't stay quiet for long, Adam. I wonder if Reuters has seen this, and has a reporter working on it."

"If so, can you find out who?"

"I can try. Reuters isn't just sitting around waiting for my call. But then, if I can get them to talk to me, I could offer some information in return. Quid pro quo. If you let me. It's your information. Well, most of it is."

Adam nodded slightly, thinking.

"Someone is watching the Somali papers, then," he said. "Or they have someone on the ground. And they knew, or assumed, it was Abukar Dualeh, based on the location of his remains. His name isn't in the piece, is it?"

"No. Twelve days is probably not enough time to establish a definite identity. Or would it be? Could they identify him by dental records or DNA that quickly?"

"I have no idea how fast that might happen in Somalia. It'd depend on what kind of records they had on the child, and I suspect they wouldn't be comprehensive. What kind of access

229

to dentists would they have had fourteen years ago, in the middle of a civil war? I just don't know. I can't even speculate."

"I can try calling Reuters tomorrow. It's unlikely I'd reach someone at this hour; it would be something like four in the morning in London. And I'd have to call head office. I have no idea how I'd reach someone in Somalia, even if I knew the reporter's name. I'll also try Agence France-Presse in Paris."

They were interrupted by Adam's cellphone ringing.

"Sergeant Davis," he answered, recognizing the number.

"Sarge," said the staff sergeant, "I have a package here, addressed to Tom Allbright. You want to be here when we open it?"

# Chapter Twenty-Seven

The box weighed next to nothing and measured a few inches square. Wrapped in brown paper, it bore no postmark or other indicator of its source. Only Tom Allbright's name decorated the top.

"How was it delivered?" Adam asked, turning it over in his hands.

"One of those small independent couriers," said Lorne Fisher, who was still in the office searching for a woman who had gone missing that day. Fisher divided his time between serving on the detective squad and as the new missing persons' co-ordinator. "The guy dashed in, according to Karpinski, dropped it on the counter and left. We're looking for him now."

"Someone paid him a bundle to do that."

"Yeah. Not exactly protocol."

Sergeant Joan Karpinski, in charge that night, popped her head into Adam's office.

"Hey, Joan. Did you see the delivery guy?" Adam asked.

"I came into the lobby just as he walked out. Very quickly. Five-foot-ten, dark jeans and hoodie. The van was idling outside; white, with a logo reading FD. Fast Delivery, maybe? He floored it when he took off, but he managed to avoid squealing the tires."

"Okay. Has this been tested yet?"

"No electronics in there. No idea if there's poison, of course. There is none on the outside. We were thinking anthrax, though, possibly."

"I'll go get suited up. Want to join me?"

"Yup," said Lorne and Joan together.

They decamped to a small room equipped with a ventilator and various other safety gear, tugged on coveralls, gloves and masks, and bent over the tiny box. Adam carefully tore open the brown paper, which revealed an equally nondescript gift box, its lid taped down.

Cutting the tape, he gently wiggled up the lid and paused before lifting it. No cloud of white powder puffed out, but a stink wafted into the room.

"Ewww," Joan sniffed. "It's going to be dead, whatever it is. Or at least rotten."

Adam slowly removed the lid to reveal a fairly large, very dead, somewhat decomposed mouse.

"He, whoever he is, couldn't find a rat?" Lorne suggested.

"That would be my guess," Adam agreed, closing the box. "Not a lot of rats in Saskatoon, unless you're doing medical research. Mice squeal, too, though."

"We'll have to tell Allbright, I assume," Joan said.

"Let me think about that. He's jumpy enough, and this might shut him up. We'll decide tomorrow. Meanwhile, keep someone on him. I mean right on top of him. And on Simpson."

"Will do, Sarge," Joan said.

Adam removed his safety apparel, swearing silently. Obviously, the RCMP in Meadow Lake knew where Al Simpson and Tom Allbright were, but he had hoped no one else did; or, that no one else on a Saskatchewan police force was involved in this mess. Which was it?

Who the hell was Charles Best?

Whoever he was, he sure as hell was in Saskatoon.

Adam returned home to catch a few hours' sleep and found Grace with her eyes glued to her computer screen.

"That's not good for the brain before bed, you know."

"Hi, love. What happened?"

"We received a decomposed mouse packed in a box and addressed to Tom."

"Ew, yuck. A threat, then. Any idea who sent it?"

"No, although I assume it's our killer. What are you up to?"

"I thought I'd do a little searching, so I'd be ready to go first thing tomorrow. I've found the news agency numbers, and I've been looking at some maps of Somalia, trying to understand where Abukar Dualeh was buried."

"As I said, not relaxing before sleep. I have a better idea."

"Do you? What?"

"Give me a minute."

Exactly one minute later, Grace could hear water running; then the fridge door opening and closing, and the clink of glasses being set on the counter. Adam reappeared, naked, and pulled her to her feet.

"Am I getting a bath, then?" Grace asked, a bit breathlessly.

"You know it. Plus, a little wine. Come on, beautiful. Let me work those neck muscles. And a few others."

\*\*\*\*\*

Bad start to the morning, Adam thought the next day, when the first person he encountered was Inspector Terry Pearson leaning against his office door.

"Terry," Adam said briefly, unlocking it.

"Adam," said his direct superior. "Long time no see. I understand you've been meddling in an RCMP file and haven't been around much."

"Have you actually read that file?"

"I thought you could bring me up to speed."

Adam powerfully wanted to roll his eyes. Was the man illiterate? No. Just bone lazy.

"The case up at Meadow Lake is intimately connected with the recent murder in Saskatoon," Adam told him. "And there are at least two witnesses, also suspects, who need protection. Ergo, meddling."

Had Terry been away? This was weird, even for him. Granted, Adam had been avoiding him, but he also hadn't been in Saskatoon much lately. He assumed the chief would have briefed Pearson.

"And you're also taking Lorne Fisher away from his missing persons' duties, as I understand it. Which strikes me as odd, considering it's your precious new co-ordinator's role."

Adam had indeed fought hard to create the position, after the events of the summer when the killer he sought had been responsible for the deaths of women gone missing. Adam felt strongly that the man would have been caught earlier had files been shared with other police forces and more closely investigated. The force hadn't had a constable focused on missing people until late that summer.

"Lorne," Adam said evenly, "was working overtime on the case of a missing woman last night when we received a suspicious package. You know he crosses over with the detective squad. And one of the murdered men was, in a sense, missing."

"You should be checking in with me when you leave town, Davis. Not to mention spending police funds on renting vehicles."

"I was on holidays when all this started, Terry. I was on the ground. You know it." Defending himself made Adam feel vaguely sick and distinctly angry. "And I did check in with the chief. You were nowhere to be found."

As usual, Adam added to himself.

"Meanwhile," Pearson continued breezily, "you were using up an awful lot of manpower on that twenty-four-hour watch on the two prisoners. I cancelled that."

"You what?"

"It's not necessary in cells. No one is going to get in there."

"You don't know that, Terry. Those two men are in serious danger, and we don't know from whom. What if they get a visitor? Someone who looks legit, but isn't?"

It had already happened, with Martin Best. Despite best efforts, if a police officer wasn't closely watching everyone who made contact with Allbright and Simpson, it could happen again.

"Well, it's my call. And I think it's ridiculous to have twenty-four-hour cover on a couple of perps."

"They're also witnesses, Terry, for God's sake. One of whom got a threatening message last night."

"Too bad so sad."

Adam thought his head was going to explode. He pushed past Pearson, still standing nonchalantly in his doorway, and headed straight for cells.

"I'm not done with you Davis. Get the fuck back here."

"Maybe not," Adam snarled over his shoulder, "but I'm done with you."

He ran down the hallway yelling for James, flew down three flights of stairs and pushed through the door leading to the holding area, his constable already on his heels. Christ, thought Adam for the thousandth time, that guy can move.

"What's going on, Adam?" James asked, in complete control of his breath.

"Terry pulled the guard on Simpson and Allbright," he said. "Let's go. It's going to take more than a few minutes to reinstate."

"Fucking asshole," James muttered.

235

"We should be looking for George Best right now, not pulling guard duty."

"Look, I'll go in there; you call Char, and then you can go and find the chief. Okay?"

"No, I'll come with you until Charlotte can get down here."

They buzzed at the door and waited until the constable in cells answered their call.

"Is everything all right in here, Duncan?" Adam asked immediately. "Simpson and Allbright?"

"Right as rain, Sarge," Duncan said. "Want to take a look?"

"Yes. Now."

The constable led the way to Tom Allbright's cell and opened the metal door to expose the by-now healthier-looking witness, sitting upright on his bed.

"Hi Tom," Adam said, as calmly as possible. "How are you doing?"

"I'm okay. How are you? Something up?"

"No, everything's fine. Just wanted to check on you. We'll talk again later."

Adam nodded to the cells officer, who locked up on Tom and gave Adam a questioning look.

"Okay. Now Al."

He moved to the cell two down from Tom's, and unlocked it for Adam, who swung the door open. Al was still asleep.

"Hey, Al," he said. "Wake up, man. It's morning. Almost time for breakfast."

"Oh, he's had breakfast," Duncan told him. "I guess he dozed off again."

Adam's head snapped around to look at the officer. "How long ago?"

"'Bout half an hour, I guess."

Adam lurched toward Al, yelling his name and shaking him, but there was no response.

"Holy hell," Adam breathed. "James, get an ER doctor right now. Duncan, call nine-one-one. Now!" he yelled at a frozen Duncan, who seemed glued to the cement floor.

Turning back to Al Simpson, Adam took his pulse, which was weak and thready, but at least it was still there. His skin was clammy, and a thin white substance scummed his lips. At first, Adam wondered if he'd been poisoned with sarin; but then, leaning in, he realized the stuff was icing. He'd ingested something sweet — pastry?

Al's body, already clamped tightly, suddenly began to shudder and spasm.

Strychnine.

Rat poison.

Adam could do nothing for him beyond CPR. He reached for his cellphone and called Charlotte.

"Char, find the chief," he said, with no greeting. "Now. He had a morning meeting; I don't know where. Just find him. And then find whoever served Al Simpson breakfast. Hurry."

"Adam, what the hell? Where are you?"

"In cells. He's been poisoned, I'm pretty sure. The doctor and ambulance are on their way."

"I'll be there as soon as I locate the chief."

The three subsequent minutes it took for the paramedics and the doctor to arrive seemed like two hours. Al's rigours became more pronounced, and Adam felt as impotent as he ever had in his life. He kept talking to his witness.

"Stay with me, Al. Help is coming."

When it finally did, chaos came with it. Dr. Brian Ashern, one of the best emergency doctors Adam had ever seen in action, pushed him aside without a word and dove at the patient. The paramedics were right behind him, squishing into the tiny holding cell, and Al was on a stretcher and out the door in a moment, headed for the hospital.

"What the fuck happened, Adam?" Ashern asked, as they strode together behind the patient.

"I don't know. I'm sure as hell going to find out. Strychnine, I thought."

"Yeah, judging by the rigours, it looks like it."

"Keep me posted. And I'll be sending an officer along the minute I can find one, to keep an eye on him."

"Not a suicide attempt, then."

"No. Where would he have found the poison? No. Someone wants him dead."

"How would someone get in here?"

"I have no idea."

"Okay. Gotta go. I'll call you as soon as I can."

"Thanks, Brian. Appreciate it."

By now in the lobby, the two men parted, and Adam turned to find Charlotte churning toward him.

"I've just checked the cafeteria," she said. "Al and Tom had the usual breakfast, same as all the other food served this morning. They're taking away the garbage the plates were scraped into, to test it. But Adam, unless one of our people poisoned him and only him — and I can't see it — well, it wasn't in the cafeteria food. And everyone else is okay, so it wasn't a big dump of . . . of what? What was it?"

"Ashern and I think it's rat poison. Strychnine."

"Ohhhh," Charlotte said. "I get it. How did he get it? And why not Tom?"

"I don't know how he got it, yet, but I think Tom didn't get a visit because he would have recognized the guy. He's seen him, although always with a hat on. Al hasn't. So, the killer sent him a little message last night, instead. Except, of course, we intercepted it." Adam paused. The killer must have known the police would examine the package. "I think it was meant for us as much as for Tom."

"The dead mouse."

238

"Yes." Adam thought for another moment. "Where's Duncan?"

"He's back down in cells. He's pretty shaken up."

"We better go talk to him."

They traipsed back down and buzzed again for the young constable, who appeared sheet-white and sweating to let them back in.

"Okay, Duncan, just have a seat. Take a deep breath. Do you need some water?"

He nodded, dumbly.

"Char, do you mind finding a bottle of water?"

Charlotte left, and Adam leaned over, forcing Duncan to meet his eyes.

"I need you to tell me everything that happened this morning. Now."

"Well, there was no backup guard, when I got here," he said. "I thought that was weird, but it's not up to me. Everything was quiet. The food came down, the guys ate, I took out the trays and the cafeteria picked them up."

"Nothing else? No one came down here, apart from the food servers?"

"Just the chaplain."

"Chaplain?"

"Yeah, the new guy. He popped in to chat with Al, see if he was okay."

"Not Tom?"

"No. He said he peeked in and Tom was asleep."

"We have a new chaplain?"

"Yeah, just started this week."

"First I've heard of it. He had ID?"

"Yep."

"Name of?"

"David Smith."

Despite the seriousness of the situation, Adam gave a sharp, sardonic laugh.

"Really. Smith?"

Horror dropped Duncan's jaw and widened his eyes. "Oh, my God," he whispered. "I can't believe it. Fuck, I'm sorry, Sarge." He paused. "But, how did he do it?"

"He brought Al a treat, apparently. Drizzled with icing, laced with strychnine."

# Chapter Twenty-Eight

Grace followed Adam out the door that morning and by eight was leaning over her editor's desk.

"Claire, is it okay if I call overseas? I want to contact Reuters and Agence-France."

"Sure. Want to tell me why?"

"The remains of a child who died fourteen years ago have been found in Somalia. I think this is a boy related to our story, and I'm hoping to find out where they're at with the reportage. If they're nowhere, I might be able to help. Unless, of course, you'd rather send me to Somalia," Grace added, raising an eyebrow.

"That's so going to happen. I think the budget can withstand a couple of long-distance calls, though. You're much further along on this than I thought."

"Well, I just learned about the boy last night. It appears that Elias Crow caught the child trying to steal from the Canadian military and sent him away. But he was beaten, afterward. He died, from his injuries or from another cause, and someone buried him out there."

"God, Grace, that's shocking. How far out are you on reporting any of this?"

"I don't know. First, we have to verify that it's the same child. And, of course, it would help if the police found the perpetrators. They're working on it. If you're good with the long-distance charges, I better get at it because of the time difference."

Claire waved her away. Grace rolled back to her desk on her wheeled chair and dialled.

A mellifluous and authoritative voice crackled from over the miles.

"Reuters. Colin Day here."

"Hello, Colin. My name is Grace Rampling. I'm a reporter in Canada, at a newspaper called The StarPhoenix, in Saskatoon. How are you today?"

"Hello, Grace. To what do I owe the honour?"

"I'm working on a story about a child, a male youth really, who died fourteen years ago in Somalia during the civil war."

She heard a grunt.

"A lot of children died during that war. What's remarkable about this one?" asked the Reuters editor.

"It could be that his discovery is behind the deaths of two men in my province."

"Oh. I see. How does that work?"

"Someone did not want his body found, and we think the men were silenced because it was."

"And you're calling to see if I know anything about this."

"I am. I searched for news items last night, and found a tiny piece on an Italian site, based in Somalia, from about twelve days ago. I wondered if you were covering it."

"We weren't, but we are now. Can you send me the URL for the story? My email is Colin.Day@Reuters.com. I'll wait."

Grace sent the email and made small talk about the weather until Day said, "Okay, got it. Give me a second to read it. My Italian isn't very good."

She could hear him click his computer keys and make small murmuring sounds as he translated the words to himself.

"Right," he finally said. "Not much to go on. You don't have a name, by chance?"

"I do. Abukar Dualeh." Grace spelled it for him.

"Wow. That'll help. How did you get the name?"

"Well, I don't know it's him, but I'm fairly sure. Off the record . . ." Grace paused. What was she going to say? *I'm sleeping with the police sergeant on the case, so I know more than I should?* Which was more or less true . . .

"I have a source," she replied, lamely.

"I see. A reliable one?"

"Yes."

"Tell me what you know."

Grace briefly explained, holding back details that would explode the story in Canada. She badly wanted to protect Adam and give him time to find the killer before he could potentially dive underground. What she really needed from Reuters was verification of Abukar's remains, and hopefully, how he died.

"That's huge," Colin said when she finished. "Okay. I have your email and your numbers. I'll be in touch as soon as I can. I wonder how long it will take the authorities to identify him."

"We were wondering the same thing. Thank you, Colin."

"Thank you, Grace. Cheers."

Grace hung up and picked up the phone again to call Agence France-Presse, where she had a similar conversation with another editor who thankfully spoke English. Grace could speak French reasonably well, but it was much easier to explain the situation in her own language.

Now what? Grace wondered. She didn't want to sit and stew, so she called Elijah Starblanket. He did not answer, which of course made her worry, but there was nothing she could do about it. She resolved to try again in a couple of hours.

As she scanned her brain, Grace realized with a nasty, guilty start that she had not yet told her father about the destruction of the shed at the lake. Mick Shaw's unwelcome appearance immediately after returning home had distracted her, to say the least; and if she was honest with herself, she dreaded the dad conversation — particularly since there were so many things she couldn't say.

Should she call him now? He had to know, obviously, and the insurance company would have to be contacted. Reluctantly, she picked up the phone for the fourth time that morning.

Wallace answered and was understandably upset, more about the danger Grace had been in — again — than anything else. Otherwise, he took the news fairly well.

"You're okay, though, my girl? Really?"

"Yes, Dad, I'm fine. Honestly."

"Try not to go back up there again until this case is solved."

"I'm not likely to."

"And you did close the cabin again?"

"Of course. The cabin itself is fine, and hopefully nothing else will happen up there."

"Oh, something is happening. I haven't had a chance to tell you. Your Uncle Howard is indeed up to his old tricks. He did put in a new request to build a cabin on the island."

"Did you tell him about Elias being the victim?"

"No. Of course not. I thought he could damn well wait until the news came out."

"But Dad, we haven't revealed the identity of the dead man yet. How did he know to try again?"

"Maybe he assumed the dead man was our hermit."

"Maybe. Or maybe he's been in touch with someone at the lake. Does he have a friend up there?"

"Good question. He hasn't been at the cabin all that often — a few times, maybe." Wallace paused. "Grace, what are you saying?"

"I don't know, Dad. I just think it's weird that he's jumped on this so quickly. It's probably nothing."

"Do you want me to ask him?"

"No! No, please don't, Dad. It could mess things up for the police. And, to be honest, for me."

"The police?"

"They're going to have to talk to him, Dad. I'm sorry. They won't be happy if he gets a heads-up from us."

"I'm sure Howard has nothing to do with any of this."

"I'm sure," Grace said, although she wasn't, entirely. "But he may know something about it."

And so, once extricated from the uncomfortable chat with her father, Grace made her fifth call of the morning, feeling her heart throbbing in her throat.

"Adam," she said, when he answered. "I have something to tell you."

"And I you, but you called, so you go first."

"You don't sound well. Are you all right? Or is something up?"

"Yeah. The second. Okay, so I'll go first. Al Simpson is in the hospital. We found him unresponsive in cells this morning."

"Oh no, Adam. What happened?"

"He had a visitor bearing poison, we think."

"That's insane. I assume we can't report that."

"Not yet, but we have to disclose when something happens in cells, so it won't be too long."

"You are taking care, aren't you Adam? This person is crazy."

"Oh, yeah. Wait until I tell you how he got in here. But you called. What's up?"

"I can't believe I have to tell you this, but my uncle has repetitioned the government to get access to Elias's island. To build a cabin."

"Where is your uncle?"

"He lives in Briarwood. Howard Rampling. I'll let you take it from there."

"Retired, or working?"

"He's retired."

"I'm sorry, Grace. I'll have to go find him right away." Adam heaved a sigh. "Even if he isn't complicit, I still might learn something."

"I know. See you tonight."

"Later, Love."

*****

"So, you're The Adam," Howard Rampling said in greeting.

"The Adam?"

"Grace's The Adam."

"Yes. Do you mind if I come in for a minute?"

Uncle Howard puffed out his lips and cocked his head to one side, apparently considering the request as something he could accept or refuse. Adam, who didn't want to threaten him with a station interview, waited.

"No," Howard said.

"No you don't mind, or no I can't come in?"

"No, I don't mind. Come through to the living room."

The man is a pain in the ass, Adam thought, more than a bit surprised that he could be related to smart, sweet, straightforward Grace. Can't pick your relatives.

"So. What brings you here?" Howard asked, once they'd chosen seats on sofa and chair.

"I understand that you've expressed an interest in building a cabin on one of the islands in Ferguson Lake."

"Yep. Tried a few years ago, but a petition persuaded our brilliant government to turn me down. Your Grace signed it, by the way."

Adam decided not to be baited by this annoying human being.

"It has come to my attention," Adam said, wondering from which withered brain cell this strange formal language was coming from, "that you're trying again."

"Is that a fact. And how did this come to your attention? Don't answer that. It's obvious. Wallace told Grace, and she told you. Well, to add to your information, this government is a little more open to progress and development. If you don't play the game, you can't win."

"If I understand correctly, the province is unlikely to dislocate an Indigenous person's home, or hunting and fishing cabin. Am I right?"

"So I've heard." Howard shrugged. "Can't blame me for trying."

"How long ago did you file your new request?"

"Well, let me see. Hmmm. I guess I don't remember, exactly."

"Mr. Rampling, I can check with one phone call. I'm doing you the courtesy of asking personally."

"Hmph. Fine. I suppose it was about a week ago."

"A week ago? Sir, did you know that the so-called hermit of Ferguson Lake's fishing hut was burned down 'about a week ago'?"

"Noooo . . . well, not at the time. Kind of convenient, eh?"

"Too convenient, Mr. Rampling. Did you know that the hermit is dead?"

Finally, a reaction. Howard Rampling turned a shade of purple that clashed with his green and red checked shirt.

247

"No."

"Did you assume it was him? I would think you've read the paper and saw the story."

"That had nothing to do with my application."

"Something did. I would advise you to tell me what it was."

Rampling had regained some of his composure.

"What might that be?" he said, in a musing tone that would have inspired a good throttling from someone less controlled than Adam.

What might that be, indeed. But the question, and a flare of anger, fired Adam's brain.

"That might be getting a little inside information. Do you know any of the cottagers at Ferguson, sir?"

"No . . . not well, anyway."

"Is that the truth?"

"Look. I promised I wouldn't say anything. It was just a remark, that's all."

Adam leaned over the coffee table, his navy eyes flashing.

"I'm going to tell you something that you will not repeat," Adam said in his most authoritative and menacing voice. "Am I clear?"

Howard said nothing.

"Am I clear, sir? You need to acknowledge my request, right now."

He nodded, finally silenced by Adam's intimidating presence.

"Two men are dead, including the hermit. Another is clinging to life. I know that whoever uttered that 'remark' is involved. If you are not, and if you want to remain that way, you're going to tell me which cottager you were talking to."

Adam already knew the answer. But he had to hear it from Howard Rampling.

"Now, sir."

Howard pursed his lips and blew through them in an odd little whistle.

"Hell. Okay. Every so often, I get together for drinks with some old army buddies, down at the Legion. One of the guys who shows up from time to time has a cabin up there. I didn't serve with him; he's a bit younger. We've gotten to know each other, as acquaintances.

"One night, he was in a fine mood, had maybe more than one or two too many. He knew — it had come up in the past — that I had my eye on that island and asked if I was still interested. I said I was."

Howard licked his lips, and his eyes opened wide.

"Holy shit," he breathed. "The guy said I should think about trying again, and then laughed until I thought his sides would split. I didn't see what the hell was so funny. I asked him why I should give it another shot, and he just said the government might be more amenable than it had been in the past."

"How long ago was this?"

"About ten days ago or so. I had all my application paperwork, so all I had to do was update it and send it along. Took just a few minutes."

Adam had to take a minute before he spoke.

"It was George Best, wasn't it?"

"Yes. How the hell did you know that?"

# Chapter Twenty-Nine

The chief of police's email awaited when he returned to the station, in response to Adam's request for a meeting. Adam seethed over Terry Pearson's actions, infantile and pompous and ridiculous as they were. Pearson risked Al Simpson's life, simply because he was pissed that his authority had been ignored.

*Fucking idiot*, Adam swore to himself, as he stomped the distance to McIvor's office. He knocked and the chief responded with a grim "come in, Adam."

"What the hell happened?" McIvor asked, even before Adam sat down.

"Pearson came in early, I gather, and pulled the detail on Simpson and Allbright," Adam said, pulling up a chair. "Two hours later, after the usual fight in my office, I found Al in rigour in his cell. It looked like he was frothing at the mouth, at first, but it was actually icing."

"Icing? Like on a cake?"

"Yeah. Someone brought him a pastry. Ashern thinks it was laced with strychnine."

"How's the prisoner?"

"I don't know. Ashern said he would call when he had news. Good or bad."

"Who the fuck was it?"

"The guy was posing as a chaplain. Do we have a new chaplain on call, Chief?"

"Yeah, we do, or at least we will. A new guy got signed up last week."

"That explains why Duncan let him in. I bet his name isn't Smith, though. Or is it?"

"No, I don't think so. Did he see the other prisoner, too? Allbright?"

"No. He made the excuse that Tom was asleep. Tom would have, or may have, recognized him; he saw him at Ferguson Lake. And Tom is much less of a risk, apart from recognition. He's not directly involved.

"But Al wouldn't have recognized him — at least, not as the killer. He had only talked to him on the phone. Tom had a message, too, with the dead mouse. They're trying to tell us all not to squeal. And there's something else."

Adam launched into a retelling of his conversation with Howard Rampling, watching his chief's face slowly set like concrete.

"Who is behind all of this, Adam? What the hell is going on?" he asked after Adam had finished.

"It's hard to say who's at the top of the chain," Adam said, slowly. "Maybe a top dog in the military, although at what rank, I'm not sure. Or possibly even the government — although we've had a few elections since all this began. But whoever they are, their henchmen are on the ground, and we have to find them first. George Best, the cottage owner, is definitely involved but I don't think he did the actual dirty work. He might be calling the shots."

"So who's the killer?"

"I have no idea. I have a pretty good description, but he's in some kind of disguise. And his name is Charles Best — George Best's dead son's name. An alias."

"Terrific," the chief said, sarcasm dripping from the word. "That makes it easier. What's next, then?"

"I have James setting up Tom Allbright with a sketch artist, hopefully by tomorrow morning. We'll take that sketch and hit the streets with it; Tom told us the guy found him when he was roaming the west side, stoned on meth. Maybe someone will recognize him, I don't know. Meanwhile, we find George Best."

"Okay. Glad you have a plan. Good work, Adam. And I'll take care of Pearson. Looks like you were right about getting Simpson and Allbright out of Meadow Lake and into our cells, by the way. It would have worked if it wasn't for Pearson. Fuckhead. And for the record, I did keep him informed, when I could find him."

"Thanks, Chief, for that. I'll keep you posted."

Charlotte and James were waiting for Adam in the incident room when he returned to the squad's third-floor home.

"I've found George Best, sort of," Charlotte began.

"Sort of?"

"He lives and owns a couple of businesses in the Saskatoon area. Both are numbered companies, but I got the provincial registry to search for his name."

"Saskatoon area?"

"He's on an acreage south of town, and I gather it's adjacent to the businesses."

"Like Al Simpson's mother's place. And what are the businesses?"

"He runs a turf-growing company and a paintball place down on Valley Road," Charlotte said, flipping the pages of her notebook. "Um. Green Summer Turf and Paintball Palace."

"The turf place won't be open right now; it's too late in the season. What about, uh, Paintball Palace?" Adam asked,

252

grinning over the ridiculous name despite the seriousness of the circumstances.

"It's open. I called, but they said the owner was away. They wouldn't confirm his name, either."

"Have you tried calling Best directly?"

"I did. No answer."

"Hell. James, do we have the sketch artist lined up?"

"Yes. Tom has agreed to describe the guy; he's definitely scared. He couldn't miss the shit hitting the fan in cells this morning. I think we're going to have full co-operation from now on."

"Okay. The sketch is job one. When we find Best, I want to shove it under his nose, and possibly up his ass. With Howard Rampling's information, we know for certain he's involved. I'll tell you about that later.

"As soon as the sketch is done, we'll need to organize another canvass for tomorrow morning. Let's call it a day."

So much for that, Adam thought, as his cellphone buzzed in his pocket. He pulled it out, to see that the call was coming from Royal University Hospital. Had to be Ashern.

"Hey, Brian," Adam greeted the doctor, hesitancy in his voice.

"Adam," Ashern responded. "It was strychnine, I'm afraid. I'm sorry, Adam. Al Simpson didn't make it."

Adam had worried about Al all day, but he found it hard to believe that his colleague, witness and prisoner would actually die. Shocked and sorry, Adam also felt frustration and anger rise. He would get no more information from him. Worse, Al was poisoned in the police station.

"Damn," he said quietly. "Were you able to test for the dose, Brian?"

"It was a big one, Adam. Could have killed a colony of rats. And definitely — obviously — lethal to one man. They weren't kidding around, buddy. They meant for him to die."

\*\*\*\*\*

Adam finally made it home two hours later after revisiting the chief, knowing the investigation into Al's poisoning would have to ramp up immediately now that the man was dead. He had seldom seen McIvor so angry.

An enticing aroma greeted him — casserole? he wondered, sniffing the redolent air — but no Grace. His heart thumped. Too many things had happened for Adam to assume all was well . . . but there was the food in the oven. Calm down, he told himself.

"Hey, love, I'm home," he called.

"I'm in the bedroom, Adam."

Relieved to hear her voice, he walked down the hall and found Grace at her computer, scanning online news stories from Somalia. He peered over her shoulder as he kissed her neck.

"No news, yet?"

"Nothing further, no. It's only been a few hours since I called the European agencies, though."

Grace snapped down the screen of her laptop and stood up to kiss Adam on the mouth, then gazed at him.

"What's up?" she said, taking his tense face between her hands. "Hard day?"

"Al Simpson died in hospital today."

"Oh, God, Adam. I'm so sorry," Grace said, tugging him in and holding him close. After a few moments, Adam could feel his whipcord muscles begin to release.

"Thank God for you, Babe," he said. "No matter what happens at work, everything seems all right when you touch me."

Grace seemed to be rendered speechless, as she tightened her grip on Adam's waist and shoulders. He felt something wet on his neck.

254

"Are you all right, Grace? Are you crying?" He tried to look into her face, but it was buried next to his cheek.

"Yes," she said, gulping back a small sob. "Thank you for saying that. Are you hungry?"

"I wasn't until I smelled whatever you're cooking. I wish I'd been home to help. I'm sorry about these late hours, Grace. I don't know when that will change, though. Can you put up with it?"

"Don't worry about that, Adam. We'll cope. One day we might even get a holiday." She gave him a small, crooked smile that told him more than her words.

"As soon as this case is solved. You're right; we need a break. Okay?"

She nodded, sniffed. "Yes. Let's eat, before the meat turns to leather."

Adam helped Grace serve the chicken casserole, salad and wine, and finally broached the subject of Howard Rampling.

"I saw your uncle this afternoon. Are you sure you're related to that guy?"

Grace laughed. "I know. He's a bit of a pain, isn't he? How did it go?"

"Well, I think he's an opportunist who doesn't much care if other people are hurt or displaced, as long as he gets what he wants. But I don't think he's directly involved in this mess. On the bright side, he confirmed that George Best is in this up to his neck. That part was helpful, especially on the premeditation side. George told him to reapply to the province for permission to build on the island. He didn't say why, but it happened very shortly before the fire."

"I didn't know Howard knew George."

"Apparently they know each other from the Legion. Your uncle was in the army, too."

"That's right. I'd forgotten. He served for a few years before I was born, in the Gaza Strip as a peacekeeper, I think. Was he being a jerk?"

"At first, yeah, he was. Once I'd explained how serious this was, and how two people were dead — now three — he was a little more forthcoming."

"Have you found George yet?"

"Not yet. We know where he lives, and that he owns two businesses on Valley Road. One of them is a paintball place. Makes a certain amount of sense, if he misses military action. But we couldn't reach him by phone, and his employees say he's away."

"What will you do now?"

"Tomorrow, Tom Allbright will help us create a sketch of Charles Best, whoever the hell he is. And we keep looking for George."

"I'll pester the European news editors in the morning. Maybe they'll have learned something by then."

\*\*\*\*\*

Adam paced like a panther eyeing cornered prey as Tom Allbright directed the court artist's pencil in his cell. How long was this going to take? Adam asked himself. He wanted to be back on the street, likeness in hand, right now.

Charlotte appeared bearing coffee, and instead of talking Adam down as she usually did, she joined him on his back-and-forth journey.

"How long is this going to take?" she asked.

"I was just asking myself that question. The artist said half an hour, forty-five minutes. He wants to make sure he's got it

256

right, and that Tom got it right, too." Adam checked his watch. "It's already been forty. Gah."

When the artist, name of Ward Collins, finally appeared fifteen minutes later, he presented Adam with not one, but two sketches.

"What's this?" Adam asked, as he took the sheets of paper. "Two?"

"Turns out your prisoner . . . ah, witness? . . . saw your fake chaplain for a couple of seconds through the window as he left. So, we've done two sketches, one of the baseball cap-wearing guy, and one of the dude in priestly garments. Not bad for an hour, eh?"

"Thank you. That's fantastic. I sure appreciate your time and effort, Mr. Collins."

"Don't mention it, Sarge. Anything I can do."

Adam shook his hand, turned, and with Charlotte right behind him, took the stairs two at a time to the incident room where James was already waiting. Adam put the two sketches side by side on the table, under the bright lights.

"It sure as hell is the same guy," said Charlotte, looking intently at the two little works of art.

"It sure as hell is," James agreed.

Looking back at them were two versions of the same man: dark, tall, lean but not thin. The man in the cap had a partial tattoo snaking out from under one sleeve; if it existed on the chaplain, fully clothed to the cuffs and collar, it could not be seen.

"But there is a difference," Adam said, peering closely. "Look at the guy in the baseball cap. His shoulders look like they've been installed with rebar. The so-called chaplain's don't; he's not stooped, but he's also not on military parade. He knows how to change his body language. If it's the same guy. And the nose . . . something different there . . . and he's wearing glasses."

"Right," Charlotte said. "Brothers, maybe?"

"Twins, more like," James suggested. "Apart from the posture. Of course, we can't see the top of the first guy's head. We don't know if the hair's the same."

Adam stared at the sketches, trying to get his brain to release a small thought lurking in a groggy cell. He knew he had not seen the man in the cap before. Why was an alarm ringing in his head?

"Okay, let's get these copied and hit the street. Char, if you would, keep looking for George Best. James and I will take the same canvass we did last time, and I'll see if I can get Fisher and Jones to help."

James took the sketches out for copying, as Charlotte nodded and returned to her desk. Ten minutes later, James and Adam were back on the street.

They started, as they had the last time, at Harbour House; but no one answered to the bell nor a vigorous pounding on the front door. Adam tried to peer inside, but the shades were snugly drawn.

"We'll come back later," he said. "They may be out on a rescue."

"What's next?" James asked. "It might be a bit too early for the bar. Even the Barry."

"I guess it is a little early. Let's try the Sally Ann first, see who's around."

The Salvation Army men's residence was only two blocks away. Five minutes later, Adam was greeting the captain at the front desk.

"Hello, Andrew. How's it going?

"Not bad, Adam. Hi, James. Haven't seen you two in a while. What's up?"

"I'm looking for this man," Adam said, pushing the sketch of the cap-wearing man across the high counter. "He was in contact with another man, a meth addict, named Tom Allbright,

258

who was a regular on the street. I think you recognized him during our last canvass, when Joan and Lorne came by?" Adam asked, producing the photo of Tom.

"Yes, I've seen Tom around. He stayed here a couple of times. This guy, though . . . I don't think I know him, no."

"Okay. How about this man?" Adam brought out the second sketch of the chaplain.

The burly captain peered down again, adjusting his glasses. He looked up with his eyebrows meeting over his nose.

"Same guy? Brothers? What's going on?"

"It might be the same guy. We're not sure. That's why we're showing you two sketches."

"Master of disguise?" Andrew looked again, back and forth between the two photocopies, and shook his head. "I don't know. He does look familiar. The priest could be one of several who come here to counsel — or convert — our guests. They all look the same in their collars, given similar hair colour and stature."

Adam's eyes widened. It had never occurred to him that the impostor who poisoned Al Simpson might actually be a priest. It was unlikely, but he would have to check.

*They all look the same.* Why did that chime in his brain?

"Could I have the names and parishes of those priests?" Adam asked.

"Of course."

Andrew scrabbled in a drawer for paper and pen, then brought out a slim black book. He wrote for a moment, checking back and forth.

"Phone numbers, too?"

"If you have them."

Andrew finished scribbling and handed the paper to Adam. Reading it, Adam blinked in surprise. There actually was a David Smith on the list. He'd have to apologize to Duncan.

"You should ask Father Cey," Andrew added. "He might know who you're looking for."

"We were just at Harbour House. It's locked up. Do you know if he's away, or out on a rescue?"

"No, I don't. We didn't call for a rescue, anyway. I'd heard the house was closed yesterday, but I didn't think it would still be today . . . Adam? What?"

Adam had suddenly leaned forward, bracing his hands heavily on the counter before him, his face a mask of shock and disbelief.

# Chapter Thirty

It had only been twenty-seven hours since Grace had
contacted the European news agencies. Did she dare
call again so soon, to see if there had been any progress
in identifying the child's bones in Somalia?

She chewed her lip, reached for the phone, drew her hand
back. Five minutes later, she did it again.

"Oh, hell," she muttered.

"What's the matter, Grace?" asked Lacey McPhail,
overhearing.

"I'm trying to keep myself from calling Reuters again. It's
only been about a day, but I can't stand it. I want to know if
they've learned anything, or at least if they're on the story.
Should I call again? Would they just be cranky at me?"

"I'd give it a few more hours. As you say, it's only been a
day or so. Want to grab a coffee? I could use a break."

"I'm afraid to leave my desk, in case they phone."

"Didn't give them your cell number?"

"No. Too pricey. They're using the trunk line."

"I could bring you a cup."

"That would be great. And a muffin? Here . . . take this,"
Grace said, holding out a five.

"Nope. On me." Lacey grabbed her wallet and headed for the stairs. "Milk no sugar, right?"

"You rock, McPhail."

It was getting late in Europe. Grace checked the time again, as she had been obsessively doing all morning. It would be six p.m. in London, seven in Paris. How late would the editors she had spoken to be in their offices?

Trapped by the damned phone again, Grace thought. It wasn't her favourite part of being a reporter.

And then, just as she spied Lacey through the glass door juggling two cups of coffee and two muffins, it rang. Grace looked at the area code and snatched up the receiver.

"Grace Rampling, StarPhoenix," she answered, a touch breathlessly.

"It's Colin Day from Reuters. How are you today?"

"Fine, thank you," Grace said, squirming with impatience. "And you?"

"Good, thanks. I have some information for you. We're not quite there, but I do have something.

"They were unable to identify the youth by dental records. I gather a lot of the records were lost during the war — fires, and so forth — if the poor kid ever even had dental work done. So, we don't have a definite ID yet.

"But the bones belonged to a Dualeh from that village. They've tested a surviving family member. Neither of his parents are alive, which would have made this a slam dunk. Still, this kid was a Dualeh in his teens when he died, even if we can't say for sure it was Abukar."

Grace exhaled, realizing she had been holding her breath the entire time Colin Day was speaking.

"Is there any chance they'll be able to identify him? What would that take?"

"I suppose the family could testify that he went missing that night, if he was the only family member that was lost. It wouldn't be perfect, but that, with the DNA, should do it."

Grace knew in her soul that this was Abukar Dualeh. She could move forward, and so could Adam, based on Day's information.

"Could they determine how he died?" she asked.

"That's pretty certain. The kid's skull had a round hole in it. At the back. Definitely shot to death."

Oh, God, thought Grace, a wave of nausea churning her stomach. So terrible. Just like Elias.

"No bullet, though," she said.

"No."

"Any response from the army?

"We have a call in to the Minister of Defence, but no, no response so far. I'm not all that surprised, though. As you know, it usually takes a while for the government to get back to you."

"Thank you, Colin. I'm so grateful."

"No, thank you, Grace. Hell of a story. Appreciate the tip."

"When will you run something?"

"The reporter's just finishing up the first file. We should have a full story tomorrow. I'll send you the link when it lands online."

"I'd appreciate that. Would you also let me know when you've interviewed the family?"

"Of course. Take care, Grace. Thanks again."

Grace replaced the receiver, nausea forgotten, jumped from her chair and threw her arms over her head in a victory gesture.

"That was Day, then," Lacey said, a huge grin splitting her face at Grace's reaction.

"Yes. Yes, yes, yes. High five me, McPhail," she said, holding up her hand. "They can't positively identify him as that specific child, but it's so close. Close enough that I can move on this story. Finally."

Claire Davidson had leapt from her chair and rushed over to Grace's desk.

"How close?" she asked.

"DNA proves he's a member of that family, and that he died as a teenager. Reuters is going to interview his remaining family members. That should do it."

"Okay. Great job, Grace. What's your plan?"

"At some point I'm going to have to call the military and the Ministry of Defence. The police will not be happy if I do that before they've caught their killer, though. I'll call them and see where they're at."

She stopped talking. Her chocolate eyes, wide with excitement, dimmed and narrowed.

"I can't believe I'm high-fiving over a dead child."

"You're not, Grace," Lacey said, her hand reaching out in sympathy. "You're excited because you're going to solve this crime, and maybe extract some justice for the poor kid."

"Still. Excuse me."

Grace bolted for the ladies' washroom and locked herself in a stall. Leaning on the cubicle wall, she dropped her head in her hands. Sometimes, she thought, the cynicism necessary to keeping an objective distance from story subjects went too far; and the emotions, contrary to the objectivity, could be overwhelming. It was hard to manage both.

"Grace." Claire was knocking on the door. "It's okay, Grace. We all understand. It's the excitement over a big break in a story. It's not your cold, cold heart. Come out of there."

Grace sniffled, wiped her eyes and emerged from her privacy into her editor's arms.

"I feel like a jerk, just the same."

"Which is why you know your motivations are pure, and your reaction was natural. Honey, sometimes I think your heart

264

isn't chilly enough, but your empathy is also what makes you a great reporter. Don't be so damn hard on yourself."

"Thanks, Claire. I appreciate it. But . . ." Grace saw herself celebrating in her mind's eye and shuddered. "I have to think about it."

"Don't think for too long. And call Adam. I know you want to, and you should. Let's get on this story, okay?"

"Okay."

"It's the only thing you can do for that child. Or Elias."

"I know."

Grace gave Claire a small, shaky smile, and the two women returned to the newsroom, where Grace's coffee was rapidly cooling. She took a sip, gave Lacey a quick hug of thanks, and picked up the phone.

"Grace," Adam answered. His voice was thin and strained.

"Adam, I have an update. But are you all right?"

"I'm fine. Just working this case. What's up?"

"The child's DNA has been tested, and he is a member of the Dualeh family. They don't have a definite identification; there were no dental records, and his parents are dead. But it's ninety-five per cent."

She could hear Adam's heavy breathing on the other end of the line.

"That's great news, Grace. Thanks. I have to run."

"Can't tell me why?"

"I'll tell you later. Have a good day, Babe."

And he hung up.

He had never been so curt with her, in any conversation. Grace wondered what was going on, fear plucking at her brain. She hadn't been able to squeeze in a question about how to proceed, either. She picked up the phone again. It rang and rang, but Adam didn't answer. She hung up and tried again. Then she tried his office line. Same result.

*Hell.*

Frozen with worry, Grace willed her brain to clear. What should she do next? She thought back to the clues Adam had shared with her, the information he had gathered from her uncle, the names — real or assumed — of the people involved in the fire-setting and the veterans' murders. What would Adam do next? What had he said last night?

*"Tom Allbright will help us create a sketch of Charles Best, whoever the hell he is. And we keep looking for George."*

A sketch of the killer.

We keep looking for George.

Grace pushed her chair back. She threw her digital recorder and reporter's notebook in her bag, which already held her camera, and grabbed her purse. Lacey looked up in surprise.

"Where are you going? I thought you were going to make some calls about the Somali child."

"Change in plan. I'm off to interview some people who might know the bastard behind this. Or one of the bastards. See you later."

"Shouldn't you tell me where you're going? Or Claire? Is this dangerous, Grace?"

"I don't think so. It's just a business. The guy the cops are looking for owns it. I'm off. I'll call you if I need any help, okay?"

She was already halfway to the door. Grace flew down the stairs and out to her car, wondering why she hadn't told Lacey where she was going. Had she told her the whole truth, Lacey would have insisted on coming. Why was that a problem?

Grace admitted to herself that her mission could, in fact, be dangerous. She didn't want anyone else involved. But what could go wrong in the middle of the day, in a very public place?

Throwing her bag on the passenger seat, Grace jumped into the Honda and gripped the steering wheel. It was then that she noticed her hands were shaking.

Calm down, she told herself, as she turned out of the parking lot and headed through downtown, taking vague note of traffic lights and pedestrians. Fifteen minutes later, she was headed south, out of town.

It would have been a beautiful drive down Valley Road, had Grace been in a frame of mind to notice the rolling hills obscuring the horizon, a light mist scarfing the hollows and painting the lowering clouds a dusty lavender. Early autumn beauty could not pierce her focus. Her thoughts churned as her eyes kept a grim watch on the narrow highway.

She had never before noticed the turf-growing business, nor the Paintball Palace in her many forays down the road. Friends owned an acreage not far from there, near Pike Lake, and Grace had traversed Valley Road countless times on her way to visit them. Where was this place?

Finally, as she turned a ninety-degree corner, a small sign on her right came into view: Green Summer Turf and Paintball Palace, one kilometre. Odd, she thought. Why would the owners not advertise the businesses' existence with more visible signage?

*That's not good*, her brain said loudly. *Pay attention.*

She turned down a gravel road and soon saw fallow fields that had grown lawn grass earlier in the season. At least there is turf being grown here, she thought, and relaxed just a little. Half a kilometre later, she was driving into the parking lot serving a small building, not much larger than a double-wide trailer. Palace, indeed, she thought. What the hell kind of a place is this?

Should she go in as a journalist, questions at the ready? Or should she present herself as a friend of the owner, and see how far that got her?

Grace slipped her recorder into her purse and turned it on, then slowly got out of the car, looking carefully around the premises.

Parked nearby, under overhanging trees, was Adam's unmarked police car.

# Chapter Thirty-One

Adam's brain exploded in anger and confusion. Adam had trusted him, even supported him. How could he have done such things?

*Sadly,* Adrian Cey had said, *many of them look so much the same.*

That went for priests as well as for homeless people, apparently. Suddenly, it didn't seem quite so strange that Al had eaten a pastry offered by a clergyman.

On autopilot and fuelled by fury, Adam didn't pause to think. He strode back to the car and radioed Charlotte to put out an all-points bulletin. He sent James back to Harbour House, told him to call Crown Prosecutor Sanjeev Kumar for a warrant, and to wait for backup before ramming the goddamn door down.

"Where are you going?" James asked.

"To find George Best."

"Without backup?"

"I don't need backup to interview one guy in the middle of the fucking day," Adam snapped. "Get this place searched." And he drove away.

He sped down Valley Road, which carried little traffic at that time on a weekday, realizing he had no clue where Paintball Palace was located. Damned if he would turn on the siren, he thought. No way was he alerting Best to his imminent arrival, assuming he could find him.

Screaming around the corner that gave out to a berry-picking orchard and restaurant, he began to wonder if Paintball Palace and Green Summer Turf were fictional. But there was the sign, half-hidden by scraggly bushes. Two minutes later, followed by an enormous cloud of dust, he screeched into a small parking lot, stopped and flung himself out of the car.

Adam stalked to the tiny building, threw open the door and found the little front room empty. This was no palace, for paintball or anything else. The games must be staged outside.

Instead of calling out, Adam slipped behind the front desk and approached the office door on the right side. It was slightly ajar; he pushed it open, slowly and silently. Vacant.

Down a short hallway were a small, filthy bathroom, a tiny lunchroom and two more offices. Also vacant.

Adam turned on his heel and stormed out the door, wondering where the hell the staff had gone, considering the office had been left open. A breath of wind carried a possible answer. He heard the paf-paf of paintball guns, men's voices raised in simulated combat. Adam headed north, toward the sounds.

His cellphone rang. Quickly pulling it out of his pocket to silence it, he saw that it was Grace and answered.

"Grace," he said, and heard her news about Abukar Dualeh.

Those fucking bastards, he thought, and hung up on the woman he loved.

But someone had heard his phone; he must have been nearby. Seconds later, a man emerged from a nearby copse of golden-leaved trees, paintball gun aimed at Adam's chest.

"Hello, Adam," he said.

"Hello, Adrian."

"What brings you here?"

"He said, innocently. You know what brings me here."

"May I introduce you to George Best?" Cey asked, as a second man emerged. "Although perhaps you have met."

"Not exactly." Adam's hand twitched on his belt, a finger flicking the safety. Best nodded at him with a wide grin, as if he were a customer or a friend.

"Did you come for a game?" Cey asked. "You would be excellent competition. May I set you up with a gun?"

"I have a gun."

"Very funny, Adam. You know what I mean. Have you played before? It's very . . . challenging."

Before Adam could respond, Father Adrian Cey lowered his sniper-style device and fired a blue ball at his leg, aiming precisely where Adam had been shot six and a half years earlier. He knew the spot exactly; they had talked about the experience.

Pain exploded at the impact, fireworks popped in his head, and Adam reached for his weapon.

Too late. Cey had divined his next move, and fired again — this time at Adam's hand, just as Best unleashed a ball at Adam's shoulder.

Adam hardly registered that he was outmanned; he only knew he had to move, and fast. Instinct fired his legs, and he sprung to his right, landing crouched on his hands and feet before running into the trees behind his vehicle. Breathing heavily, Adam took stock, narrowing his eyes to peer into the trees.

Another ball hit him in the chest, so hard it knocked the wind out of him. Where did that come from? It must have been at close range. There was a third man, somewhere nearby.

Maybe more. This, Adam understood in a flash of clarity, was no game.

They couldn't have known he was coming. They did not expect him, but they were ready for him.

He hit the dirt and crawled away toward more promising shelter. A series of barrels had been arranged beside a small grove of larger trees. Whether they could see him, or were just firing for effect, Adam didn't know; but paint rained on him as he scrambled for the barrels, reaching for his gun. Then he heard something else, something more sinister. The crack of a pistol.

Adam's brain snapped back to the night he had been shot in the bar. Waking in the hospital, surrounded by the concerned faces of doctors. A long blur of pain and medicated confusion. Months of heavy drinking and mindless fucking. He froze in terror.

Sweating, shaking and completely disoriented, Adam fought to understand what was happening and failed. Was this reality, or the worst nightmare of his life? Unable to turn his head, his legs turned to water and he sank to a crouch, his back sliding down the solidity of the tree trunk.

Adam lowered his chin and peered down at his legs. Six or seven large yellow, blue and red splotches decorated his pants, to the point where they were no longer black. What the hell were these colours doing on his clothes? There were more on his shirt. He touched them, and felt painful bruises under the fabric, covering his chest.

I must be dreaming, he thought. If I've been shot that many times, I couldn't be alive, could I?

There's sweat or something on my face. Is it blood?

He raised a hand and drew it down his cheek. It came away covered in blue and yellow. Strange, for blood, he thought. Where was it coming from? He felt his head, ran a hand through his hair, but couldn't find the wound.

272

I must wake up now, Adam told himself. Grace will be worrying. Where is Grace?

What is that noise? Adam started violently, and almost dropped what he clutched against his chest. Shocked, he realized it was his sidearm. The noise, again. Shouting. Someone shouting his name. Grace?

No, not Grace. A man's voice, calling him. He recognized the voice. It wasn't James's, nor Lorne's. Who was it? He tried to clear his head, to search his memory, but he couldn't place the voice's owner. Adam tried to peer around the tree, to see who was there, but he found that his neck wouldn't work. He was paralyzed. Whether from fear or because he was dreaming, he couldn't tell.

*They're hunting me*, he thought.

Something buzzed in his pocket. What was that? Some sort of medical device? He patted his pocket, and the buzzing stopped. Good. Maybe he wasn't in the hospital, then. But it happened again, and Adam reached in, annoyed, to pull out a cellphone. Its screen was alight; Grace's name was spelled out in large black letters.

*Grace.*

He touched the button at the bottom of the phone, and Grace's voice suddenly came to him.

"Adam, where are you?" it said.

"Grace? Is it you? Am I dreaming?"

"Adam, you are not dreaming. Where are you? Can you describe what's around you? I'm in the parking lot. I need to know where you are."

Not dreaming? But Grace was speaking to him. She always said he was dreaming, and she was always right. Was she right this time? Or was she trying to confuse him? Why would she do that? He couldn't see her.

"Adam! For God's sake, talk to me. You're not dreaming. It's not safe this time."

"Are you telling me the truth?"

"Yes, Adam. Always. Can you tell me where you are?"

"Behind a tree."

"Good. Adam. Listen to me. You're having a flashback. You're all right, love, but you have to fight. You have to come out of your dream. You have to wake up now."

"I have to wake up now. Where am I? I'm not in the hospital. Am I in the bar?"

"No, Adam. You're in a paintball arena. They're shooting paintballs at you. Stay behind the tree, but wake up, Adam. Please, Adam, wake up."

Another shot rang out, and Adam heard Grace scream. The bullet skimmed past Adam and embedded itself in the bark of a tree to his right. Paf-paf-paf: more paintballs, two bursting on the barrel to his left.

"Goddamn it, Adam,"' Grace said, a sob escaping her throat. "Wake up. Get on your stomach, draw your weapon. I won't, I can't lose you now to these bastards. You have to wake up."

Her scream and her words crashed through Adam's paralyzed daze. Slick with sudden sweat, he flipped over onto his belly, clutched his sidearm between his shaking hands, and knew what had happened to him.

"I'm awake, Grace," he said, though a shuddering breath. "Hell. Where are they?"

"I can't see them, but I can hear them. They're to the north of me, maybe five hundred metres out. Where are you? Can you tell me?"

"I — I'm in a circle of barrels with trees around it."

"Do you have your gun?"

"Yes."

"James is on his way. I called him when I saw your car. I'm going to see if I can find them."

"No! Grace, stop. They'll kill you."

"Not if they don't see me. They don't know I'm here."

Adam continued to shake and sweat, but by now his faculties had kicked in sufficiently that he knew he had to stop Grace from venturing into the paintball arena.

"They may have heard you scream. I'm okay here. Wait for James. Get in your car and head back to the highway."

Another shot rang out.

"Go, Grace. Now!"

"No. I can't leave you."

"You must. You're not even armed."

He couldn't see Grace wildly looking around the property, hair swirling in the wind, desperately trying to spy George Best and Adrian Cey, wondering how to help Adam. But he saw her in his mind's eye, and a tear trickled down his cheek.

"Please, Babe, go. I'm begging you."

A paintball whizzed through the air and caught Grace on the arm. She emitted a cry of pain and threw herself onto the ground. They'd found her.

"Grace!" Adam yelled over the phone. "Are you okay?"

"Yes," she whispered.

"Get in your car! Go!"

Adam came out of hiding as if he were on fire, bellowing at the attackers, drawing their attention from Grace. Bullets and paintballs zipped at him, as he ran a serpentine route from tree to tree.

A flicker of movement to his right caught the periphery of his vision. He snapped his head around to see Adrian Cey dodging behind a barrel and fired.

Missed. Cey shot back, as Adam plunged to the ground and rolled, firing again.

"Fucking hold your fire! Police!"

It was James. He discharged a rifle into the air, yelling at the top of his lungs. Adam tipped his head backward from his lying position, to see six of his officers in full special-teams gear

275

running full-speed toward him. Galvanized, Adam rose into a crouch like a runner in the blocks and dove, landing in a small hollow behind a bush.

"Adam," James called. "Where are you?"

"I'm in a ditch to your right."

"How many are there?"

"At least three, but there could be more."

James found Adam hunched in the hollow, covered in paint and blood and bruises, and handed him a vest. One of the bullets had indeed grazed his shoulder; scrapes from the gravel had ripped his face and hands.

"Fuck, man, you look like you've been through a war. It's now or never, though, Sarge."

"I know. Where's Grace?"

"In her car. She wouldn't leave."

"It's not safe . . . "

"I know. What do you want me to do? Let's go get these guys."

The other officers had fanned out and taken positions at the near end of the games arena. James and Adam emerged from the hollow and Adam nodded to his team, directing them toward the trees where he had hidden in his panic.

Adam headed straight for the barrel where he had last seen Cey, but he was gone. A few metres further on stood a small hut, much like a rain shelter on a golf course but plastered with paint splatters.

"Are you there, Adrian?" Adam bellowed, as he approached. "I'm here. Let's do this."

"I believe," said the man he was hunting, "that I have the advantage, position-wise. Why would I come out?"

Cey's armed hand snaked around the corner of the hut and Adam dropped, returning fire as he landed. A muffled cry, and another shot from Cey that missed widely. Adam knew then that he'd hit him. He took the moment and raced for the

hut, gun braced in both hands, when he heard another shot —
this one at a distance — followed by a barrage of gunfire. His
officers must have found Best.

He slowed, weapon ready, as he approached. Inside, Cey
lay on the concrete floor, bleeding copiously from his leg, gun
pointed at his own head.

"Well, Adam. I suppose it had to come to this. But I will
never say a word. I will never tell you anything. Whatever you
could do to me would not come close to what I could lose.
What our country could lose. And so . . . "

Adam lunged at Cey, reaching for the loaded pistol in blind
terror that the man would shoot himself, and tore it out of his
hand.

"You will talk to me," Adam said, softly. "If you'd really
wanted to kill yourself, or were brave enough, you'd have done
it by now. This is over."

# Chapter Thirty-Two

Adam walked out of the arena bloody, stained, limping and holding his left arm cradled in his right. Sweat poured down his face, contorted in pain and remembered fear. Grace held her arms wide as she ran toward him, and he collapsed against her.

"Adam, my love, my Adam," she crooned, running her hands through his hair, over his arms, trying to determine how badly he was injured even as she soothed him.

"You phoned me," he said, incredulity in his voice. "You came, and you saved me. You saved my life, Grace."

James and Lorne had found Adam with Adrian Cey moments later. They dragged the fallen priest away, Adam following, exhausted and distraught, worrying about Grace. Other officers had engaged in a chaotic battle with George Best and the third shooter. Both had gunshot wounds; all three men were loaded into ambulances under guard.

"Why did you come alone, Adam? What were you thinking?" Grace asked.

"Only that I would come to speak to the employees, for information, to see if I could find Best. It made sense, at the time." He paused, and looked quizzically into her face, as if a drawer had opened in his mind. "What are you doing here?"

"I had the same idea. I was also worried about you. You were very short with me on the phone, mister." Grace touched his cheek. "That's not like you."

"I'm sorry about that . . ." Adam started, but Grace cut him off.

"No. It brought me to you, even though I didn't know for sure you were here."

A fourth ambulance spattered gravel as it tore into the parking lot. This one was for Adam, and Grace wondered if he would allow the paramedics to load him in or take him to the hospital. James waved them over to his sergeant.

"How are you, sir?" one of the medics said as he approached Adam.

"I'm fine," he growled back.

"Do you mind if I take a look? I'm afraid you're sporting rather a lot of blood and other indications of injury."

Adam growled again, which brought Grace into the conversation.

"Love, please let them look at you. You're a mess, frankly. Please."

"Sergeant?" the medic chimed in. "My name is John. May I take you to the ambulance, since you obviously don't need a gurney, and check you over? It won't take long."

John, Grace thought, was doing a masterful political job with Adam, who relented and allowed himself to be led away. Grace followed, noticing a slight limp in Adam's gait. Relieved that he was permitting the medic to evaluate his wounds, she knew that the physical injuries would be nothing compared to the mental ones.

John started to unbutton Adam's shirt, but Adam waved him off and attempted to do it himself until he groaned in pain.

"I guess you'll have to, after all," he said, resigned.

"I'll be gentle," the medic said, with a small smile.

He drew back Adam's shirt with remarkable gentility and slipped it off his shoulders. Adam's sculpted chest displayed a rainbow from the paint that had seeped through his shirt, along with several blue and black bruises and a hole bleeding red from his shoulder.

"Damn," John swore quietly. "I'm sorry, Sarge, but we'll have to take you to the ER for that shoulder."

"I'm not going to the fucking hospital," Adam said, voice rising.

"I'll be there with you, Adam," Grace said, hoping to forestall an episode. "It will be all right. It doesn't look too bad; you shouldn't have to stay for long."

John probed the shoulder, triggering a wince from Adam.

"It'll need stitching, at least. I think the greater threat would be infection. Seriously, Sarge, I'd go if I were you."

"Fuck," Adam swore loudly, shaking his head. "Fuck."

James overheard the language in his sergeant's big voice and came over.

"I'll get Fisher to drive your car back to the shop," he said, distracting Adam with prosaic details. "And Joan can take Grace's, if she wants to go with you. Grace?"

"That would be great, thanks, James," she said, handing over her keys.

"Did you take a chunk out of Best?" Adam asked.

"A small one. Just enough to take him down. He'll be fine."

"Not after I'm done with him."

"Okay, Sarge, let's go. Sooner the better, eh?" John suggested.

"Grace . . . I don't know if I can do this."

"You can, Adam. You can. I'll be right beside you."

During the trip back to Royal University Hospital, John finished his check of Adam's rigid body and started an antibiotic drip, as his patient hung grimly on to his sanity. It wasn't until

Adam was lying in an emergency room bed that he finally lost control.

Stripped to the waist and waiting for the doctor, he shivered violently and cried out involuntarily. He heard his own voice and turned his head.

"Grace," he whispered. "Help."

Grace, seated beside him holding his hand, crawled onto the bed and over his body. She wrapped her arms around him, holding him as tightly as she dared, as if for dear life.

*****

"Anne," Grace said the next day, seated in the psychologist's cozy office, "what am I going to do now?"

After a round of powerful antibiotics, a cleaning and stitching of the ravaged shoulder and treatment for scrapes and bruises, Grace had taken Adam home. She had helped him shower, fed him and put him to bed; but of course, the night was terrifying, for both of them. The dreams came one after the other, and Adam awakened weeping, thrashing and sweating several times.

"It's a setback, for sure," Anne said. "Would he return to counselling? I think it would be a good idea."

"I've asked him. He's considering it. In his heart, he doesn't want to go back to the drinking and — oh, God." Grace stopped, unable to speak around the lump in her throat.

"The prowling, Grace? Is that what's worrying you?"

She nodded and dropped her eyes.

"He didn't have a lot of support in those days, if I understood your story correctly the first time you came in. Now he does. As far as I can tell from your description of him, he's very strong. He's done very, very well until now. Keep everything as normal and routine as possible at home, and don't try to avoid the subject. Tell him you love him and will be with him all the way through this. If indeed you will be."

Anne gave Grace a sharp look.

"It's a commitment, Grace. Are you up for this?"

"Yes," Grace got out. "I am," she added more adamantly.

"Okay. I had to ask. You've got to be sure."

"I'd never leave him, Anne."

"Do you want me to have a chat with him, or would that be uncomfortable for you? Would you see that as inappropriate?"

"No, that would be fine with me, if it is with him."

"Good. Bring him in tomorrow at ten. Unless he can do it under his own steam?"

"I don't know yet. We'll see."

When Grace returned home, Adam was in the kitchen, thirstily downing a glass of water. Not whiskey. So far, so good, she thought.

His drawn face and limp posture frightened her; she wondered if he would slip into a darker place and shut her out entirely. Tentatively, after preparing dinner, she asked if he would agree to counselling with Anne. He leaned across the table, took Grace's hands in his, and asked her to look into his tired, sad eyes.

"I will do anything, everything it takes to be with you," he said. "Having you in my life has made me see a future, a real future, maybe even free of these dreams. I will fight, Grace. I will heal. I will be the man you deserve."

"Oh, Adam, you already are. You always are. Just because you have fears and terrible memories doesn't make you less of a man. It makes you human."

"I don't know what to say," Adam said. "I'm so grateful, Grace, that you're mine."

He fished in his pocket and drew out a tiny, wrapped box.

"I didn't forget," he said, rather proudly. "Happy birthday, beautiful."

It was the last day of September. Grace had almost entirely forgotten about her own thirtieth birthday, apart from a brief flicker of realization early that morning. Unreturned messages lurked on her phones; she had spent the entire day involved in Adam.

"Ohhh," she breathed. "In the middle of all of this, you remembered?"

Grace threw her arms around Adam's neck, remembering his injured shoulder a second too late. Yet he barely flinched. He drew his head back to look into her brimming eyes, then kissed her softly but deeply.

"Open it, love."

Her fingers shook as she drew away the pretty paper, and she took a deep breath as she touched the velvety lid.

"Just the box is lovely," she said.

"The suspense is killing me," Adam said, sounding more like himself.

Grace opened the lid to reveal his gift, and her lips opened to say something; but she was speechless. Her eyes widened as she drew the item from its silk nest.

The goldsmith had created a perfect, tiny magnolia blossom, fashioned from rose gold with a diamond gleaming in its centre, suspended from a delicate matching chain.

"It's so beautiful," Grace whispered, awed at the lovely thing.

"Not as beautiful as you, but the man tried," Adam said, a little overwhelmed by Grace's reaction. Shyness was not one of his personality traits, but he felt it now.

A chaotic and passionate few moments ensued, Grace weeping in Adam's arms and kissing his neck, Adam muttering endearments in her ear.

"How did you . . . where did you . . ." she finally asked.

"I asked the goldsmith on Second Avenue if he could make such a thing. He claimed he could. Apparently, he told the truth. You do like it, Grace, don't you?"

"Oh, Adam, it's breathtaking. It's incredible. And one of a kind, then?"

"One of a kind, my love. Like you."

A knock at the door interrupted another teary kiss. Grace got to her feet and reluctantly went to answer the door.

"Happy birthday, sister," said Hope Rampling. "I was getting worried. Do you know I've called you four times?"

"No, I didn't. I'm sorry, Hopey. It's been a crazy couple of days."

"Is everything all right?"

"Not exactly," Adam said, walking up behind Grace. "Your sister has been busy saving my ass. Come in, Hope."

Hope stared at Adam's bulky, obviously bandaged shoulder and the scrapes on his face, then threw her arms around him.

"Are you okay, Adam? What happened?"

"Long story. Let us get you a glass of wine. I'm so glad you came over, Hope. It hasn't been much of a birthday for Grace."

"Untrue," Grace said, managing a smile. She hadn't yet put on her new necklace, so she dragged Hope to the table, picked it up and held it before her eyes.

"Wow," Hope said. "God, that's beautiful. Put it on, Grace. Let's see."

Hope's appearance was the perfect thing. They told her an abridged version of the previous day's events, ate dinner, drank wine and a semblance of normalcy saw them through the evening.

"What's with the magnolia thing?" Hope asked Adam. Grace was glad; she'd always wanted to ask that question, too, but had never found a good time.

Adam blushed.

284

"The folks took us to Florida one year for a holiday. There were magnolias everywhere, and I thought the flowers had the most beautiful petals I'd ever seen; soft, thick, a rich warm white. Grace, well, her skin reminds me of them," he ended, simply.

Hope gave him a look that made him blush again, matching the pink of Grace's cheeks.

As she left, Hope, fully aware of Adam's PTSD, quietly asked Grace if he was going to be okay, and if there was anything she could do to help.

"I don't know yet, but thanks, Hope."

"Let's do a birthday thing with the family on the weekend, okay? Mom's been calling you, too."

"Eek. I better call her back."

"No. I'll call her and tell her you'll call tomorrow. You look like you could keel fucking over. Get some rest. Okay?"

"Okay," Grace said, relief flooding her. "Okay. Thanks, Hopey."

"Just take care. Of him, and of yourself."

\*\*\*\*\*

Adam did manage to drag himself to Anne Blake's office the next morning.

"It's very nice to finally meet you, Adam," she said, reaching out to shake his hand. "I'm so glad you've come. Please, take a seat."

"It's very nice to meet you, too. Grace says you're a genius. I need one, right now."

"That's kind of her. I wouldn't say that, but I hope I can help you."

"How?" Adam asked. "I thought I was getting better — well, I was, with Grace's help — but I . . . I really fell apart out there, Doctor."

"First of all, call me Anne. And I'm a PhD, not a medical doctor. Tell me what happened."

Adam explained, to the extent he could, that when the paintballs began to fly his mind returned to the night he had first been shot. He had reacted appropriately at first; but then he'd been purposely hit in the same place where a bullet nearly cost his life six years ago, and he had frozen in fear. For a while, he didn't know whether he was dreaming.

"Have you done cognitive behavioural therapy before?" Anne asked.

"Yes."

"Was it helpful?"

"Yes. Well, fairly helpful, yes."

"I think we should continue with that. Exposure therapy is another avenue we could try, but you've just been exposed to a threat that triggers your PTSD."

"I need to get back to work, Anne," Adam said. "Fast."

"Well, I'm glad to hear you're anxious to go back. That's a good sign. But maybe it's a bit too soon?"

"Maybe it is. But doing nothing will drive me crazy, and I have to get on this case. Can you help me?"

Anne regarded him thoughtfully.

"Would you consider entering a semi-hypnotic state? I've had good luck with other patients, but some flatly refuse to try it."

"Why?"

"It can be frightening. But it can also have a very good outcome. It's up to you, Adam. Some people who exert a great deal of control over themselves and have a considerable amount of control in their careers are not amenable. They feel the potential loss of control is more than they're willing to risk. I think you may be one of those people."

Adam laced his hands together, dropped his eyes and bit his lip, a trickle of sweat running from one temple. Anne simply waited until he raised his head and nodded.

"If you think it might work, I'll do it. I'll do anything to get back to work, but more importantly, to stop scaring Grace and to have a normal life with her."

"I wondered if you'd say that. Let's begin."

# Chapter Thirty-Three

Anne Blake slowly, gently talked him down, taking him to a quiet place in his mind where he felt safe. Powerful. In control. Adam floated in the hayloft at his parents' farm, watching straw dust fall through a sunbeam, listening to the livestock snorting below.

Remember this, she said. This is where you belong, where you can escape to, at any time. Any time, Adam.

She moved his brain, then, into the line of fire. Six years ago.

"Where are you, Adam?"

"In the cruiser. There's a fight at a bar downtown."

"What are you thinking?"

"Shit, not another one. Same bar, over and over again."

"Are you there yet?"

"Yes. Going in."

"What do you see and hear?"

"Lots of noise. Men shouting and throwing punches. Smoke in the air. Stinks. The bartender looks freaked out. Oh, God. Look out!"

"What's wrong, Adam?"

"The guy is packing. I know it. He's reaching for something. It's a gun. There's never been a gun before. Just fists and knives. Why is there a gun now?"

Then Adam shouted. "I've been hit! Fire in my shoulder. God! Fire in my leg. I'm down. Officer down."

He flinched and thrashed, then stilled.

"Are you conscious, Adam?" Anne asked.

"No. I don't remember." He was quiet for a moment. "I'm awake again. I'm in the hospital. There are people staring at me, stabbing me with things. I don't want to be here! Let me out of here!"

She watched him carefully, as he twitched and reacted to the scenario.

"All right, Adam. Think, now, about leaving the hospital. About going back to work. About meeting Grace. Think about being a survivor. You survived. You survived then, and you survived again."

She brought him back to his bed of hay in the barn's loft. Calmed him and returned him to reality.

"Breathe for me, Adam. Breathe normally. Where are you?"

"I'm in your office."

"Yes. Good. How do you feel? May I take your pulse?"

"Yes."

She reached over to take his wrist under her cool fingers and found his heart rate was almost normal.

"How did you find the exercise, Adam?"

"I won't lie. It wasn't great. But now . . . I feel a bit tired, but better." Adam paused, took stock, searched his brain. "Much better."

"Would you like to do this again? I would recommend it. It will be a while before you recover entirely. You've been through a very serious, recent, significant event, on top of the initial one."

"I can't say I'd be looking forward to it, but yes. How often do you think it will be necessary?"

"Let's try once a week. We can also try some other things, such as eye movement desensitization. We can talk about that next time. But, Adam, if you feel the demons are too close, call me immediately. You don't need to go through that, certainly not alone."

Adam wanted to hug Anne, kiss her hand, bow before her. He leaned forward instead, searching her eyes with his, and simply said, "thank you."

*****

"Should you be here?" Charlotte asked the moment she clapped eyes on Adam striding into the office. She jumped out of her chair and stood, legs planted, right in front of him.

"Charlotte, my sister in crime, my saviour of sanity," Adam said, smiling down at her. "That remains to be seen. Right now, I am all right. I'm back in therapy. And I'm back in action. Where are we with Adrian Cey?"

Charlotte gave a small cry and launched herself at her sergeant.

"Adam, I was so worried," she said, clearly not caring if the entire squad saw her hugging her boss. "I'm so glad to see you."

Adam hugged her back with his right arm, for a moment, and whispered in her ear.

"Thank you, Char. For everything."

They released each other, tears in both pairs of eyes, and nodded. Back to business.

"He's not talking, of course."

"Do we have a twenty-four-hour watch on him?"

"Yes, Adam."

"When can I interview him?"

"Whenever you like. He's had lunch. And yes, before you ask, I checked him fifteen minutes ago. Alive and not poisoned."

Adam chuckled at that.

"No, I suppose he'd be fine on that score, since he was the poisoner. That being said, you never know. How is his leg?"

"Not bad. If it was, he'd still be in the hospital. He's on antibiotics and painkillers, and a doctor is checking him twice a day."

"Okay. Give me an hour to get my head around the approach and check my messages. Interview one?"

"That works. See you there."

Adam started to head for his office but stopped as another thought occurred to him.

"Char, has Tom Allbright seen him in a lineup yet?"

"Yes," she said, with a wide grin. "Identified him as both the guy who approached him on the street, and as the fake chaplain. You're good to go."

Adam exhaled. "Fantastic. See you soon."

He unlocked the door to his office and sat heavily in his chair. He did feel better, but he wondered how he would respond when confronted with Adrian Cey. He had trusted the man, supported his cause, even liked him. A part of Adam felt betrayed. But he knew Cey wasn't at the top of the chain. He needed him to talk.

What was the chink in his armour?

The phone rang, breaking into his thoughts. The chief.

"Adam. How are you, man?" he asked when Adam picked up the receiver.

"I'm doing all right, Chief. News travels fast around here. I just got in fifteen minutes ago."

"Well, thank God it does, since you didn't call me."

"I was going to, Chief."

"I'd like to have a chat with you, soon as possible. When would be good?"

"I'm interviewing Father . . . ah, Adrian Cey right away, and I need to prepare. Later this afternoon? Tomorrow morning?"

"Either works. Let me know when you're finished with that son of a bitch."

"I will. Thanks, Chief."

"Adam," McIvor said gruffly, clearing his throat. "I'm very glad you're okay. Very." And he hung up.

Adam, rather moved by his chief's words, returned to his musings. Did Cey have family who might be threatened? What did he care about, if anything? And who was his leader, if indeed Adam was right and there was someone above him, calling the shots?

The phone rang again. Grace.

"Babe," Adam said, answering. "How are you?"

"I couldn't wait until tonight, Adam. How did it go with Anne? Should you be in the office?"

"Short form, it went well. Very well. It was hard, but . . . I'm all right, love. I'll tell you about it later. Are you all right?"

"Yes," Grace said, choking back a small sob of relief. "I also wanted to tell you I've heard back from Reuters. They've interviewed the Dualeh family. They confirmed that the bones were Abukar's. He was the only one who went missing that night. I think we've got it."

"Holy shit," Adam breathed. "That's great news. And perfect timing. I'm interviewing Cey in a few minutes. Thank you. Love you. See you at seven?"

"Yes. Love you, Adam."

As Adam hung up, he reconsidered his decision to interview Cey immediately. The impersonating priest struck him as an intelligent, frightening psychopath. Would George Best be an easier target? He called Charlotte.

"Char, where's Best right now? Is he here, or in the hospital?"

"They kept him at RUH, Adam. He was worse off than Cey."

"Let's go see him. Call off the interview with Cey and make sure he knows we're talking to his partner. I doubt it'll make him sweat, but I'll take any advantage I can get."

"I'm on it, Adam. See you downstairs in five."

"Give me ten. I have to look something up."

Twenty minutes later, they were at the hospital looking for Dr. Brian Ashern, hoping for an update on Best's condition before confronting him. They found him in the ER.

"How's Best, Brian?" Adam asked, after pleasantries were exchanged.

"He's all right. Maybe a little stoned. Claims to be in a lot of pain, and probably is. Shot in the hip bone, and yeah, that's going to hurt. But he'll survive."

"Can we talk to him?"

Ashern considered, then reached for and flipped open a chart lying on the ER's triage counter.

"Okay. Fifteen minutes, though. No more."

"Yes, Doctor," Adam said. "You're the boss."

"Yes, I am, Sergeant. I'll take you to his room."

George Best, who stood well over six feet, had a barrel chest, a rounded belly and a closely cropped ash-blond fringe encircling his balding head. Stern eyes and a grimly set mouth were normal for him, but he appeared considerably less aggressive lying in a hospital bed with several tubes snaking in and out of his body.

Adam intended to try the oldest trick in the police book.

"How are you today, Mr. Best?" Adam said, as politely as he could manage.

"How does it look like I'm doing?" Best growled, slurring his words.

Adam ignored his question.

"This is Detective Constable Charlotte Warkentin. We are here to ask you a few questions, if you don't mind."

"Fuck off."

"I'm afraid that's not going to happen."

"I'm not talking to you."

"Let me talk to you for a while. Let me tell you a few things you may not know. For example, I know that the bones of Abukar Dualeh have been recovered in Somalia. Looks like your boys didn't bury him deeply enough, Major."

Adam paused. Best grunted but said nothing.

"Also fascinating about this discovery is that the boy — and he really was just a boy — was shot to death, in the back of the head. No bullet was found in the skull. That sounds very much like what you did to Elias Crow, wouldn't you say? And also similar to Martin Best. Why, I wonder, did you decide to murder your own nephew?"

"I didn't kill Elias or Martin," Best said.

"Really. I understand from Adrian Cey that you did."

"Is that a fact. I wouldn't kill my own nephew."

"You were complicit in his death."

George's eyes clouded. "Not by choice. Cey ran that whole scenario. He already had Charles's ID."

"I see. Why was the good father snooping around Ferguson Lake looking for Crow? You must have known where he was."

"No. I didn't. And I didn't kill Elias."

"No? You did set fire to the shed behind the Rampling cabin. You tried to kill us."

George Best, at his best, might have been able to control his reaction; but lying relatively helplessly in the hospital and thoroughly drugged, his eyes betrayed him. Adam saw the glint of truth. Best did set that fire.

"It's too bad," Adam continued, "that you're stuck here. Under guard, of course, but there are ways of getting past the police. Adrian proved that when he poisoned Al Simpson in the station cells. I keep asking myself how high the stakes were for him to risk it."

That hit home; Adam could see it in Best's reaction. He moved restlessly, head tossing on the pillow. Clearly, he didn't want to die here. Adam surreptitiously checked his watch; seven minutes to go. Come on, come on, he said silently. Spill it.

"I have enough evidence, sir, that my next move will be to approach the military and the government for someone to interview on this case. Believe it."

"Fucking Adrian," Best finally spat. "He's the killer, not me."

"But you helped him, did you not?"

"Like I had a choice."

"You set him up with a false identity, that of your own deceased son, which helped him get your nephew out of the hospital. Your paintball business is really a cover for your little gang, isn't it? Including Adrian. What else did you do?"

"I set him up with the fake identity when he got out of jail. They did get him for conduct unbecoming; he led the raid. He needed a fresh start, and I had little choice. The guy's a freaking loose cannon. I never knew if he or Phi . . . he would make good on his threats to expose me.

"I knew Elias was somewhere around Ferguson, at least in Meadow Lake Park. Incredible how tight-lipped the Allbrights and Ramplings were. We bought the cabin so I could watch for him — and I knew about the fishing shack. But no one seemed to know where his cabin was. Not even Tillie Allbright; I thought she'd know, because she was tight with Starblanket. Maybe she did know, and just wouldn't say.

"So Cey went up to see if he could find it. He couldn't, at first; you saw yourself how well-hidden it was. He thought he'd ask around, in disguise as a salesman. He didn't get much, so he moved on to Tom and got enough that he was able to find the place. Elias wasn't there, though. He caught up to him at the shack. It almost worked. It would have, if you and fucking Grace weren't there that weekend."

"Do not," Adam said evenly, but with ice in his tone, "ever call her that again."

He paused, glaring at the man.

"Did you think no one would notice the fire?"

"Unlikely. Cey is good at fire. It would have burned fast and hot, and at three in the morning, would have been out before anyone saw it. It's quiet up there at that time of year. It was too bad that it was necessary."

"I don't see why. He could have bashed in the door and shot Elias."

"True."

And Adam saw his way in to Cey's psyche. The man was a showoff. Fires. Disguises. Risks. Delusions of grandeur?

"Then he removed the ammunition, so no one would know it was military ordnance," Adam continued. "He didn't want to use a civilian gun, because that wouldn't have been as satisfying, would it? It had to be his regiment sidearm. And it's easier to remove full metal jacket; it doesn't break up like regular ammo."

"I guess. I don't know. He's a freak."

"Was he the unit chaplain in the forces?"

Best gave a harsh laugh.

"Fuck, no. He was a medic and trained in explosives. He's not a man of the cloth," Best said, the last words dripping with contempt. "He's a scary son of a bitch."

"So I gather." Adam thought for a moment. "A medic. That's why he knew how to remove bullets from bodies. Quickly and efficiently. Right?"

Best just nodded.

"And he would have had access to the dope," Adam continued. "Mefloquine, codeine . . . anything else?"

"Yeah. He shot everyone up before we went and doled out the other shit while we were there."

"On whose orders?"

"That," said Best, raising his head in emphasis, "I will never tell you. Go ahead, get it out of Cey. Good luck with that. But I won't tell you."

Ashern came back into the room; Adam's time was up.

"Thank you, Mr. Best. I trust you'll have a quiet and safe night." Adam emphasized the last two words before he turned, nodded to Charlotte, and left the room.

"Have we let Cey stew long enough, do you think?" Adam asked Charlotte on the way to the car.

"Sure. Let's give him a go when we get back. Do you know how you're going to approach him, Adam?"

"I think so."

\*\*\*\*\*

Adrian Cey sat back in his uncomfortable chair, legs spread widely, a supercilious grin playing at the corners of his mouth.

The oldest trick had worked with Best; Adam had presented what he knew, along with the lie that Cey had fingered him, and the older man had coughed up to save himself. It wouldn't help him much from a legal standpoint, but it might save his life — and Adam was sure he didn't want to die. Best would be arrested for conspiracy to commit murder and attempted murder by setting the shed afire at the Rampling cabin; he had already been charged with the attack on Adam at the paintball arena.

Painball, more like it, Adam thought.

297

But he still refused to name the person at the top. Adam had some ideas, but they all seemed too incredible. He needed Cey to crumble. And he did have a coup de grâce in his pocket, courtesy of James's search of Harbour House. Would it work?

Adam regarded Cey, wondering how he had been taken in by him. Wondering how Al Simpson had been taken in, as well; Al would likely have known the medic. Perhaps Cey's disguise, and the context of a priest coming to visit, fooled Al. Perhaps he ate the pastry before he recognized him. Perhaps he thought Cey really was just coming to visit. Al didn't know he was the killer.

Quite the actor, Adrian Cey.

"You had me fooled, Adrian," Adam said submissively, sadness in his voice, as he sat across from the prisoner. "I believed in you. You were doing great things, things we couldn't do. I don't understand."

"Really, Adam? I thought you were smarter than that." Cey smiled at Adam but said no more.

Shit, Adam thought. What was going on at Harbour House? It hadn't occurred to him that Cey was . . . what? Dispensing drugs, maybe? He thought the man was keeping an eye on Tom Allbright and Martin Best from his vantage point on the west side. He'd have to investigate that later.

"Maybe you over-estimated me, Adrian."

"Maybe I did."

"But I do know you were the medic for your company in Somalia," Adam said. "You never were a priest at all, were you? Handy, though, to pretend you were, to keep an eye on your post-trauma vets. Didn't Martin recognize you?"

"I don't know what you're talking about, Adam."

"Maybe he did, but he didn't think you were going to kill him, did he? And it didn't matter with Elias. By the time you got to him, he was going to be dead in seconds. You're brilliant, Adrian. You had it all figured out."

298

"Interesting theory."

"Not smart enough to be the kingpin, though. Or not powerful enough. You were someone's little slave, weren't you? Shooting up your men with mefloquine like they told you, and lots of it. Experimenting on your own soldiers. How much did they pay you to do that?"

Cey bristled. The smile disappeared, and the corners of his mouth went down. He eyed Adam.

"You know shit," he said.

"I'm sure you thought it was important work. You knew why they'd chosen that drug. They wanted to see just how apeshit those men would go. Good in theatre, maybe, but not in peacekeeping. But Somalia was a very good place to test it. No one would give a damn what happened over there. Such a backward country.

"We know differently now, though, don't we? The Shidane Arone murder showed us that. And now, Adrian, you're the fall guy. Cleaning up the mess. Killing the witnesses, the ones who knew right from wrong. Lucky for you they had PTSD, so badly they couldn't come forward. But when they found that child's remains, everything changed. I think I know why."

During this speech, Cey's face had turned into a mask of rage.

"You know shit," he repeated. "I will be exonerated. I will be repaid for my efforts. My friends, Adam, are in high places."

"Too late, Adrian."

"You don't know who my friends are."

"I do know that you're the most disposable man in the plan, apart from George. The bottom of the barrel. Why else would you be doing the dirty work?"

"I'm talking about one of the highest authorities in the country, Adam. I have connections. They'll never let you get to me. You'll be dead first."

"Why did you kill Al Simpson?" Adam switched topics. "Did you think he'd roll over and give us a list of all the Airborne soldiers? And all his superiors? He was one of the men who buried Abukar. Did you threaten him with a summary trial? Were you still pissed that he fucked that up? And why didn't he recognize you?"

"No comment."

"We've found his body. We've interviewed his family. We know for sure that Abukar Dualeh was killed by your men. Someone dug a bullet out of that child's brain. It will be in the paper tomorrow. It was you."

Cey leaped to his feet, placed his hands on the table and screamed into Adam's face: "You're lying."

But Adam was not. He knew Grace was almost ready to publish.

He reached into his pocket and drew out a velvet bag with a drawstring, once the home of a bottle of whisky. Pulling it open, he allowed the bullets inside to fall clattering to the table in a metallic rain.

"Your trophies, I assume, Adrian."

"How did you find them?" Cey screamed.

"They were at Harbour House. Not hard to find. You couldn't resist having them nearby, could you? Bad move, Adrian."

"I'll deny it! I'll say they're not mine. You have to stop it! Stop the story," Cey shouted. "It'll fuck everything up. He won't be in, and all of this will have been for nothing."

"Be in?" Adam asked.

"They'll court martial him." Cey was ranting now. "It'll all be for nothing. I tried to protect him. I did everything they wanted. I even took the fall in a summary trial. You can't put my name in the paper. They'll know. He'll know."

"Who will know?"

"He's going to change everything," Cey hissed, eyes bright and sly. "He'll make the military a real force, not just a ragtag bunch of fucking peacekeepers. He'll bring back the airborne, the joint task force. I'll be part of it again. This time, I'll have power. I've been promised. Think about it, Adam. A warrior force."

Adam was thinking about it, urging his brain to unearth a name, or at least a rank. Who was going to change everything?

He thought about all the names he had searched earlier that afternoon . . . the majors, the generals, the high-ranking men from the early-to-mid 1990s who had been fired. It couldn't be any of them; they had long since disappeared in disgrace and wouldn't return to the public sphere.

It was someone who survived the purge, someone still active, someone who managed to dodge the mess and avoid public condemnation.

Then it rang in his brain. What Best had said: "I never knew if he or Phi . . . he would make good on his threats to expose me." Adam thought it was just a splutter, a break in the sentence.

No. Now he knew. He decided to take a shot. Only one thing made sense.

"I'll contact the government, then. I have to get in touch with the Ministry of Defence anyway, to tell them what you've told me, and what George told me." Adam stood up, as if to leave the room. "Goodbye, Adrian."

"That won't get you anywhere," Cey said, the arrogant grin returning to his face.

"I thought you might say that," Adam said. "Thanks, Adrian. That's exactly what I needed to know."

Cey paled. "How did you figure it out? That it was Richard Phillips?"

Adam smiled. It had to be someone in the ministry; he just wasn't sure who, until today. He almost couldn't believe it.

301

Between them, Best and Adrian had slipped up. Given him a name.

*Got him.*

"I didn't, but now I know. The new Minister of Defence. Who else could it be, with that kind of power?"

# Chapter Thirty-Four

**Murders, military drug abuse linked
to Minister of Defence**

October 3, 2007
Page One

By Grace Rampling
and Lacey McPhail
of The StarPhoenix

In 1993, a fifteen-year-old boy named Abukar Dualeh was murdered by Canadian soldiers near Belet Huen, Somalia, for attempting to steal from the Airborne Regiment's supply tent.

The Airborne was in Somalia on a peacekeeping mission during that country's civil war.

Last month, Dualeh's remains were found in a sandy grave uncovered over time by the desert winds. The discovery of his body has recently led to the murders of three other men, all of them former soldiers and two of them suffering from post-traumatic stress disorder (PTSD).

Implicated in the killings is Richard Phillips, a former officer commanding (OC) with a once-promising political career. The prime minister, who announced the installation of Phillips as the new minister of defence just last month, has suspended him from caucus and stripped him of his role, pending an investigation. The RCMP have taken him into custody.

Elias Crow, a member of the northern Raven River Nation, was shot in the back of the head outside his burning fishing shack in mid-September. Two days later, Martin Best was found on an acreage near Saskatoon, shot dead in the middle of the back. In both cases, the bullets were removed from the men's bodies.

Crow had attempted to save the boy's life after finding him on the military base in Somalia. Martin Best was one of the two men assigned to bury the youth after he was killed.

A week later, RCMP Sergeant Al Simpson from the Meadow Lake detachment was poisoned with strychnine in police cells and later died in hospital. He was the other soldier who buried Dualeh.

Charged with the murders is Adrian Cey, alias Charles Best and alias David Smith, who served as a medic in Somalia. Cey had become well-known in Saskatoon as the priest who started Harbour House, a charity and haven for homeless people and addicts. Police are investigating whether Cey was also experimenting with drugs on the people in his care. He recently signed on as a chaplain for the police service under the Smith alias.

Also charged in the cases, with conspiracy to commit and attempted murder, is George Best, a major with the military during the Somalia peacekeeping mission. Best owned several businesses in and around Saskatoon, most recently Paintball Palace and Green Summer Turf on Valley Road south of the city. Charges are pending against an unidentified third man, who was involved in an attack on Det. Sgt. Adam Davis of the Saskatoon Police.

Phillips had a long and decorated history with the Canadian Armed Forces, spending part of his career as Officer Commanding with the Airborne. During that time, soldiers were dosed with mefloquine, an anti-malaria drug that had been previously proven to cause hallucinations, dizziness, insomnia, aggression and other severe side effects. The soldiers under the command of Best were particularly targeted with high doses of mefloquine, as well as codeine and other drugs which have not yet been identified. The experimental mixture of drugs caused serious mental health problems, likely leading to the murder of Dualeh and an attack on his village.

Interviews with former soldiers indicate that Phillips was part of a military command interested in learning whether the drugs would increase aggression in theatre. The soldiers in the Somalia peacekeeping mission were a testing ground to see if the drugs would work, before the forces were sent into a war zone. The government of the time was aware of the experimentation but did not intervene to stop it.

Phillips was elected in Ontario in 2004 and was long thought to be a natural choice for minister of defence. Those interviewed said he planned to push for reinstatement of the Airborne, which was disbanded in 1995 after the murder of Shidane Arone, also a Somali youth.

Reuters, the Europe-based news agency, has interviewed the Dualeh family in Somalia and shared its notes with The StarPhoenix. Abukar Dualeh's DNA identified him as belonging to that family. A brother and a cousin have testified that he was the only member of the family to go missing the night of the attack on their village.

Further charges are pending against two other members of the Airborne command.

The life of Elijah Starblanket, Elias Crow's uncle and stepfather, was also threatened, but he escaped to a neighbouring reserve. Starblanket had been warned by police to abandon his home.

"Elias returned from Somalia a broken man," said Starblanket. "The mefloquine, the codeine, the abhorrent drug testing on Canada's soldiers, and the directive of the army commanders that stealing was a capital offence, all led to his PTSD and ultimately his death. I call on the government to ruthlessly weed out and punish the men who caused this, and who are responsible for my family's grief."

Crow will be laid to rest on the Raven River Reserve. Best's body will be returned to Manitoba, his home province, and buried there. Al Simpson is survived by his wife, Gillian, and children, Jason and Jennifer; his mother, Margaret Robertson; a sister in Calgary and her family; and numerous cousins. A service in his memory is planned for next week in Saskatoon.

Simpson, had he lived, would have been charged with aiding and abetting Best and Cey. However, the charges would have been mitigated by the threats against his mother's life.

*Continued on Page 4.*

\*\*\*\*\*

"Elder Starblanket, it's Grace."

"How are you, Grace? I saw your story in the paper. Well done. Thank you. And please call me Elijah. I've stopped calling you Miss Grace. It's only fair."

Grace laughed. "It's hardly the same thing, but thank you. I just wanted to say how glad I am that . . . that you're all right."

She cleared her throat. She was already not just fond of Elijah, but also felt a sense of awe at his kindness, knowledge and courage. She was deeply relieved that the police had persuaded him to leave his home, and that he had escaped harm when a package arrived for him.

"When is the funeral? Have you decided?" she asked.

"On the weekend. We will be glad to at least have that closure."

"I'm so sorry, Elijah. Elias was a wonderful human being. I will always be grateful to him."

"Thank you for that, Grace. And for your incredible work on this story. I hope to see you again soon."

"I hope so, too."

# Chapter Thirty-Five

Adam had been forced to postpone his chat with Chief Dan McIvor for a couple of days. Once he had scared hell out of George Best and backed Cey into a corner, chaos ensued. Chasing the clues and information all the way to Ottawa was a new experience for Adam, and he had to admit it was equally exhilarating and exhausting.

Finally, he was knocking on the chief's door.

"Come in Adam. Sit down. I see you brought coffee," McIvor said, holding out his hand for a steaming mug. "Thanks. How the hell are you feeling?"

"Not too bad. Shoulder is starting to heal, and the hand is pretty good now. Chief, I should tell you I'm back in therapy. I kind of . . . well, broke down out there. It was worse than I let on at the time. Grace connected me to a psychologist, and I think she's really helping me. But you needed to know."

"I'm glad you're feeling better, and good for you to explore more therapy. Great work on the case. Kind of puts us on the national map, doesn't it? In a good way, this time."

Adam understood that the chief was referring to a previous time in the police force, under a different command, when Indigenous people were not treated well. A few officers had taken men outside the city in the depth of winter and forced them to walk back at great risk to their lives. It had, of course, hit the national news.

"I guess it does," Adam said. The publicity was not important to him.

"One thing I don't understand," McIvor said, "is why Simpson accepted the pastry from the so-called chaplain. Didn't he recognize him?"

"We'll never know for sure. Maybe he didn't; it had been fourteen years, and Cey was disguised. Maybe he trusted Cey from their time in the army. He may have just accepted that the man visiting him was the chaplain, and the slight disguise did the rest. And I'm sure Cey had a Plan B if Al didn't accept the food."

"How the hell did he know where Al was? And that the detail on him had been removed?"

"He didn't know about Pearson removing the detail. He wouldn't have known we had one in the first place. He was enough of a risk-taker he didn't care. He just figured out where Al was; he called the Meadow Lake RCMP and was told Sgt. Simpson was away. Where else would he be? And if he was wrong, he would have simply kept looking."

"Right. Well. I didn't call you in to chat about the case, Adam. I haven't announced this yet. I thought you should be the first to know. I fired Terry Pearson last week."

"Holy shit, Chief. You've managed to keep that quiet."

"I want you to take his position."

Adam stared at his boss, in a state of considerable shock. It took several seconds for him to respond.

"Thank you, Chief. But are you sure I'm the right person for the job? It's not like I have the perfect temperament for inspector."

"You're wrong about that, Adam. You have exactly the right skills, sensitivities and personality. If you're referring to the PTSD, I'm not all that concerned. You've managed very well, and it's the one thing you will have to try to overcome. You can do it, Adam. I know it. Goddamn it, man. I see in your face you're thinking of turning me down. Don't do that."

"I appreciate your confidence in me, Chief, and I'm honoured by your request. But I do have to think about it. I have to know I can do it."

He stopped and grinned at McIvor.

"You really fired Pearson? How did it go?"

"He swore and stomped around and called you some very bad names. Oh, and threatened to sue for wrongful dismissal." McIvor chuckled. "Let him try, especially after that disaster in cells with Al Simpson. I must say, it's great to know I'll never have to fight with him again. Adam, think hard. I want you to take this promotion. You're the best goddamn crime solver on this force. Say yes."

"I'd really like to talk to Grace about it first. If that's okay."

"Yes. Of course. Don't wait too long. I need a fucking inspector."

Adam thought of little else as he drove to Hope's house for Grace's birthday party. Should he accept? Could he do it? Would it take him off the street more than he'd like? What would Grace think about it?

He arrived at Hope's only a little late and just in time for dinner. Hope, Grace and their mother Sandra were zipping around the kitchen, carrying platters of roast beef, potatoes and vegetables to the table. Sandra was telling her daughters about their grandmother's progress after her hip surgery; she was doing very well. Wallace and Grace's brother David opened wine bottles as they congenially argued about politics and the Dean of Law's curriculum adjustments.

Grace gave a little squeak of joy when Adam appeared, and ran to welcome him with a hug.

"Hi love," Adam said, once again experiencing shyness now that he was in the fold of her family. He didn't know them well yet, apart from Hope. She had been a constant, stalwart protector that spring while her sister lay frustrated and helpless in the hospital, healing from being attacked outside the local gay nightclub. Ferocious little thing, he thought, a smile curling his lip. Hope was a darker, shorter, slightly rounder version of her sister, with the personality of a lioness. He loved her.

"Adam, come in, come in," Wallace said, holding out a hand. "Let me get you a drink. Wine, whiskey, beer?"

"A short scotch, if you have it, please. Thank you, Wallace."

Adam took his drink, smiled his appreciation, and joined the conversation.

"What's this about the dean? Has he been making changes again?"

Wallace the lawyer and David the law student launched into the curriculum problems, as they saw them, and Adam tried to pay attention. He had another mission tonight.

Over dinner, the chatter turned to Hope's new adventure. A social worker, she had recently decided to adopt a foreign child, furious as she was about the conditions in overseas orphanages. Many of her clients were from other countries, and she heard constant horror stories.

"Adam," Grace said, catching him up on the news, "Hope has found a child. She is going to Thailand next month."

"That's wonderful, Hope; so exciting," Adam said, putting an arm around her for a quick hug. "Are there pictures?"

"I was hoping you'd ask," Hope said, jumping up and leaving her dinner to cool. The photo was attached by magnets to the fridge; she snatched it down and brought it to Adam. "Isn't she beautiful?"

"She is, Hope. She really is." Adam looked down at the tiny girl, clad in a threadbare pink dress. A quiver connected his heart to his brain. A child.

"How old is she? Two, maybe?"

"She's three. You can see how small she is. I have to get her out of there." Hope emitted a tiny sob, followed quickly by a crooked smile.

"What's her name?"

"Lawan. It means 'beautiful.' As she is. Should I give her an English name, do you think?" she asked anxiously.

"Lots of time to think about that, Hopey," Grace said. "We can talk about it and decide on the right thing to do. Don't worry; the main thing is to get the adoption done, right?"

"Yes, you're right, Grace. I do think of her as Lawan." Hope swallowed. "Okay. Time for cake!"

Thirty candles created a fair amount of heat atop the chocolate cake, decadently stuffed with mousse and iced with espresso butter cream. Grace laughed at the small fire and blew it out in one breath.

"There," she said. "No boyfriends, Adam. As you know." Grace gave him a slightly mischievous, slightly sympathetic smile.

Adam looked a trifle abashed. "I know, love."

After the cake was consumed and the dishes were either washed or stowed in the dishwasher, the Ramplings moved into the family room, ready for more wine and conversation.

"I can't wait to have a niece, Hopey," Grace said quietly to her sister. "Anything I can do to help, please let me know. I mean it. Please. I want to be involved."

Adam overheard, and his knees went weak. He kept a close eye on Wallace, and when the older man took a break to visit the bathroom, Adam rose, muttering that he needed a glass of water.

When Grace's father emerged and came through the kitchen, Adam swallowed hard, turned and said, "May I speak with you privately for just a moment, sir? It's about the cabin."

\* \* \* \* \*

"Grace."

"Yes, Adam."

"It hasn't snowed yet."

"Yes, I've noticed. And?"

"Well, I was thinking. The last time — the last two times — we were at the lake were not exactly relaxing. It's been . . . God, Grace. It's been insane, hasn't it? And I won't be able to take more than four or five days off for a while. There's so much more to do on the case, especially on Cey's homeless shelter. I feel a bit strange asking you this, since it's your cabin and not mine, but what do you think about heading up for a few days? Forecast is for above seasonal."

"We'd have to close up the cabin again," Grace said, with heavy emphasis on the final word.

"I know. I'm getting good at it. No problem, as far as I'm concerned."

"It's a lovely thought. Are you thinking Thanksgiving? Or next weekend?"

"As soon as possible, if you can get the time off. Again."

"Well, considering the last two trips ultimately produced hundreds of inches of newspaper copy, I think Claire will be okay with it. I'll check on Monday. And I could maybe visit Elijah. It would be wonderful, assuming nothing else happens."

"Fan-hitting shit does follow you around. It follows me around, too, but I'm a cop. I'm used to it."

"I'm a reporter. I'm used to it, too. Although I'll admit this year has been a little much."

"Let's see," Adam said, preparing to tick off the events of the last several months. "You found the dead bishop. Then all hell followed, and someone decided to bash you on the head. Then you were on the scene when they found Sherry Hilliard, murdered in her basement. And all hell followed. This time, you couldn't just stay in bed; you had to go flying across the lake to find your friend. And more hell followed."

"And you solved all those cases."

"With your help."

"You would have, anyway."

"I'm not so sure about that."

"Silly man," Grace said, throwing herself at him and covering his face with kisses. "Beautiful man," she whispered.

*****

The next Friday, Adam and Grace followed their lake trip routine. Buy the food and wine. Load the truck. Drive hell-bent for the lake, Adam behind the wheel. Open the cabin, now minus its burned outbuilding. Turn on the power. Bring in the luggage. Head for the water's edge, drinks in hand.

"Water's down, a bit," Grace said, frowning.

"Just a bit, Grace. Autumn rains are coming."

"I wonder who's up? I don't think the Allbrights have returned. They'd be dealing with Tom, maybe finding him a lawyer, I would think. I must call Tillie when we get back."

They were silent for a moment, staring over the water, remembering the fire, the death of Elias, the flames that nearly burned down the cabin, and may have injured or killed them, as well.

"Adam," Grace finally said. "Why did you want to come back up here? It can't have great memories for you."

"Oh, but it does," Adam said, a smile in his eyes. "I remember a long, peaceful canoe ride. I remember delicious dinners and drinks on the deck. And I recall love in the afternoon, and love in the lake. And I know you love it here. So, I do too."

"Adam," Grace breathed, then kissed him.

They had not made love regularly for some time, as Adam healed both physically and, to some extent, mentally.

"I want . . . can we . . . Adam?"

"Yes. Maybe not in the lake, though. It is October."

They barely made it back to the cottage before passion inflamed them. Grace carefully removed Adam's shirt, taking her time with the shoulder, before uncarefully attacking his chest and stomach with her lips, teeth and tongue.

"I want you," she said huskily, unbuckling his belt. "I want to kiss you, bite you, lick you everywhere."

Hearing that, Adam was rendered speechless and caught his breath as her lips travelled lower. He could only stand a minute of it, knowing then how much he, too, had missed their loving. Drawing her up gently to her feet, he lifted her, as he loved to do, and bore her to the bedroom.

Adam madly pulled off Grace's shirt and jeans, kissing her everywhere he could reach, and they fell together on the bed, bodies writhing against each other, skin to skin, lips to lips, feeling every soft hollow and hard muscle.

A moment later, Grace, aroused to the point of no return, bucked and cried out from the simple friction of body against body. Amazed, Adam rode the wave, then entered her in a long, slow, careful thrust.

"Is it all right, Grace?" he panted, worried that her spasms were too strong for his entry. "Does it hurt?"

"No," she said. "No. Yes. God, it's unbearable . . . don't stop, Adam."

But Adam did stop, just holding Grace as he paused, inside. "Show me, tell me when," he said.

And she did, a moment later, her hips rising and falling in the rhythm of fresh arousal, then increasing in intensity until Adam tensed.

"Come with me," he said. "Now."

\*\*\*\*\*

The sun had long ago left the sky by the time Adam and Grace rose from their lovemaking and began to prepare dinner. Adam's heart started hammering halfway through the grilling of the steak. From the deck, he watched Grace through the picture window, bustling and humming happily to herself as she threw together the salad, opened a bottle of Shiraz and checked the potatoes.

There was no other. There had never been another. There never would be.

My brave, beautiful, generous, sexually overheated, wildly sympathetic and sometimes goofy Grace. Her golden, almost innocent, loving heart. He smiled at his own thoughts.

"Adam, how far out are the steaks?" she called to him.

"Two minutes, Babe. For medium rare."

"Perfect. I'm salivating. They smell so good."

"You're perfect," he said.

"Aw, Adam. You are."

Silly, loving talk in the haze of afterward. Adam lived for it.

Yet he was quiet over dinner, listening to Grace's update on Hope's adoption of Lawan and the follow-up story she was planning on the disgraced politician, Richard Phillips.

"I'm starting to think he's crazy," she finished.

"Crazed with power, certainly. Why do you think so?"

"He reminds me of a mad scientist, in a bad way. Thinks he can mess with people's minds for some bizarre vision of the greater good."

Grace took her last bite of steak. Adam didn't say anything.

"Honey, are you all right?" Grace finally asked, a bit anxiously. "You're quiet tonight. Sorry if I'm being intrusive . . . but is everything going okay with Anne?"

Adam took a sip of wine, inhaled deeply and sat up straight.

"Everything is going really well with Anne. Grace, I have something to tell you — to discuss with you. I waited until now, because I wanted a distraction-free moment. Well, hour or two."

"What is it, Adam? Has something happened?"

"Yes. The chief fired Terry Pearson two weeks ago."

"That's great news. He's such a jerk. And?"

"McIvor has asked if I'd like to take on his position."

"Babe! Congratulations. I'm not all that surprised," she said. "I've thought for a while that the chief had his eye on you. I didn't think it would happen quite so soon. That's wonderful, Adam."

"I haven't accepted yet. I wanted to talk to you about it first. I'm not sure I'm the right person for the job, Grace. I'd have many more people under me; can I do it? I can't let them down. What if I crash and burn?"

Grace leaned over, sympathy written on her features, and placed a hand on his arm.

"It's completely, totally up to you. Whatever you decide, I'll be right behind you. But I believe you can do it, Adam. People follow you, wherever you go, whatever you do, and that's a sign of a leader. And your good, strong heart — that's why they should follow you. Don't turn it down because you don't think you can do it. You can. You'd be genius."

"Thank you, Babe. But think about it. It's very important to me that you're absolutely sure."

"It's more important that you're sure, Adam."

Adam slipped to the floor from his chair, and from his knees, looked intently into Grace's eyes.

"I'm hoping," he said, voice dropping into a husky bass, "that you'll make those decisions with me. Those, and more. All of them. Forever."

"I'm so honoured, Adam. Of course. I'm always here for you . . . "

"Grace. I'm talking about forever. I cannot imagine my life without you. I know it's only been a few months, but there is no doubt. I admire you. I want you. I love you. I know you'd be taking on a lot, with me, and I'm sorry for the hard nights and the worry and, sometimes, the danger. And the jealousy. I'm working on it.

"I want it all, the babies and the home life and the making love, with you, just you, forever."

He stopped talking, and searched Grace's face.

"Can you, will you . . . marry me, Grace?"

Fat, juicy tears rained from Grace's eyes, the dark, enigmatic eyes that had intrigued Adam from the moment he met her. Only recently had he begun to learn to read them. Even now he fell into their gaze, rapt and waiting for her response.

Grace continued to stare at Adam, as if she did not quite understand his words. A flicker of fear that she might say no thumped in his heart. He reached up to touch her cheek.

"Please say yes, Grace."

Grace took his face between her hands and kissed him softly, as she had the very first time.

"Yes. Oh God, Adam, yes. My love, my Adam."

Then they were in each other's arms, weeping together, holding on hard, hearts aching with joy and the bittersweet knowledge that life would bring so many things. Happiness. Heartbreak. Hard times and perfect times. Life.

Many minutes later, Adam realized he had forgotten something. He slipped two fingers into his shirt pocket, and delicately drew out the symbol of his love for her. Holding her left hand, he slid the shining, shimmering thing onto her fourth finger.

Grace gaped at her engagement ring, as if it might disappear. The diamond spat fire under the light, set in yellow gold that warmed her skin. The band scooped up on either side, the ends fashioned into flower petals with tiny diamonds sprinkled into their folds.

"It's . . . I'm speechless. The word 'beautiful' doesn't do it justice. Oh, Adam."

"Take it off for a second, Grace," Adam said.

"Never."

Adam laughed. "Look inside, Babe."

A puzzled look crossed her face, but she did as Adam asked. Inside, on the widest part of the ring under one of the petals, was a minuscule engraved cottage, identical to the Rampling cabin. On the other was the goldsmith's mark, along with the tiny words, Yours Forever. Love, Adam.

"The same goldsmith who made my pendant," Grace said. "It's amazing. How did he manage to engrave the cabin? So tiny, so perfect. When did you . . . Adam, when did you have this made?"

"When we came back from the lake the second time. Grace, I've known since the day I met you that you were the only one. I had to wait, though. I didn't want to presume that you could learn to love me in the same instant. But after the fire, after the madness, I couldn't wait any longer. I want to always be with you, protect you, experience everything you do.

"And, I was so afraid you would associate the bad time — Elias and the fires and Tom's attack, all of it — with me, and not want to come here anymore. This place is in your heart, your mind, your very self. I want to be there, too. This was the only place to ask you to be mine, forever."

"Adam, you are inside me like no one else, like nothing else. You are my heart; you are in my soul."

They stood, then, and held each other, and kissed for a long time, sweetly, gently, murmuring unintelligible words of love. Adam finally drew his head back and looked into Grace's tear-stained face.

"You will marry me, then."

"I think I've made that clear, yes."

"Is it too cold to go skinny dipping?"

"Definitely."

Adam's phone buzzed. He couldn't believe it. Now? And how had he forgotten to turn it off? He reached to do so, but Grace stopped him.

"It's probably very important, Adam. They wouldn't call you otherwise."

"I'm not answering this phone right now, Grace."

"Sounds like a text notification to me. Just check it. We're not going anywhere. Except maybe back to bed."

"You're kidding."

"Well, if you're going to be the new detective inspector . . ."

Adam sighed, and looked down to see it was, indeed, a text from James. His eyes widened.

"What is it, Adam?" Grace asked.

"There's been a death at the Canadian Light Source. The synchrotron. A scientist has been killed."

"Oh my God. How did it happen?"

"James didn't say. He did say he could handle it until we got back."

"Murder, I assume."

"So he says."

"Here we go again."

"Yes. But not now." Adam scooped Grace into his arms. "Now, we're going back to bed."

# Notes and Acknowledgements

Northern Saskatchewan is a spectacular place. Forests, lakes, rivers and wildlife contribute to its beauty, and I have loved the area all my life.

One of the lakes is my second home. It is not Ferguson Lake, which does not exist. Ferguson, aka Fire Lake, is an imaginary place nonetheless based in reality. It has been named for a certain resident who deserves to be honoured for his dedication to conservation and peace. Raven River is also fictitious.

Some elements of Fire Lake do refer to actual situations. For instance, there was a hermit who made his home on the shores of a lake, and it was partly his story that inspired mine, although this work is entirely one of fiction apart from some of the realities surrounding the Canadian peacekeeping tour in Somalia.

I am grateful for the support of so many people who put up with my plot musings, grumpy moments after hours of writing and abandoned plans in the name of authorship.

First among them is my alpha reader, life support and plot-filler, my husband Ken. Thank you, you wonderful spousal unit, for everything. Always.

To my editors:

Tory Hunter: Thank you for clear comments, definitive direction, speed and brilliance.

Lori Coolican: Thank you for your knowledge, patience and Gracefulness.

CeCe Baptiste: You inspire me and make me better in so many ways. Thank you.

To my beta readers: I have listened to all of you, and Fire Lake is much improved because of your input.

To my family: Thank you for supporting and loving me despite this crazy new adventure.

To you, gentle reader: Thank you for your time and your readership, not just of this book, but all the books.

# The Adam and Grace Series

## Adam's Witness

When reporter Grace Rampling stumbles onto a grisly crime scene while on a routine assignment, she abruptly finds herself at the centre of a police investigation into the death of a Catholic bishop.

Evidence points to a troubling hate crime as Grace finds herself central to the case — as a key witness, a suspect and even potential victim. Lead investigator Detective Sergeant Adam Davis is thrown by the fierce attraction he feels toward Grace that, if acted upon, could throw the entire case into jeopardy.

With Grace at risk and off limits, Adam races to unravel an increasingly disturbing mystery, while he struggles to both protect and resist the woman of his dreams.

# Broken Through

**Winner: Best Mystery, Indie Originals Literature Competition**

*Based on a true crime.*

*A dead dog. A smashed car. A wild storm . . . and then, a violent death.*

The quiet streets of a Prairie city have rarely seen such brutality. Tough crime reporter Grace Rampling is covering the case until it suddenly becomes very personal: a close friend is on the front line of danger.

Grace's lover, Detective Sgt. Adam Davis, is forced to return home from a conference, confront his PTSD and find a murderer before he, or she, kills again. And as Adam knows, a psychopath never commits just one crime.

Made in the USA
Monee, IL
31 December 2020